A NOVEL

KATHERYN'S SECRET

T 20615

LINDA HALL

Multnomah Publishers® *Sisters, Oregon*

KATHERYN'S SECRET
© 2000 by Linda Hall
published by Multnomah Publishers, Inc.

International Standard Book Number: 1-57673-614-8

Photograph by Jake Pajs/Tony Stone Images
Cover design by Kirk DouPonce

Printed in the United States of America

Multnomah is a trademark of Multnomah Publishers, Inc.,
and is registered in the U.S. Patent and Trademark Office.
The colophon is a trademark of Multnomah Publishers, Inc.

For information:
MULTNOMAH PUBLISHERS, INC.
POST OFFICE BOX 1720
SISTERS, OREGON 97759

Library of Congress Cataloging-in-Publication Data
Hall, Linda, 1950–
    Katheryn's secret/by Linda Hall
       p. cm.
    ISBN 1-57673-614-8 (alk. paper)
    1. Women novelists—Family relationships—Fiction. I. Title.
PS3558.A3698 K38 2000
813'.54—dc21   99-057291

00 01 02 03 04 05 — 10 9 8 7 6 5 4 3 2 1 0

To my children, Wendy and Ian

ACKNOWLEDGMENTS

Although the fictional Sullivan family of Maine in no way resembles the real Hall–Hammill family of my husband, I thank my sister-in-law Ruth Barbin for loaning me boxes and boxes of mementos from my mother-in-law's family; shoe boxes full of photos; binders full of her poetry; plus her journals. All of the unsigned poetry in this book, notably the "Old Shoes" poem, was written by my late mother-in-law, Eiliene Hall.

Thank you to Earl Hintz of *Latitudes and Attitudes* magazine for reams of information about the green flash.

Thank you to my editor, Rod Morris, for helping me to become a better writer.

And most of all, I thank my husband, Rik, for his faithful support and love.

ONE

The flashlight dimmed. I looked down at it in surprise. Didn't I just put new batteries in? I cursed out loud a couple of times and then rammed the thing against the cement wall. Hard. All I succeeded in doing was cracking the plastic casing. The quality and quantity of light did not change, but remained a dull trickle of pale yellow. I muttered to myself and kept picking my way down the basement steps. When I reached the bottom I held onto the wall with my left hand and used the pinpoint of light to look around. This is where she said she'd be, that mysterious middle-of-the-night caller who had awakened me from a sound, albeit short, sleep a little more than half an hour ago. "Underneath the barn," she had said.

"Underneath the barn?" I didn't know barns had an underneath.

"Just take the steps down at the side of the building. I'll be waiting."

I poked through bits of straw and hay and dried manure and wondered if this whole thing were a practical joke concocted for my birthday. Except my birthday was seven months ago. Well, the joke was on me. Here I was up to my sneakers in crud with a weak flashlight, looking for what? I shook my head realizing that I should have had it examined long ago.

The weird middle-of-the-night muffled voice had talked about life and death and how I was the only one on the face of the earth who could help. Yeah, I bet you say that to all the girls.

But there was something about that whispery voice, something familiar when she woke me with, "Summer? Summer Whitney? I need to see you."

I'm naturally curious. That's what makes me a good private investigator. I knew I'd never sleep anyway, not after a call like that, so I got up. At 3:42 with only about two and a half hours of sleep under my belt, here I am pulling on my black jeans and turtleneck, grabbing my flashlight, my revolver, stuffing my blond hair under a black knit cap and setting out for the mysterious farmhouse with its mysterious basement where I was supposed to meet this mysterious caller.

Something was foul and it was more than just the cow patties. I could smell it. I could feel it. Call it instinct but suddenly I knew I was not alone in this basement. I felt that familiar chill which is half excitement, half dead-awful fear.

Carefully, as silently as I could, I aimed the thin flashlight beam around the room. I whispered "hey" a few times. No answer. Finally, the tiny bean flickered onto a face. The face was attached to a body, the body of a woman, hanging by her neck from the rafters. Dead. And I knew exactly who it was....

Sharon Sullivan Colebrook hit SELECT ALL, then pressed DELETE. For several minutes she stared at the empty screen, the cursor blinking in the top left corner. She was excessively tired and even the bones around her eyes ached. Beside her on her desk was half a cup of cold coffee in a Skull and Crossbones Mystery Reading Group mug.

She sat in the fading light of a Tuesday evening in spring in the fair-weather city of Victoria, British Columbia, Canada. Her husband Jeff Colebrook was working late at the newspaper, and she had the entire evening to write. An entire evening spread out before her, but still something was nibbling at the edges of her thinking. She couldn't concentrate, couldn't get her mind around another Summer Whitney adventure. She rubbed her forehead. Outside, lights were beginning to flicker on here and there among the houses in the city.

She and Jeff lived on a quiet street in the Oak Bay area, a house they never would have been able to afford had it not been in the Colebrook family for generations. Jeff's parents lived here until they moved to the lake full time. Her office was in a second-floor room in the back overlooking a small backyard, Jeff's boyhood room. She ran her hands through her hair and reclasped the wispy ends into a ponytail.

It was the phone call that was making her like this, all jittery and headachy, unable to work. Her husband had said she should go. "Why not?" he had said. "What's keeping you? I'll even come with you."

"You will?"

"Sure. We could make a vacation of it. I've always liked Maine."

"You hate Maine."

"No, I love it. Really, I do."

It was not as though she had never gone back. When the odd book tour took her through New England she always visited her aunt. The two would sit on the screened-in porch, iced teas balancing on the wide arms of their wooden chairs, and look out at the ocean while they talked. She always made it a point, too, to at least get in a meal with her father, who lived in Portland, Maine.

Once they had gone even as a family. More than a decade ago, she and Jeff and their then eleven-year-old daughter Natasha had driven across the country in an old Dodge van that kept breaking down. They stayed in a motel in Beach Haven, Maine, despite protests from her father that he had plenty of room.

A snapshot of Natasha and her latest boyfriend Jordan was pinned to the corkboard next to her computer. The two, clad in khaki shorts and wool sweaters, were sitting in some café in France, mugs of beer on the table in front of them.

Sharon was twenty, younger than Natasha now, when she had dropped out of Bible college and headed for western Canada. She had applied for and been accepted into a journalism exchange program in Vancouver, B.C. Upon graduation, she got a job at the *Vancouver Sun* where she met and married Jeff, also a reporter. A few years later the couple and their small baby moved to Victoria where Jeff took on the job of assistant editor at the Victoria *Times-Colonist*. When Natasha was ten, Sharon wrote her first novel, a sprawling family saga dealing with the war years and beyond. It sat in a drawer. Then she wrote her second novel, a whimsical look at the newspaper business. It also sat in a drawer. Her third, a light detective story featuring a private investigator named Summer Whitney was picked up by a publisher of mysteries in California. That story launched a series that had met with moderate success among readers of the genre.

Sharon took off her glasses and pressed her fingers against her eyes. Would this headache never go away? The phone call had come late last week. She had been sitting here at her computer when she learned that her aunt had died, leaving everything jointly to her and her brother Dean. She had gripped the receiver feeling suddenly ice cold. "Katie's dead?"

"Yes, ah, you didn't know?"

"No, I…this is news to me."

"I'm sorry. I thought you would have known. She died peacefully in her sleep about two weeks ago. She was quite elderly, you know."

"Yes, I know."

"Mrs. Colebrook?"

"I'm still here."

"It looks like you and your brother are her sole heirs." The lawyer cleared his throat. "We were, ah, wondering if you could give us the phone number for Dean Sullivan. It's not noted here."

"I don't have a number for him."

"Address then?"

"I'm sorry. I don't know where he lives."

"Ah, I see."

"Is there anything else?"

The lawyer cleared his throat again. "Well, ah, yes there is—the house in Beach Haven, the one called Trail's End in Miss Sullivan's will. It would be helpful if someone could come out here and go through it. Either you or your brother. We could put the entire thing up for auction, but I'm sure you'll be wanting to go through the house yourself. It's worth quite a bit being oceanfront. And there may be some family things you would want to keep."

"My father's out there."

"Yes, we know that. But he has declined."

Sharon sighed. "It's probably out of the question, my going. Now, I mean. I have my work. A deadline."

Later, when she had told Jeff, he had smiled widely and congratulated her. "If your writing won't make us rich, maybe rich relatives will!"

Sharon hadn't smiled, hadn't returned his embrace, hadn't responded even when he began talking on and on about the two of them flying out to Maine and "making a vacation" of it.

"It might take a while," was all she could say. "We might have to be there a while."

"So, what does that matter? We can take the computer and I can work from there. So can you, for that matter." He winked at her. "Maybe the place will be good for the old creative juices. You can have Summer Whitney solve that old family murder."

"What old family murder?"

He put his hands up. "You're the one always telling me that your Aunt Katie used to go on and on about some murder."

"Oh that."

"What, 'oh that'?"

"My Aunt Katie was a teller of tales, Jeff."

Sharon gazed out the window now. A soft spring rain was falling. She could hear it on the rain gutters. Jeff was right, of course; they could go. Natasha was still traveling around Europe with her boyfriend, and who knew how long they'd be gone? Maybe a trip away would be just what she needed to get her thoughts together for this new book. Still....

TWO

WHEN SHARON WAS EIGHT YEARS OLD, Katie took the poker from beside the fireplace, raised it high above her head, then brought it down hard on the hearthstone, so hard that the gray slate cracked all the way from the front of the fireplace to the outer edge of the hearth. Sharon heard it happen, so loud was the snap, like the crash when she and Dean dropped shells and rocks from the second-story window just to watch them break apart on the pavement.

"Katheryn!" yelled Sharon's father, rising. "What in heaven's name was that in aid of?"

"Watch your language, Mack," said Hilda quietly from her chair, the Bible opened on her lap. "This is the Lord's day after all." Then she turned to their sister. "Why did you do that? Why on earth, Katheryn!"

But Katie had already seated herself on the loveseat by the window, her hands folded properly in her lap like a lady, her vision fixed on a place outside. Then she said rather wistfully, "Do you suppose this was the way the murder was accomplished? Something hard? Metallic? Like a fire poker?" She winked at Sharon when she said this. That's what Katie was like. Shocking. Outrageous. Totally inept at some things, but gloriously competent at others.

It had been one of those bitter midwinter Maine afternoons when snow drizzles down miserably from a slate sky. Only a small fire burned in the grate, and the parlor in Trail's End was cold and damp. Aunt Katie used to say that when you felt a chill, that was a ghost. Sharon was sitting on the couch, still in her Sunday dress, her doll's blanket covering her bare legs, her feet with the fringed, flowered socks and the black-buckle shoes jutting up from the bottom. She had been looking at the snow and the ocean and wondering about ghosts when Aunt Katie cracked the slate hearth.

Hilda had risen then, the Bible on her lap slipping to the floor with a soft thud and a rustle of pages. She gasped as the Bible fell, picked it up quickly, and pressed a white handkerchief to her forehead. Sharon's mother put the tops of her fingers to her mouth, and looked over at her husband. Only Grandma Pearl and Sharon's brother Dean seemed unaffected. Grandma Pearl, asleep in her rocker, mouth open, stayed that way, right through the crash. And Dean, who lay on his stomach in the corner of the room, calmly put his hands to his ears. Then, just as quietly, he went back to drawing his intricate pictures of little army men and tanks around the edges of his Sunday school paper, the depictions punctuated with lots of *pow*s and *oh no!* and *arghs*.

Sharon's father cleared his throat and said, "Katheryn, why fill the children's heads with that talk? And on the Lord's day. The Lord's day, Katheryn."

"Oh, Sharon doesn't mind, do you, Sharon? And look at Dean, he hasn't moved an inch, didn't even hear me, most likely."

The stiffness had returned to Hilda's spine. "That's enough!" Then she reached for the little bell on the mantel and jangled it for the house girl. "Doreen, dear, it's time we had a repast of sorts." Her voice was loud, shrill. Dean put his hands to his ears again.

Sniffling loudly, Doreen, a skittish girl, nervously poured tea, spilling some.

Sharon had forgotten about that day more than forty years ago, but her aunt's rubberbanded letters, their edges brittle, retrieved now from the bottom drawer of her desk where she had kept them all these years, were bringing it all back. She could almost smell the room the way it was then, the seaweed smell of empty crab shells and moist sand, the saltwater dampness of the place in winter. If Sharon closed her eyes she could see Hilda, rigid, corseted, twisting her white handkerchief, the edges of her lined mouth turned down in a frown. Sharon also remembered the way Katie clapped her hands playfully like a child, as if this were all a joke, something to lighten a dull Sunday afternoon at Trail's End.

Sharon pulled a letter postmarked October 14, 1981, from the center of the pile. There was a time when once a week without fail Sharon would receive a letter from Katie. A few years ago the letters became irregular, and then infrequent. "Eyesight is failing in this old gal," she wrote once, which was about as close as Katie got to complaining about her health. Or talking about herself at all, come to that.

Sharon tried to remember the last time she had seen Katie. Probably three—no, four—years ago when she had hurried through New England on a book tour. Together the two women sat on the porch and talked about the state of the English language. At that time Sharon sensed there was something her aunt wanted to tell her.

Sharon unfolded the letter and read a few penciled lines:

There was a time when there were no houses up against the beaches, when trolls and fairies could walk around on top of the sand undisturbed by sunbathers and lifeguards and people trying to bodysurf the waves. But when the people came and built their houses and carted off the sand for sandboxes all over New England, the trolls and fairies had to move underground....

Sharon smiled. Trolls and fairies. Two of Aunt Katie's favorite creatures; the fairies always good, the trolls always bad. According to Katie that was the unchangeable order of things. "But couldn't there be a good troll?" the child Sharon would ask, but Katie shook her head. "Trolls are bad."

And so trolls became Sharon's monsters. In her nightmares they had huge warty heads, fuzzy hair and lips, and teeth that dripped green blood. When she would awaken afraid in the night, her thoughts were that the trolls had come up from the ground and were under her bed, behind the curtains, in her closet, holding fireplace pokers high above their heads.

"I'm going to talk to that sister of mine," Mack would say in the doorway, frowning. "This has got to stop. These stories. Giving her nightmares. This can't go on."

This was one more proof, according to her father, that "stories should have no place in the Christian home." They were allowed to read true things only: biographies of missionaries, stories from nature, passages from the Bible. Nothing of the sort that Aunt Katie delighted them with. What her parents didn't know was that Sharon read stories, books and books of them that she sneaked home from the library, under the covers of her bed.

"What's Summer up to now? Still hanging out under the barn with dead bodies?" Jeff had walked into her office carrying a stack of mail and a sandwich. She smelled pastrami.

"No. I have no idea. I should be writing, but I'm looking through some of these old letters of Katie's."

"You kept them?"

"Yes."

Jeff sat down beside her. "She lived a full life, Sharon."

"I know, but I should have—I don't know—been there more, somehow."

"Sharon, you live clear across the country, and you did write faithfully."

"I know, but...."

"And when you were in Maine, you always visited."

"Maybe I should go to Maine, clean up her house, for my aunt's sake."

"As I've said before, I'll go with you."

Sharon looked at the darkened screen of her computer. "But then there's my book. I should turn the computer on and work on it, but I don't have an idea in my head, not one, for my next Summer Whitney adventure."

"What happened to the body in the barn?"

"Scrapped it. Deleted it."

"Deleted it completely?"

"Right off the face of my computer."

"I liked that beginning."

"I'm thinking of including Katie in my next book." She said it off the top of her head. "I have all these letters."

Jeff took a bite of his sandwich. "The eccentric old aunt meets the wild and woolly Summer Whitney. Sounds like a sure thing."

She shrugged, pushed her glasses up on her nose. "Right now I'm just brainstorming; it's just thoughts, random things."

"Maybe you can get some ideas for your next mystery when we go out there." He pointed to his sandwich. "You want a bite?"

"No thanks." She wiped her hands on the thighs of her jeans. "Is that the mail?"

"Yep."

"Anything worthwhile?"

He put the sandwich on the desk and methodically went through the envelopes. "One power bill, one phone bill, one letter offering us a platinum MasterCard, if we act now. Oh, and we can get eleven CDs or twenty cassettes for a buck ninety-nine; some company offering the lowest long distance rates in the history of the planet if we sign up before the fifteenth; a letter from Maine; a postcard from Natasha—"

"Natasha? Let me see."

The card featured a stone castle on a muted Irish hillside.

Hi Mom and Dad,

Having a great time. Ireland is beautiful. Jordan and I are thinking of maybe staying here for a while. Well, no, not in this castle, ha ha, but maybe in Ireland. We might see if we can find work. Mom, I saw Fallen from Grace *here in a bookstore. I actually did! The manager says he's read it and really loves it! Just thought I'd tell you.*

Love, Tash.

"I didn't even know your books were in Ireland."

Sharon turned it over. "So, it's Ireland now."

"They must be all over the world."

"She's going to stay over there in Ireland. Well, that's news."

"Nice of the manager to like your book."

Sharon sighed. "And what about her schooling? Tell me that."

"Everybody likes Summer Whitney."

"Those two, just wandering around the countryside without a thought to their futures."

"If we brainstorm, maybe together we can come up with an idea for your next book."

"She's twenty-two, Jeff. By that time I knew what I wanted to do with my life. I had it all planned out. I had goals and things I was working toward. What has she got to show for herself? One year of university, with none too great marks, I may add, and two years of traveling around the world with that boyfriend of hers."

"Maybe your aunt's murder story would do well as a Summer Whitney book. I think the idea might just fly."

She sighed loudly. "Jeff, you're not listening to me."

"You're not listening to me, either, and I started this conversation."

"I'm worried about Natasha."

"She'll be fine. And she wouldn't call traveling around wasting time."

"Why are you sticking up for her? You agree with me."

"I know I do, but the more we nag the more she's not going to listen to us, Shar."

She looked at him: at his long, slouchy body, legs wrapped around the stool; at his eyes slightly droopy behind his glasses; at his hair, unruly and falling forward onto his face; his smile. After more than twenty-five years of marriage, she still couldn't resist that smile.

"I worry about her, though," said Sharon as she went through the mail, filing the bills, throwing out the junk mail until finally she said, "Well, I guess that's it."

"What about this one?" said Jeff, holding up a small square letter by the corner.

"I don't need to read that one." She knew what it would be: a long diatribe from her father about her latest book, noting with appropriate page numbers all the places where she had used what he called "ungodly language," quoting appropriate verses for her to look up if she still had her Bible.

"You want me to read it?"

"Go ahead. Be my guest."

He opened it and read it aloud:

Sharon,

I am writing to inform you of the death of my sister, Katheryn, your aunt. She died peacefully in her sleep out at Trail's End. I did not phone you because long distance is expensive and this death was not entirely unexpected, she being of an advanced age, and you not being one much for family. Katheryn is buried in the family plot near Portland, should you wish to know. Odd to think that I am the last of the Sullivans now, the very last of the line.

Mack

"Oh," said Sharon. "I'm not one for family? I'm not one for his type of family is what he should be saying."

"Sharon…"

"I mean it, Jeff. He didn't call. Just this letter. And 'the last of the Sullivans,' what's that all about?" She bit her lower lip. "There's Dean, or has he completely forgotten about his son?"

THREE

Katie Sullivan loved stories; that's probably the first and foremost thing that anyone can say about her, that she loved a good yarn. She had lots of stories in her arsenal; tales of magic potions and shipwrecked sailors and ghosts and murders and children gone missing only to turn up later on the other side of the continent in the company of fairies.

Her favorite, however, involved an intricate crisscrossed underground highway of caves and corridors and secret rooms beneath the sands at Beach Haven, Maine. It was down there that a constant battle between the good fairies and the bad trolls was being waged. Directly above, bathing-suited sunbathers lay on their blankets and ate hot dogs and drank lemonade out of thermoses. Katie loved the idea that these sunbathers had no idea any of this was going on a mile beneath their blankets.

If anyone scoffed at these stories, Aunt Katie would merely shake her head, her short curls fluttering around her face, and say, "But look at the tides. Just look at them. There's your proof. You need nothing else." She never said exactly *how* they were proof of it, but that was enough for us.

We would dig, my friends and I, and our holes would get quite deep, the sand cooler and darker and wetter down there. Once we spent all day digging and ended up with a hole that we could actually stand up to our necks in. But we never found the trolls and fairies. How deep was a mile? None of us really knew. A lot deeper than our plastic pails and shovels were capable of excavating, that much we figured out. Still we tried, and while we would dig, the perpetrator of these stories would sit under a beach umbrella beside us delighting us with even more tales, gesturing with large, expressive movements of hand and arm.

Katie, as she was known to almost everyone, was born Katheryn Susan Sullivan on May 10, 1912, in Portland, Maine, the middle daughter of Pearl Esther and Gerard Boyd Sullivan. When Katie Sullivan died, just a month short of her eighty-eighth birthday, her personal library contained hundreds of books. She loved the fantasy of C. S. Lewis, George MacDonald, and J. R. R. Tolkein, but she also read mystery and loved the classic horror of Edgar Allan Poe, and had many signed, first editions of Stephen King.

Katie, however, didn't inherit her love of books from either of her parents. Both Pearl and Gerard were convinced that the reading of fiction would warp the mind. The only book allowed in the Sullivan home was the Bible. It is said that when Katie was a young girl, one morning she smilingly regaled her parents with the tales of David from the Old Testament, omitting the names. Her horrified mother wanted to know where she had read such trash. "The Bible, Mother!" Katie said clapping her hands.

That was a gesture of Katie's. After telling a story, she would place her palms together, fingers pointing straight up, and then clap them together three times very fast. It was a gesture reminiscent of someone trying to bring a meeting to order or a director calling the actors onto the stage. On Katie, it seemed a call to play.

It was the story of the murder, however, that engendered the most reaction. She would bring it up innocently enough, at the Sunday dinner table or during Sunday afternoons in the parlor. She would get a look in her eye and say something like, "I saw the green light this morning, and it reminded me of something. I'm thinking of writing down the part about the murder. You know the murder I'm thinking about?" We didn't know what green light she was referring to, but before we had a chance to ask, she would clap her hands and say, "Do you think Pastor Harley's hair's a rug? I'm fairly certain that it is. I think you should talk to the elders about it, Hilda."

Once, Doreen dropped an entire tray of food when Katie said, "Once there was a boy who died and his body was left right on the beach, right out there where it happened. Fortunately for him Mildred came by."

We heard it,—dishes, food, glasses clattering to the floor, the sound of shattering glass in the kitchen. Hilda scowled across the table at her sister. The only Mildred I knew was the garden scarecrow, an old store mannequin Katie dressed in suits and gloves and propped up between the rows of tomatoes to keep the gulls away.

Today Beach Haven, Maine, attracts tourists from as far away as Quebec, New York, and Toronto and features condos, beach cottages, craft shops, cafés, deep-sea fishing expeditions, and sailboat charters. On hot days, sunbathers lie blanket to blanket, their radios tuned to light-rock stations, while lifeguards perch high above them on wooden stands. When Katie was a child there was none of that, only miles and miles of empty sand. It was there, I am sure, that Katie came up with her stories of trolls and fairies living beneath her.

Trail's End was the name of the Sullivans' beach home located there. I can find no record of how it came to be called that, because it wasn't the end of any trail that I could ever see, but for as far back as I could remember it was called Trail's End.

Every Memorial Day, the entire family would move into the house where they would stay until Labor Day. Early on Mondays Gerard would take the train back to Portland where he worked as a banker. And every Friday he would return to Beach Haven. When Gerard Sullivan died in 1948, the three women, Pearl, Hilda, and Katie, moved into Trail's End permanently. My parents, Mack and Rose, married in 1952 and moved into the Sullivan home in Portland.

ır ır ır

Sharon read over what she had written, smoothed her hair through her fingers back into a ponytail, and glanced at the time readout at the top corner of her computer. She gasped. She was supposed to meet her friend Carolyn in just fifteen minutes in downtown Victoria for lunch. She shut down her machine, then called Carolyn's cell phone and told her she was running late. In the bathroom she ran a quick comb through her straight hair, outlined her lips with pink, smacked them a couple of times, grabbed her jacket, and left.

"I'm glad you called," Carolyn said when Sharon arrived. "I was scrambling to get here on time myself." They were seated at a table by the window overlooking the bay.

"Problems?" Sharon asked.

"Oh, just the usual hoop-jumping. You'd think I'd be used to it by now. Maybe it's me. Maybe I'm too stubborn for my own good, but I'm sick of bowing to the department head: Yes master, yes master. Anything else you would like? And do you want cream with that coffee? How about some arsenic on the side?"

Carolyn, a high school teacher, and Sharon's closest friend, was working on a Ph.D. in history.

"You're almost done, though. Your thesis is written, you're practically out of there."

"It's bowing to their little idiosyncrasies. I'm fed up." Carolyn took a long drink of water and waved her hand. "Ignore me, Sharon. I'm just having a bad day, or as my students would say, a bad hair day."

Sharon grinned. "Your hair looks fine."

"My hair." She shook her head. "That's yet another topic of conversation which shall go untalked about."

Their waitress came. Both ordered chicken Caesars.

"Anything in particular?" Sharon asked after the waitress left.

"Had another run-in with his highness. Just before I got here."

"Sean Fowler?"

"Doctor Fowler to me. And to anyone else who happens to cross his path today." She shook her head. "That little smile of his, the condescending way he folds his hands and looks over at you over the top of his glasses. I just can't understand why they would put someone with the people skills of a troll in charge of an entire department."

"Funny you should mention trolls," Sharon said. "I've had a few encounters with trolls this morning, too."

Carolyn raised her eyebrows, and Sharon told her about her aunt. "You must be a lot like her."

"I'm flattered at the comparison, but I'm not that eccentric. Compared to the stuff she used to do, I'm really very boring."

"What's happening with that TV thing? You hear any more about it?"

"Oh that. Nothing will come of that."

"You told me there was a company interested in making a television series on your books. I wouldn't say that's nothing."

"It's a long way, an incredibly long journey, from producing a pilot and actually having a series air on a national network. Plus, I'm not exactly a household name. I have no idea why they chose me."

"Someone must have liked your books, though."

"I'm not counting any chickens before they hatch."

"You're being too modest. So who's going to play Summer?"

Sharon laughed. "If Summer gets 'played' at all, I'm sure they won't let me in on the decision."

Their salads arrived and while they ate, they discussed in great detail who, among all the actresses they had ever seen, would make the best Summer Whitney and why.

Outside their window a slight breeze ruffled the water in the bay and the sun shone on the tall masts of the boats moored there. It was only March, but people were walking along the water's edge, jacketless and in sandals.

"Don't you love it here?" said Carolyn putting her chin in her hands and gazing out to where crocuses bloomed along the side of the wharf. "Do you know Winnipeg's in the middle of a blizzard today?"

A few moments later Sharon said, "You remember all those many years ago when you first decided to go back for your doctorate, how you said you were feeling stifled and needed a change?"

"Oh, the incredible stupidity of some decisions."

"I'm starting to feel that way. A bit. Maybe. I don't know."

"What do you mean?"

"It's something I think about. I hate to admit it, but I'm starting to get bored with Summer. She's just too perfect, solves every crime that comes her way—"

"Well, of course she does, you nimwit. She's a fictional detective with this amazing body, boundless energy, and smart. And everybody loves her. They're even going to make a weekly television show on her escapades, and if they choose the actress I picked, it will be a raging success."

Sharon smiled wanly. "I don't know. Maybe it's me. But I have this feeling I should be doing something else, like writing something big and important. Literature. I don't know. I'll get to the end of my life, and all I'll have to show for it is a plastic grocery bag full of pulp fiction."

"Make that two plastic grocery bags. You want to write literature?" Carolyn leaned forward, her fork in midair. "Let me tell you something about literature. You walk into any bookstore—are books of literature on the front bestseller shelves, where all the mysteries are? No. Books of literature are in the very back of the store where no one ever goes. People take courses to read literature. People just read mysteries."

"Yeah, but my mysteries aren't exactly on the bestseller shelves, either."

"You'll get there. I have great faith in you."

Sharon said quietly. "I've got this idea. Just the germ of an idea. I started on it this morning. I'm thinking of writing about my aunt. Memoirs. Fictionalize her life. I'm trying to remember some of her stories."

"The trolls?"

"That and more."

"A book? Maybe?"

"I don't know. The lawyer wants me to go out there and sort through the house. I'm thinking of working that into a trip I have to take. At the end of the month I have to go to New Brunswick on a Canada Council thing. Signing books, speaking to a mystery writers group in Fredericton, I don't know what all. Then I'm thinking of renting a car and driving down to Maine for a couple of weeks."

"Maine can be pretty dismal this time of year, I'm told."

"I know what Maine can be this time of year, Carolyn. I grew up there, remember?"

"Ah yes, our landed immigrant come late to these Canadian shores. Jeff going to go with you?"

"He's hoping to be able to get the time off from the paper and meet me there."

"You could visit your father then."

"Great, Carolyn, any more brilliant ideas?"

"Yeah, let's get that waitress to bring us more coffee." She raised her cup.

FOUR

THREE WEEKS LATER SHARON WAS FLYING eastward above the clouds toward Fredericton, New Brunswick. Jeff would meet her the following week in Maine. "We'll keep in touch by e-mail," he said, unhooking his little portable computer. He showed her how to hook the computer and modem up in the hotel room in Fredericton. He wrote step-by-step instructions on a little piece of paper he tucked into the front pocket of the computer case. He offered ideas and suggestions for the Katie project, as he was now calling it. "You'll have to talk to the people who knew her. Neighbors, you know, and friends. Maybe they'll come up with stories for you, too. I'll get one of the old Dictaphones from the office for you to use. You'll need help doing this kind of thing, Shar."

"Jeff." She placed her hands, one on each of his shoulders, and looked at him. "Think about it. Where did we meet? At a newspaper. And how did we meet? I was a reporter. You were a reporter. We were reporters together. I think I know what I'm doing here."

"Times change, Sharon. You've been out of the loop for a while. Everything's all high tech now."

She got up on her toes to kiss him. "But it's still writing," she said.

She was glad he would be there. On the infrequent visits to Maine, Jeff played peacemaker between her and her father. While Sharon did the bookstore rounds, Jeff took her father out for the afternoon. What they did, what they actually talked about, Sharon never asked.

It was quiet in the cabin of the airplane. For a few moments Sharon listened to that peculiar whir of recycled air, the flight attendants' voices sounding thick and far away, conversations wading through the artificial air as if through water. Beside her, still buttoned up in a gray, woolen coat, a man leaned his head against the seat back, folded his hands on his lap, and closed his eyes. On the other side of her a chubby-faced girl who looked about fifteen had her face pressed against the window. She had with her a large backpack which she held protectively across her lap, her baby fingers, nails polished to a high pink gloss, gripping tightly to its edges.

When her tray was cleared, Sharon got out one of Katie's letters. She had brought them all with her. In the course of the last two weeks, she had read them all at least twice. She had also started a notebook which she had labeled, aptly enough, "Katie." In it she was jotting down memories, remembrances, bits and pieces of stories Katie told, as much as she could remember.

My dear Sharon,

Last night a troll came right up the stairs, one at a time. I could hear its feet splatting on the steps, grunting the way trolls do. As it got closer I could also smell it. I'm not as nimble as once I was, I'm eighty-two next birthday, you know, but I rose as quickly as I could to shut my door and place the back of a chair underneath the handle. Just in time I did this, for had I tarried a moment longer, the troll would have forced his way into my room....

My dear Sharon, I was asked to tell a story at the local children's hospital, my storytelling ability well known in the senior's quarters, and that's how I began. Now, as you may recall, I've told that story, or thereabouts, many, many times down at the nursing home, and no one has raised so much as an eyebrow. None at all. Well, the nurse in charge of the children nearly threw a fit. And that woman, who was more than three hundred pounds, well maybe I'm exaggerating—well, if I am it's only slightly—she came onto me telling me that my story would frighten small children, and that I was not welcome to come back. Her face turned into this delightful shade of red. "How can you scare the children so?" she asked me.

I was stunned, and have decided that I shan't tell my stories to children. Not anymore. I'm not good with children. It's probably just as well that my life worked out in such a way that I never had any of my own....

Sharon folded up the letter and smiled. When she was a child she would occasionally stay at Trail's End for a week or two with her grandmother and two aunts. If Aunt Katie happened to be the one who was assigned to look after her, she would flutter about the kitchen asking if Sharon needed a drink or a cookie, and then she would fling herself into a chair and say, 'Sharry, I'm just not very good at this. How about we do this—if you want something to eat, you just tell me. And I'm not even going to be worried about ruining your appetite or eating the right foods or anything. Whatever you like for lunch you can have, okay? Just don't tell Hilda or your parents. And you can fix it yourself, okay? I'm not good at fixing things, either."

Unlike Dean, who found both aunts foreboding and begged not to have to stay there without his mother, Sharon loved the freedom of being with Katie and the conversations they had—Katie talking to her as if she were an adult, an equal. And while Dean found the tension between the two sisters unbearable at times, Sharon found it entertaining and amusing. She often acted out their stories with her dolls:

"No, I will not go to church on Sunday evening. I don't care if Pastor Harley is going to do magic tricks from the pulpit or stand on his head. I go once a Sunday, and that should be good enough for anyone's soul."

"How dare you talk about magic! As if he would do magic tricks. Don't you have any idea what the Good Book says? Disgraceful to say that about a man of God!"

The plane lurched suddenly, and the girl at the window put one nail-polished hand on the back of the seat in front of her.

Sharon turned. "This your first time on a plane?"

"Yes."

"They're quite safe, you know."

"That's what everyone's been telling me."

"Where're you off to?"

"Toronto."

"Big city."

The girl nodded.

"Been there before?"

"No."

"So what's waiting for you in Toronto?"

"Our youth group is going there. On a mission project."

"Oh. And what will you do on this mission project?"

The girl shrugged. "Lots of stuff. Mostly talking to street kids. Helping out in the youth shelter. Cooking, doing the lunches for them. Our youth group's raised money for the shelter. For blankets and things."

Sharon put the letter down and looked at the girl, at the straight line of bangs above the eyes, at the sincerity in those eyes. "Have you done this kind of thing before?"

"Nope. We're getting orientation when we get there."

"And this is with your church?"

"Yeah. My church and another church are setting it up."

"Is the rest of your, uh, youth group on the plane?"

She shook her head, clutched at the table, swallowed visibly. The seat belt sign flashed on. "No, it's spring break. I had to go late because I had these tests I had to take for college. Why's the plane doing this?"

"They say there's a blizzard underneath us. See those clouds down there?"

The girl placed one palm on the small oval window and looked down, eyes wide, mouth open.

Long after the girl disembarked in Toronto, and long after Sharon had landed in Fredericton and was met by a member of the local mystery writers group, she thought about the girl's innocent face. Scenes from her own teen years came to her; she with the others in Young

People's, dressed in their Sunday clothes, carrying armloads of tracts, driving down to the shore to witness, going door to door with "religious surveys," memorizing Bible verses, and always aware that the list of things a Christian couldn't do was far longer than the list of things he or she could.

FIVE

IT WAS RAINING. And it matched Mack's mood perfectly. He was sitting in his living room in Portland, a bowl of soup on the coffee table in front of him, the television tuned to the weather channel. He hadn't walked over to Mona's Café today for lunch, as he usually did. The dampness would get to his knees. And his eyes were getting so that he didn't trust his driving in rain anymore. Katie's eyes went in the end; so did Hilda's. He had heated up a can of chicken noodle soup on the stove and found an old box of crackers on the top shelf.

He picked up the TV remote and turned up the volume. There was no end in sight for the rain, he learned, which was socking in the entire East coast.

This television was new—not new, but new to him. It had been in Fred and Sylvia's family room until two years ago.

"Would you like it?" Fred had asked one day after church.

Mack stared at him.

"The television. You're welcome to it. We just bought one of those new, big jobbies. But this one works fine."

"Television is of the devil." Mack had said it quietly.

"Come on, Mack." Fred had jostled his arm. "There are lots of Christian programs on television now. Really good ones, in fact. It's not of the devil, any more than books are of the devil or music is of the devil or art is of the devil."

So Fred had brought it over that afternoon, set it up, and the next day Mack had ordered the cable package that included the weather channel. Now, that was the only thing he watched. He still couldn't bring himself to watch Hollywood movies. He glanced up at the framed photo on the mantel and said out loud to his long-dead wife, "Rosie, I do hope you are enjoying the sunshine where you are, because here the rain has gone on too long. Too long. It's on a day like

33

today, Rose, a day like today, that I wish I was done with this place, and with you again."

He stirred the soup to cool it and smiled to himself. Fred would rebuke him for talking like that.

"You've got a lot of life left in you, Mack. What're you doing going on like that for? Why, I'm surprised you aren't out there taking out the ladies. Nice-looking guy like you." And then Fred would wink at him.

When Rose had died, his two children, Sharon and Dean, had been teenagers. Despite the help the church gave, the covered dishes the ladies brought over, the desserts and offers to wash the dishes, Mack had been overwhelmed.

When the children grew and left home Mack thought of remarriage. Honestly, he did. He even told Fred that. Well, that was all Fred's wife Sylvia needed to hear. Suddenly she was introducing him to every Christian widow lady in Portland. But none was like his Rose. What did he expect? An exact replica? "You're too fussy, Mack," Sylvia would say playfully, touching his arm. "Altogether too fussy."

And Mack would laugh, make a joke. "No one could live with me, Sylvia. I'm too set in my ways."

And so, Mack settled into his life of working in the bank like his father, the only job he'd ever had, and living in this house, his parents' house, the house he grew up in, the house he had raised his own children in. He had his job at the bank, his church and choir, walking to Mona's for lunch, and watching the weather channel. Fred and Sylvia brought over home-canned tomatoes and fresh-baked bread on occasion, and he still went over there for Sunday dinners occasionally.

Sometimes the part of his life that had included Rose and Sharon and Dean and weekly Sunday visits to Trail's End seemed like something he had dreamed a long time ago, someone else's life he had read about.

Rose had been gone for almost thirty years. He closed his eyes and tried to remember the way she looked when he had fallen in love with her, all that mass of flaming ginger hair and those laughing green eyes. In the picture on the mantel, her hair had darkened to a satiny auburn, and she kept the unruly waves at bay with handfuls of bobby pins.

The lawyers had told him they were trying to find Dean. Maybe that's what was bringing on this sadness. After all these years, what would he be like? Didn't I do the right thing, Rose? Didn't I? You would have agreed with me in sending him away, wouldn't you?

A small part of him on this rainy day longed to see his son, longed to hold him, like he had done all those long nights after Rose had died, cradling him in his arms, this almost-grown son who couldn't stop crying. When Rose had died, everyone pitied Sharon—"a girl needs a mother," they would say. But it was Dean who was the most injured.

He hadn't seen Dean since their last and final blowout right in this living room, right in this exact place. Mack had gripped the cloth at the back of the couch, this very couch, with one hand and with the other pointed a shaking finger at him. "You're on your way to hell, son!" And Dean had yelled back just as fiercely, "If you're not there, hell will be a pleasant place! I'm no longer your son." He had left. And was gone. More than twenty years had passed.

Katheryn told him that Dean had ended up out in California. He never asked her how she knew this.

The entire North American continent was displayed on the weather channel now. Mack leaned forward, his hands on his knees. Oddly, it was the weather channel that helped him feel closer to his lost children. When he would hear of heat spells and raging fires in California, he would wonder if Dean was experiencing any of this. When the cameras would scan the houses and streets, he would look for his son among the milling crowds. He had no idea what Dean even looked like anymore. Was his hair still carrot blond? Or had it darkened like his mother's?

And when he saw rainstorms in the Pacific Northwest, he thought of Sharon, just across the border in Canada. It was not as though he never saw his daughter. When Sharon came out east on that book business of hers, she would call him and they usually ended up eating hasty dinners in some restaurant of her choosing. She never stayed overnight in the house. "The publisher puts me up in a hotel. No sense putting you out," she would tell him. "It would be no trouble," he always said, but it was as if she hadn't heard.

The crackers were stale and the soup bland. He shook in more salt. He should have walked to Mona's and gotten himself a decent lunch, despite the rain. He liked it there. If she wasn't busy, Mona would come and sit across from him. She had soft gray hair which she tied back under long, colorful scarves. It gave her a slightly foreign look. There was a tinge of eastern Europe in her accent. She told him that her husband had died some years ago and to keep herself from "going crazy in my head," she had started this restaurant. She was someone to talk to. Someone different from his church friends. Someone he could be honest with and it didn't matter. He had told her all about Dean once, and all she had done was cluck her tongue and say, "Well, youngsters these days, they make up their own minds, don't they? There's no help for it, either, is there?"

When the phone rang, Mack assumed it was Jeff with an update on tonight's plans. That's the kind of word Jeff would use, update.

It wasn't Jeff. It was Fred asking if he needed a ride to prayer meeting.

Mack touched his face. "Uh, no, um, Sharon and Jeff are in town. Taking care of Katheryn's business. They're coming by. We're going out to dinner somewhere."

"Well, that's great. I'd say that's worth missing prayer meeting for one night. How's she doing these days, anyway? You must be so proud of her."

"She does all right."

"Sylvia just read her latest, *Fallen from Grace,* I think it was. She enjoyed it. You tell Sharon that, you hear?"

"Okay."

"Now, you have a fine night tonight."

"Maybe if we're finished in time, I'll get them to drop me off at choir."

"Don't you worry about choir, Mack. You're the most faithful member we've got, if you miss now and again, that's perfectly all right. Now, you give that daughter of yours a big hug from me, hear? You tell her old Uncle Fred says hi."

"Okay."

He had known Fred all his life. Mack had met Sylvia even before she and Fred started seeing each other. And then when Fred started dating her, it was only natural that Mack meet Sylvia's best friend, Rose. They had stood up for each other in their respective weddings, had children at about the same time, and had even, on occasion, taken vacations together. If he closed his eyes he could see all of those children, Dean and Sharon plus Fred's four—Diane, Steve, Chuck, and John—chasing around at Sunday school picnics, or dressed as angels and shepherds standing in uneven rows at the front of the church on Christmas Eve.

Three of Fred's children were on the mission field now, and one son was a minister in Connecticut. Now, that was something to be proud of.

Rain blew sideways against his house. Mack turned up the volume on his television and finished his soup.

SIX

"WHO ORDERED UP THIS WEATHER ANYWAY?" the motel manager said to them.

Jeff laughed. "Not us. Daffodils were blooming when we left Victoria."

The manager grunted. "Not like that here. Whole coast is socked in. For weeks now. Maybe you two'll be the good luck charm to bring us some spring sunshine or something. One can only hope."

The Drift Inn Motel was one of a group of motels on Beach Haven's main road, a block from the beach. Sharon knew the motels along here hummed in the summer. Now the only one with a lit vacancy sign was this place. The rest of them were shut up and dark.

"You'll be staying a few days?"

"At least. If that's all right."

"You're my only guests right now. Not much happening this time of year. I'm giving you my best room, the one on the end. By the way, the name's Russ," he said extending his hand. Jeff and Sharon shook his hand in turn. From a wall board behind the counter he picked up the key to room 14 and handed it to them. While Jeff filled out the requisite forms, Sharon found herself drawn to a small, framed watercolor that hung on the wall beside the key rack. It looked like a sunrise over the water, but the predominant color was green.

"That's a pretty picture," Sharon said.

"Oh that. Yeah." The manager grabbed a yellow rain slicker from a hook behind him. "Here. Let's go. Follow me."

As they made their way through the downpour, he yelled, "Cable's not hooked up; don't know how many channels you'll get on the box."

"That's okay," Jeff said.

"The room on the end's my biggest. Has a nice big desk in it. And a lamp you can move over by the desk. You've got a computer with you, you say?"

"Yes," answered Jeff loudly over the rain. "I'm hoping to do some of my work from here."

"Oh yeah?" He looked at them. "You can do that, can you?"

"Sort of, for a while anyway."

"What kind of work you fellas do? If you don't mind my asking."

"I'm a newspaper editor. My wife's Sharon Sullivan Colebrook, the mystery writer."

"Mysteries? You writin' one about this neck of the woods? Lots of mystery here, I tell you. Stuff goes way back round here. Here's the room, by the way." He fumbled with the key.

"Actually, I'm here to see to the estate of a relative," Sharon said.

"Oh yeah? You said the name Sullivan; would that be any relation to Katie Sullivan?"

Sharon nodded. "She was my aunt. You knew her?"

"Your aunt?" His face momentarily clouded. "Most people round here do know her, as a matter of fact. Quite a character. Well, here's the room, such as it is. Whew, it's some raining out! I had Doreen turn the heat on, but it still feels cold. Here, let me check it. Well, she turned it up, but not near enough. Here, this'll warm up the place in no time. And there's the lamp over there. There's a plug underneath it somewheres. And the TV over there, and the bathroom in the corner there. Shower, no tub. You fellas need more hangers? I can get more if you want."

"Doreen?" Sharon said.

"Huh?"

"You said the name Doreen. Who's Doreen?"

"Doreen Cutcheon, my sister. I'm Russ Cutcheon."

Sharon regarded him. "Is she the same Doreen who worked for my aunt? I remember a Doreen when I was small."

"Think so. She worked for Katie and them over at Trail's End, as well as for a lot of other people around here. She lives here in the

39

motel now. I'm sort of taking care of her, if truth be told."

"Taking care of her?"

"A bit of a sad case, that one. They're calling it early Alzheimer's. So, I do what I can. Most days she's good."

"Oh, I'm sorry to hear that. She couldn't even be that old."

He shrugged and looked away from them.

When Russ left, Sharon looked around the place. It was a cottagey room with fresh, white walls and rugged barn boards surrounding the windows and doors. Along the wall above the beds were glass-framed pen and ink drawings. It was obvious that the artist who had drawn these had painted the odd green sunrise that hung in the lobby. The first was a lighthouse, the second was a small house with the sea in the background, and the third was the side view of a young woman kneeling in the sand. Her feet were bare, and she was bent over as if praying. But on closer examination Sharon saw she held a tiny clamshell in her hands. Her face was barely visible behind her long hair, which fell forward.

Jeff talked while he hooked up the computer and dragged the floor lamp toward the desk. He plugged in the modem and started up the machine to make sure it would work. When he was finished, he stood back like an artist admiring his work.

"There," he said. "We're all set up. You can run around the state, visit lawyers, and dig up the buried treasure in that old house while I stay here and work."

"You're not going to help me?"

"Of course I'm going to help, but I do have a paper to run." He looked at his watch. "We're also going to have to get a move on if we intend to pick up your dad in less than an hour."

She looked away from him.

"There's going to come a time when you'd wished you'd spent more time with him, you know."

"I doubt it." She unpacked sweaters and shirts and dresses and shook them vigorously before hanging them in the tiny closet. "Oh great. Not enough hangers. Why is there never enough hangers?"

"The manager said he'd bring some."

After a while she said, "There are times I blame him for my mother's death. I really do."

"Who?"

"My father. That's who."

"Sharon…"

"He kept her on such a tight rein. She wasn't allowed to do anything, go anywhere without his permission. He wouldn't let her work or earn any money of her own. And she couldn't have any friends unless they were church friends." She sat down on the edge of the bed, hugging Jeff's brown sweater.

"A lot of women didn't work then," Jeff said. "My mother didn't, and it wasn't for any great religious reason. It was a cultural thing, the whole June Cleaver thing."

"Well, my church turned that cultural thing into a religious thing. I'm nervous about being here. About seeing him again."

Jeff sat down next to her and put his arms around her.

Forty-five minutes later they were standing at the front door of the house Sharon grew up in, the house her mother died in, the house her father now lived in.

Mack opened the door, squinted at them, and then ushered them in out of the rain.

"Sure is raining out there," said Sharon, managing a smile.

Mack grunted.

Jeff extended his hand. "Good to see you, Mack. Really good."

To Sharon, her father looked older and more bent. The older he got, the more he grew to resemble Grandma Pearl. There was that same sag to the jaw, the pouches there, the fuzzy white hair. When he turned sideways, she could see the bones of his face, his gray skin taut across the forehead.

"How have you been?" Sharon said.

He shrugged. "'Bout the same."

Sharon looked around her. Nothing had changed at all since the last time she was here; nothing had changed since she left for college; nothing had changed really, since her mother had died. Still that faded picture of her on the mantel, the only photo there; none of her or Jeff or Dean or Natasha even though she had faithfully sent school photos of Natasha every year since kindergarten. There was just the one. Always just the one. She felt a catch in her throat.

The one astonishing surprise was a small color television balanced on a TV tray in the corner. Jeff nodded toward it. "Is there supposed to be any break in this weather?"

Her father's face brightened. "The whole eastern seaboard's socked in. There's a low pressure trough right on top of us that will not budge. Not a breath of wind. Not a breath."

Jeff nodded.

"Just above us, in Canada, this low pressure system's causing major blizzards. The jet stream is irregular, too, followed by a warm front of even more unstable air. Odd for this time of year. The result is no end in sight for the rain."

Jeff looked at Sharon and raised his eyebrows.

Mack rubbed his nose. "Strange weather all over. A frontal low is forecast to move in after this, leading to even more rain. Even more rain."

"Lovely," Sharon said.

"It's let up slightly now," Jeff said. "If we make a run for it, we can get into the car and get to that restaurant before they cancel our reservations. Mack, you sit in front."

"You staying in Portland?" Mack said on the way to the restaurant.

"We found a motel in Beach Haven," said Sharon, leaning forward from the backseat.

"You could've stayed in Portland, you know. At my house. There are rooms. You could've."

"We know," Sharon said. "We didn't want to inconvenience you."

The restaurant was a bright, noisy place that featured a many-paged, glossy menu offering large portions of just about everything. Mack seemed overwhelmed by the choices and in the end found Yankee pot roast on the last page.

"Doubt it'll come close to Mona's, though," he said.

Jeff raised his eyebrows. "And who, pray tell, is Mona?"

"A restaurant I sometimes eat at."

"Oh."

Their salads came.

"Choir's tonight," Mack said.

"Oh?" Jeff said.

"Starts at 8:30. Right after prayer meeting."

"You want us to get you back on time?"

"If you wouldn't mind."

"No problem," Jeff said.

"Don't know why I go, though. They do all this new music now. Doesn't make any sense to me. No sense at all. Some of it. Guitars, drums. In church, even. Can't get used to the new church. I try, but I can't."

"You've been in the *new* church twenty years," Sharon said.

"Fred doesn't mind the new stuff, though. Told me we need to have an open mind. Christians going to movies. Dances, even. It's just not right. An open mind. More like a perverted mind, if you ask me."

"Fred's still around?" asked Sharon lightly.

"Yeah. Where else would he be?"

Sharon turned to her husband. "The Smith kids, Fred and Sylvia's—I know I've told you about them. Steve Smith, he was my age. Diane was a year younger, the same age as my brother. Chuck was older than me by two years, and John was the baby. The two of them, Diane and Dean, were a thing for a while in high school. We all thought they'd end up together. Then they went to different colleges."

"And your brother got himself involved with those godless people and left us." Mack's voice was quiet, almost a whisper. "He and Diane should've gotten married. Look at what he missed out on. I should've insisted on it. I should've."

"I'm sure Diane feels she made a good choice," Sharon said.

Mack took a forkful of salad, made a face. "This is bitter stuff. Whatever happened to regular lettuce?"

"This is good, Mack," Jeff said. "It's romaine and radicchio."

"They expect you to eat this?"

"Maybe we should've gone somewhere else," said Sharon, looking around her helplessly. The people at the next table were noisily gulping huge mugs of beer and laughing loudly. At another table, a baby was crying insistently. The place was bright, loud, overwhelming.

"We'll go to Mona's next time," Jeff said. "We'll give this restaurant one chance, and if it doesn't make the grade, we switch, okay?"

Mack grunted. "Diane is home."

"Diane?"

"She and her husband are home on furlough from the mission field. Her husband spoke at church on Sunday. You should've heard him. Both of you should've. Can we get some water here? This service is terrible. How can they expect you to eat this stuff without water?"

Jeff raised one finger for the waitress.

When three waters arrived, plus the pitcher, Mack declared that the water was too warm and that they, all three, needed more ice. Jeff winked at the waitress who replaced the pitcher.

Mack turned to Sharon. "You should look her up."

"Who?"

"Diane. We were talking about Diane."

"We were talking about water and bitter lettuce and ice. The subject of Diane was a long time ago."

Jeff touched her hand under the table.

Mack grunted, mixed the salad around in his bowl without eating it. "Diane is a fine Christian lady. You could learn a lot from her."

Their meals were served. Yankee pot roast for Mack, clam strips for Jeff, and chicken Parmesan for Sharon.

Jeff leaned forward. "Mack, did you know that they're going to make a television program based on Sharon's character of Summer Whitney?"

Sharon shot him a look.

Mack sighed loudly. "Most of television is vile. Most of it is."

Later, after they had dropped her father off at his church and were on their way back to Beach Haven, Sharon stared out the window at the rain. "Why did you tell him about the television show?" she asked. "He hates television."

"He has a television, honey."

"That surprised me. We were never allowed to have one when we were kids. I had to go to girlfriends' houses if I wanted to watch television. It's so vile, you know."

"Sharon..."

"Nothing is ever good enough for him. Did you notice that? Not the salad, not the water, not his son, not his choir music, not his church, not television, not me. Especially not me. I never was, and I'm not now."

"Sharon, he's an old man. He's set in his ways. You remember that *Grumpy Old Men* movie? That's how I think of him. We'll never change him, so we just accept him the way he is and laugh about it later."

"I find it hard to laugh, Jeff. Most fathers would be proud of their daughter if someone was making a television program of her books." She watched the windshield wipers and unconsciously began tapping her fingers to their rhythm. "A sweet woman like Diane would never write for television."

"Maybe you should look her up," Jeff said. "If she was an old friend, I mean."

"In your dreams."

Just before they unlocked the door to their motel room, Russ Cutcheon called, waved, and ran toward them.

"Been thinking about something," he said when he caught up. "You going to check on Katie's things, you should talk to Cos. That'd be the first place I'd go. If it were up to me."

"Who is Cos?"

"You don't know who Cos is?"

Sharon shook her head.

"He was Katie's boyfriend."

SEVEN

"HER BOYFRIEND!" SHARON LAUGHED as she undressed for bed. "My eighty-eight-year-old maiden aunt had a boyfriend?"

"Shows you can never tell about people," said Jeff grinning. "Come here."

"My spinster aunt had a boyfriend." She sat down next to him on the bed.

"I always wondered about that," he said. "How those sisters never married and lived all those years with their mother after their father died."

"That's what women did then. If they didn't find husbands, they stayed at home with their parents."

Jeff looked up. "Listen to that rain. I love the sound of rain on the roof."

"You are into this, aren't you?"

He put his arms around her. "I think it's good for us to be here. We needed this. I know I did. Beginning to feel burned out at the paper."

"Burned out. I know what you mean."

That night as Sharon lay next to her husband on the queen-size bed, the rain clamored relentlessly against the motel. There was an excitement in the storm. An electricity. She could feel it, a physical thing almost, reaching out to her, drawing her back here. A fearful thing.

Jeff was gone when she woke the next morning. It was still gray, but the downpour of the previous evening had played itself out and was now a gray mist that hung suspended in the air.

When she got up and went to take a shower, she saw the note—"Gone to get coffee. Back soon"—written in soap and encircled by a heart on the mirror. She grinned, had her shower. Back in the room she turned on the local news while she dressed.

She was dying for a cup of coffee and wondered where Jeff had gotten to when he walked in with an elderly man who had pure white hair and a large pink face and carried a cane.

"Sharon, meet Harold Cosman, Katie's friend. Mr. Cosman, this is my wife, Sharon."

He inclined his head. "Ah yes, Ms. Colebrook. I've read all your books, every single one of them at least once, most of them twice. It is indeed a pleasure." He extended his hand.

She took it and laughed. "I've never met anyone who's read my books twice!"

The man had a large nose and ears which gave him a whimsical, clownish look, as if he found the world a curious and funny place to be.

"Oh, but they are fine, indeed."

"Thank you."

"And you are thinking of writing the biography of Katie?"

"Oh no, nothing of that sort, really. Maybe a short article. I'm here mainly to clear up estate business."

"Well, that is good, indeed."

"Right now I'm trying to remember her stories. Katie and I wrote quite regularly until she lost her eyesight."

"Oh yes," he said, leaning on his cane. "She told me as much. Told me a lot about you, in fact." A smile crossed that wide, comedic face. "Katie was a very good friend of mine. Indeed, my best friend, if I may be so bold. Her passing has left a great void in my life."

"I'm so sorry, Mr. Cosman."

The tips of his large ears reddened. "Please call me Cos."

"I have a suggestion," Jeff said. "Why don't the two of you head on down to the motel coffee shop, and while you're doing that," he patted the computer, "I'll check in, see if they're managing to put out a paper without me."

"Will you join us later?" Cos asked.

"Depends on how much I've got to get caught up here. But you go. Reminisce about Katie."

"Capital idea," Cos said.

"Then I could finally get my cup of coffee, which I see you didn't bring me."

He grinned at her.

Cos opened the door for Sharon and with a sweep of his arm invited her to walk through first. They were the only ones in the small coffee shop, and Mr. Cutcheon himself waited on them.

Cos asked for tea, and Sharon ordered the breakfast special, with a large coffee as soon as possible.

"Wouldn't you like something to eat?" she asked.

"Oh no, dear, you go right ahead. I've had my fill already."

"I hope you don't mind if I eat in front of you. I'm absolutely famished."

"Not at all."

"Do you know Doreen, the motel manager's sister?" Sharon asked.

"Oh my, yes. She cleans for me."

"She worked for Katie. I guess she works here, too. I remember her as a girl, or a teenager, really."

"Oh my, time does fly, does it not? She cleans for me now, a few times per week."

"Russ Cutcheon told us she's suffering from Alzheimer's."

"What?"

"He said she has the beginnings of Alzheimer's."

Cos looked around him. "Oh my, I don't think so. I hadn't heard that. She seems fairly normal to me, but you know she has always been a bit fluffy."

Sharon smiled. "I'm just curious. How did my husband find you?"

"I'm not that terribly difficult to locate. Everyone in Beach Haven knows everyone else. My house is three houses down from Katie's on the beach."

"North or south?"

"South."

"The Kohler place?"

"The very one, indeed. Needing a place of solitude after my wife's passing, I jumped at the chance to buy it."

Their drinks came. After they had creamed and sugared them to satisfaction, Sharon asked, "So how did you come to meet my aunt?"

"Oh my." He smiled his clown smile and said, "That does take me back a bit."

"How long?"

"Oh well, now. Ten years, yes, an entire decade. Yes. It was Mildred who brought us together."

"Mildred?"

"I had just moved here and was out for my morning constitutional along the beach, and saw a woman standing in her garden. She was wearing a blue suit and holding a handbag. How curious, I thought to myself. I must go and meet this woman who stands unmoving in an old-fashioned blue suit."

"The famous blue suit," Sharon said. "Katie always dressed that scarecrow in a blue suit."

Cos grinned. "You can imagine my astonishment when I discovered this wasn't a woman at all, but a plastic dummy." He laughed, a merry, giggly sound, and his ears wiggled. "Then Katie came out and told me this was Mildred and that Mildred keeps the gulls from pecking at her plants."

He leaned back and placed his hands on the woolen fabric of his knees. They were large hands, like his ears. His feet, too, Sharon noticed, were long and slender, encased in brown wing tip shoes. It was as if the core of his body had shrunk, leaving his extremities large and overgrown.

"If you've known Katie for ten years, how is it that I've never met you? I visited Trail's End whenever I was in the area. I must have been to Trail's End at least a half a dozen times in the last ten years."

"Katie was a private person. A very private person, indeed. Surely you remember that about her?"

Sharon nodded. The manager brought her food, and she began to eat while Cos continued.

"She never talked much about herself. But the stories, that's how she revealed herself. Through her stories." He held his teacup in midair. "One of the things I used to do for her—she found it difficult to get out much, especially at the end—was to pick up old *Ellery Queens* and *Alfred Hitchcock* magazines at Gus's Used Books out on the highway. She was addicted, utterly, to the mystery genre. She got a lot of her own stories there. Those elderly folk down at the nursing home where she told stories loved her. She kept that up, too, every Friday night until a month before her passing, I might add. The seniors used to think she made them all up herself, but more often than not they came from books and magazines. She'd take a Stephen King story and change the names, the gender of the individuals and voilà, she'd have a new tale!" He giggled again. Sharon couldn't help but smile.

"She drove those poor nurses crazy, every last one of them." He spilled a few drops of tea on his rubbery fingers. "She was a practical joker, our Katie was. She had one pretty little nurse all in a flutter two years ago when she told her there was a dead body in the garbage can in the laundry room and that she'd better see to it. Well, the place went crazy. The police came in swarms, finally questioned Katie, who was sitting there looking ever the sweet old lady, calmly saying, 'But Officer, it was all a part of the story. Can I help it if the nurse actually believed me?' That poor little nurse was afraid of Katie until the day she died. She'd see Katie coming and turn tail and head the other direction. Never knew whether or not to believe anything Katie said to her after that."

Sharon laughed. "What a character! She used to say and do things at the most inappropriate times. I remember one calm, quiet Sunday afternoon she struck the fireplace and broke the stones in front of it."

"And they remain cracked to this day."

Sharon put her fork down. "Did she ever talk about why she did that?"

He looked at her, his mouth working. Sharon waited. But Cos looked away from her, past her and out the window to the rain. He began talking then about the trolls and fairies, remarking on the finer points of their description, waving his fingers and wiggling his ears as he described the pathways under the sands.

Sharon played with the edges of her napkin.

"That murder," he said, "the one accomplished with the fireplace poker, was nothing more than a story, told in a similar vein to the trolls and fairies."

"I thought as much."

"Some would call our Katie a gossip and a cutup. And nosy. Oh, was she nosy. But possessed by a storyteller, nosiness is called curiosity. We talked a lot about that, she and I, about how naturally curious minds must learn to rein in their curiosity so that it becomes socially acceptable." He looked at her. "And she told me you possessed that gift."

Sharon grinned. "A nice way of saying that I'm nosy? My problem was questions. I asked too many of them. Plus, I *was* nosy. I still remember being caught by my Aunt Hilda—that was Katie's older sister—rummaging through her top drawer. Ever after that she called me a nosy parker."

"Oh my."

"I didn't find anything of interest. Just pairs of gloves and dozens of those pressed white handkerchiefs she used to carry. And hat pins. An entire container of hat pins. That's what found me out. I pricked my finger and it bled all over a handkerchief."

"Oh dear." He chuckled again. "Curiosity is a good thing; nosiness is quite another, considered gauche, even though the two are cousins of each other. Storytellers don't see things the way others do.

Katie loved to embellish things, the murder story for example. She found something that got a rise and used it to its utmost."

"Hilda once sat me down on a kitchen chair and told me that Katie was dangerously close to insanity because she couldn't tell the difference between what was real and what was not. She could see that I had those same proclivities, she called it, and wanted to warn me."

Cos raised his eyebrows and looked at her. "But my dear, it's the storytellers, it's those people who have the firmest grasp on reality. They are the ones who can see life through many different sets of eyes."

"Yes."

Russ cleared their table and asked if they wanted more coffee or tea.

"Oh no, not for me," said Cos, placing his hand on top of his cup.

"I'm finished, too," Sharon said. She rose, then turned to Cos. "It's been nice meeting you, even though my husband never did make it."

"Maybe we shall meet again." He inclined his head slightly.

"Oh, I hope we shall."

On her way out, Sharon thought she glimpsed a swish of blue at the doorway, someone running. Someone who'd been at the door of the coffee shop, listening to their entire conversation.

EIGHT

TROUGHS AND FRONTAL SYSTEMS, lows and air masses with their pulsating pink arrows; these were the things that leant form and order to Mack's life. It was a certain, unexplained comfort to him that the outrageousness of storms and the unpredictability of wind could be explained by diagrams and lines with their arrows, ever moving patches of gray upon a board; the sense and order that it made on paper.

Sometimes Mack imagined his own onward moving life as lines on a weather map with their sharp edges, diamond points in the direction of thrust, or little red nubs, all in a row in retreat. A world governed by unchangeable patterns. He thought of Dean. He thought of Hilda. The stories Katie told. His father. The newspaper article he had carefully cut out all those long years ago and had kept folded in his wallet. The questions unanswered. The death of his beloved wife. If only these things could be so easily diagrammed, so easily explained.

Mack couldn't explain his fascination with the weather, couldn't name it, couldn't define it, rarely admitted it; but in his circle, which was not large, he had come to be known as somewhat of an expert.

It had started with the weather channel, that earnest questioning, that leaning forward and turning up the volume. He found himself repeating new information to Mona, who would nod her head to the side, her silk scarf grazing the table, or to Fred, or to the back row of men in choir. Occasionally, one of the altos might turn around and say, "But isn't this early for snow?" to which Mack would reply, "Not if you're paying attention to the jet stream; not if you're taking that into consideration."

He knew how to read the diagrams. He could distinguish the various patterns of clouds and knew what they forecast. He could read an isobar chart with accuracy. He could stand outside, gaze up at the sky, feel the weather on his face, and predict with fair accuracy when the storm would hit and how hard. On more than one occasion his forecast was more accurate than the weather bureau's. Mona told him this was a gift. He said it was just common sense.

For Christmas last year Fred had given him two books about the weather. One was a glossy, colorful book for the layman titled *Weather for Every Day.* It featured full-page photos of hurricane-devastated towns, sailboats thrown up against rocks, their masts snapped like toothpicks, houses piled one on top of the other, windows shattered like cut candy. He studied the pictures of tornadoes, of crops devastated, sea winds, icebergs. In a chapter titled "Unexplained Weather Phenomena" he saw pictures of a house that a tornado had turned top to bottom, yet left everything else around it, including the front porch, perfectly intact.

The other book was a college textbook on meteorology. "Something to sink your teeth into," said Fred chuckling.

This one was slower going, more detailed, and sometimes Mack had to reread chapters a number of times before he finally understood them. He blamed it on his age. "Getting too old to learn new things, Rose," he would say out loud. "Things just don't stay in the old noggin' the way they used to."

Sometimes he took the textbook to Mona's and drank tea and ate biscuits served to him by one of Mona's granddaughters. He would puzzle and puzzle over a paragraph or a chapter, then a few days later pick up the book and begin where he left off, and suddenly it would make sense.

The satisfaction this gave him, this pride in learning, worried him in another way. Sometimes he wondered if he was putting his weather book ahead of his Bible. So, he would try to balance them out in a kind of rhythm, a chapter of the weather book, followed by a chapter of the Bible, followed by another chapter of the weather book. He was always making deals with God.

In front of him the weather channel was on, the volume low. There was going to be a description with pictures of "sea state" in a few minutes. The last time he was at the RiteAid, he'd purchased a spiral notebook in which he jotted down interesting weather facts. He was planning to take extensive notes on sea state.

The phone rang.

"Mr. Sullivan?"

"Yes?"

"This is Doreen."

"Yes?"

"I'm calling about Sharon, Mr. Sullivan."

A pause while Mack opened to a new page in his book, his yellow Bic pen at the ready.

"Mr. Sullivan? Are you there?"

He craned his eyes toward the television screen. "I'm here."

A very old and trusted method of estimating wind speed at sea is the Beaufort Wind Scale. This nineteenth-century invention...

"Will she be staying at Trail's End, do you know?"

"Who?"

"Sharon and her husband."

Force Zero is calm air. The sea is like a mirror...

"I don't know."

"Thing is, I'm wondering if I should go down there and clean it up. Air it out a bit, I mean, for them. I'm thinking it's going to be some dank in there by now. What with all this rain we've had."

"I don't know anything about their plans."

Force One is called light air by sailors with its scalelike ripples across the surface of...

"They didn't tell you, then?"

"No."

Force Two is called a light breeze. The crest of waves do not break...

A pleasant picture was on his screen, a small sailboat gently gliding across the water with full sails.

"I just wanted you to know that I'll be heading on over to Trail's End. If anyone sees me."

"Okay."

Force Three is called a gentle breeze...

"Just so's if anyone says anything like that they saw me there or anything, it's just me cleaning up the place for your daughter and all, in case anyone should ask or see me in there."

Mack shook his head and let a breath out of his mouth.

Force Four winds are called a moderate breeze by sailors. These are large wavelets with crests just beginning to break and waves still less than one meter...

Mack reached for the TV remote and inched the volume up a bit.

Doreen was still talking. "Actually, I was just telling you so's you know."

"Fine, fine."

"Just in case you see your daughter."

Force Five is called a fresh breeze. Small waves become larger, and there is a slight chance of spray...

"Fine," Mack said. He could never figure out Doreen. She lived with her brother now, in that motel of his. But ever since Hilda had died she had phoned him, once, sometimes twice a week. At odd times of the day she'd call to say she was sure Trail's End was haunted, or did Mack know that Katie wasn't taking care of the place? And what should be done about it?

A strong breeze on the other hand...

"Is someone there with you? I don't want to disturb you, Mr. Sullivan, if someone is there with you. I hear voices."

He sighed. "No one's here, Doreen. Is there anything else?"

She paused. "Well, actually, I'm not so inclined to go over to Trail's End."

"Then don't."

In near gale conditions the sea heaps up. Foam from waves blows across the water...

"But the place may need cleaning up."

"Trail's End is not my responsibility."

"Hilda died in that place. Gives me the creeps just to know that."

Mack absently rubbed the loose skin around his throat. A whole lot of people had died in that house: Pearl, Gerard, Katie. Why single out Hilda?

Gale conditions occur when the wind reaches speeds of thirty-four to forty knots and wave height reaches four to five meters. At this height and wind strength, the Coast Guard will often issue a warning for small craft...

"The heebie-jeebies, sir, if you must know."

Mack grunted.

"See though, thing is, I'm supposed to. Lawyers hired me to keep it clean."

Force Ten indicates a very strong gale, with winds reaching forty-eight to fifty-five knots and wave heights reaching nine to twelve meters...

"'Cept I'm too scared to go over there. Not without anyone there no more."

"Do whatever you want to do, Doreen."

"But I don't want to go there, not under the circumstances. It's the angels come back for revenge, Mr. Sullivan. God's judgment. God come to destroy me. What do I do, Mr. Sullivan? What do I do now?"

Hurricane force winds are catastrophic winds with phenomenal wave heights. Ten minutes of hurricane force winds are the equivalent of all the world unleashing its nuclear weapons all at once...

NINE

THE OFFICE OF HOBBS AND SON was in a suite on the second floor of brick office buildings in downtown Portland. Beneath them was a chartered accountant, a real estate firm, and a wholesaler for hair salon products. Roman Hobbs, the lawyer, reminded Sharon of the Pillsbury doughboy. It was rare for her to be able to look a full-grown adult male straight in the eyes. Everything about him was round: pug nose, wide eyes, little hands with pudgy fingers. She found herself wondering idly if he bought his suits in Boy's Chubby.

"Ah, Mrs. Colebrook. We were awaiting your arrival." He rocked on his heels and placed his fingertips together in front of him.

By "we" he meant himself and his father, a somewhat larger man who belted his pants high on his pronounced belly pouch. He appeared in the doorway carrying a file folder. It appeared that Roman Hobbs and his father were the only two attorneys in the firm Hobbs and Son.

"Ah, yes, the paperwork. It's all here," said Roman, taking the file from the elder Hobbs. "The will's been verified, and we have hired the services of Doreen Cutcheon to keep the beach house clean. She is the only one with a key at this point. Now what remains is to locate Mr. Dean Sullivan, your brother, I believe."

Sharon nodded.

"Sit down, please, and we'll go over the terms with you."

Sharon sat.

"We are doing the requisite things," Roman Hobbs said. "We are placing ads in major newspapers in California—we were told that is where he might reside."

"You haven't heard anything?"

"It's early yet, Mrs. Colebrook. Or do you prefer Ms. Sullivan?"

"Mrs. Colebrook is fine. Sullivan Colebrook is the name I write under."

"Very well, then."

"What happens if you can't find him?"

"Oh, we usually find people in cases like this, especially when they're due to inherit. But if the need arises, we will not be opposed to hiring a private investigator. We have, on occasion." He placed his little sausage fingers against the straight edges of the papers. "Odd that no one would know where he is, though."

He said this last part more to himself and in an offhand way, but Sharon felt the strong rebuke.

"That was something between Dean and our father. That's why he left. I was already married at the time. I don't know what precipitated it."

He looked up at her. "Ah, I'm not commenting on your particular situation. Oh, I've seen all manner of family circumstances in this work. There's nothing that would surprise me. Nothing at all."

"I'm sure there isn't."

"In any case, we shall let you know the moment we locate him."

"Thank you."

On the drive back to Beach Haven she thought about her brother. She hadn't seen him since 1974. No letters. No colorful postcards. No e-mails. No phone calls. No exchange of Christmas or birthday gifts with "I hope this fits. I saw it and immediately thought of you."

What if that efficient little Roman Hobbs did find him? Would Dean want to see her? She had always felt it was partly her fault that he'd left in the first place. But could he still hold a grudge after all this time, after so many seasons had passed?

When their mother had died, Sharon had begun making her plans to leave. She had to leave, had to get away from her suicidal brother and her stern father. Bible college was a church-accepted way to leave, so that's what she decided upon. When she found Bible school more stifling than home, she decided she needed to go much farther. Vancouver, British Columbia, seemed a good choice.

"It's only temporary," she had told her father. "Six months, a year at most. Not many kids my age get this kind of opportunity."

The Sunday she left, she and Dean sat next to each other in church. During the sermon she looked at his knees, knobs poking through the black cotton of his pants, his head bent down. Their father, in a maroon choir robe, sat in the back row in the choir loft. Sharon sang the hymns; Dean merely stared at the hymnal, his mouth a grim line.

> *Yes, we'll gather at the river*
> *The beautiful, the beautiful river,*
> *Gather with the saints at the river*
> *That flows by the throne of God.*

Sharon sang lustily, as the song demanded. She could afford to. Her plane ticket—one way—was in the top drawer of her dresser. She had already decided that no matter who she married, she would always include the name Sullivan in her byline. There would be no doubt who she was and where she had come from. She would make a name for herself, and she would show them. She would show them all.

At home a little chicken was sizzling away in the oven. Her last offering. Since her mother died, Sharon had done all the cooking. No one had asked her to take on this responsibility; it was just expected. She was stirring frozen peas into boiling water when Dean came into the kitchen.

"You're lucky to be leaving," he said.

"Dean, you're twenty, why don't you leave, too?"

"I'm thinking about it, but I can't."

"Why not, for heaven's sake?" She stirred the peas vigorously.

"Things are all upset with me. Things are not right with me." His voice was practically a whine, and Sharon found herself growing impatient.

"Is this about Diane?"

"It's got nothing to do with Diane."

"I know you guys just broke up, but you'll find someone else."

"This has got *nothing* to do with Diane."

She tapped the wooden spoon against the side of the pot. "Things are never right with you, Dean. You're always upset about something. You're always whining about something, and everyone's getting a little tired of all your suicide attempts."

Dean turned and left the room. He didn't come down for lunch, which she and her father ate in silence. He didn't come to the airport with them to see her off. A few years later she heard from Katie that he had moved to California.

The rain was blinding and viscous as she headed south, and she didn't know which was inhibiting her vision more, the rain on the windshield or her tears.

She steered the little rental car onto the road that led to Beach Haven and began to look on the horizon for the ocean. As a child, she always felt a particular thrill when they could finally see it. She and Dean would have contests about who would see it first. The one who saw it first got to be the first to run down and put his or her feet in.

At the top of the rise Sharon stopped the car and stared at the wide expanse of gray sea, flat and dimpled in the downpour. Remembered pictures played across her vision: she and her brother building sand castles; she and her brother collecting shells and crabs and snails; the time they collected a bucket of snails, placed them on the table in the sunporch, and by morning, the snails were crawling all over the furniture, the door sills, the floors, the row of old *National Geographic*s in the bookshelf. And the way Hilda screamed at them, and the way Katie laughed and clapped her hands at the whole thing.

She put the car in gear. Trail's End, bleak and empty, was ahead of her. Still that barn red color with white shutters. Still that American flag hanging limply on the front porch. She wondered why no one had thought to bring it in.

Closer to the house she saw a face in the second-story window. She stared up, puzzled. And then remembered. Doreen had been hired to keep the place clean.

She knocked at the back door a few times and called loudly. When Doreen didn't answer, Sharon unlocked the door and walked in. The back door opened onto a hallway. To the right was the kitchen and the tiny room attached to it that Doreen had lived in. Ahead of it was the dining room. To the left was a bedroom, small bathroom, and beyond, that the parlor. A sunporch ran the entire length of the house at the front. Unheated, it was shut up during the winter with layers of clear plastic covering the large windows.

Sharon tried the light switch. Nothing. She'd have to get the power turned on if she was going to go through the place and pack it up.

"Hello? Anyone there? Doreen?" No answer.

She entered the parlor. The door to the sunporch stood open, and she walked toward it. Out on the cold sunporch she shivered as she looked through the crinkled plastic to the ocean below.

She had a strong sensation, then, of someone standing directly behind her. She turned around quickly.

"Doreen?"

She was alone. Back in the dim parlor she faced the fireplace, the one Katie had scarred. Next to it was the rocking chair where Grandma Pearl had sat for hours. Still the same chair. She could almost see Grandma Pearl there, rocking slowly, the way she did, foot tapping to some melody only she could hear, a brown blanket across her knees. She stared at the chair, and a shudder began somewhere in her spine. It was rocking, ever so slightly, back and forth, back and forth. She forced herself to walk toward it. She put her hand on it. No, it wasn't rocking, not moving at all. Just another trick of light and shadow. Like the face in the upstairs window when there was clearly no one here.

She turned away from the chair and looked at the fireplace. Above it on the mantle was a pink ballerina music box that had been there as far back as she could remember. If she wound it up, the ballerina would dance to a tune she could never quite identify. And there was the bell Hilda had used to summon Doreen. On a whim, she picked it up and rang it. It had a tinny, metallic sound. Doreen did not come running. Next to it was the Westminster chime clock that gonged every fifteen minutes. It was stopped now at quarter past four. Above the fireplace hung a dark painting of the Last Supper. She blinked at it. No, I am not going crazy, she said to herself. There is no one rocking the chair, there was no face in the upstairs window. No, the eyes of the Christ figure are not following me as I back away.

She bumped into the wall separating the stairs from the parlor. Since her childhood, there had been major structural changes to Trail's End. After Grandma Pearl died, Hilda and Katie had rented out the top floor, and to provide a separate entrance for their guests, the stair-well had been walled in with flimsy wallboard.

Underneath the stairs was a small closet. This, too, was walled in. When Sharon and Dean were small, this storage area was full of boxes and trunks which they climbed over and on top of to get to the trea-sures—porcelain-faced dolls with soft, cloth bodies, and a hinged wooden box full of lead soldiers.

She opened the door in the paneling and ascended the darkened stairs. When Sharon was small, framed photos had lined the wall going up. Pearl and Gerard; the two little daughters, Hilda and Katie, in matching sailor dresses; Hilda and Katie with their baby brother, her father. The photos were gone now.

She entered the front bedroom, the room where Hilda and Katie's sister, the aunt she had never met, the one they called Little Mary, had died of pneumonia. Sharon had heard the story often. "She was a beautiful little girl," Hilda would say choking back a sob. "Only seven-teen when God in his gracious mercy took her home to be with him." And then she would dab a handkerchief underneath the rim of each eye, carefully, one at a time.

"I've seen her ghost," Katie said once when the three of them were in this room together. "Haven't you seen it, Hilda? Haven't you? I would have thought you'd be the one to have seen it, that she would come to you first." And Katie grinned, showing all her teeth.

With one swift movement Hilda walked right up to Katie and slapped her hard across the face. Sharon, who was sitting cross-legged on the bed brushing her doll's hair, gasped. Then Hilda pointed a finger at Sharon and said, "And you'd be wise, young lady, to not repeat what you saw here. Imagine, your aunt tarnishing the memory of our dear sister like that!"

The room was neatly made up now, like a motel room, the sheets and blankets tight around the edges, paintings on the walls, the chipped porcelain jug and bowl on the bureau. She checked the closets; they were still packed tightly with Katie's clothes.

There was an old-fashioned dressing table and chair with a gilt-edged comb, brush, and mirror set on top of it. Sharon sat down and looked at her reflection, distorted in the ancient glass. To the right was a small vase with one dried red rose. But the most plentiful thing around the room was the books. Sharon saw all of her own, all fourteen Summer Whitney mysteries lined up in order in a bookcase underneath the window. There were shelves devoted to mystery, horror, shelves of contemporary novels, some biography, some poetry, some art books, and many hardcover novels.

The other three bedrooms were the same, neatly made up, nothing out of place. She glanced into the room where she had seen the face, but it was empty. A trick of light and shadow. Like the rocking chair and the eyes of Christ.

There was a tiny bathroom upstairs that was really a converted closet, built when they needed a bathroom for their renters. It, too, was tidy. Old medicine bottles were lined up in the small medicine cabinet behind the mirror: iodine, Mercurochrome, Vicks, aspirin, camphorated oil, Hilda's blue bottles of BromoSeltzer and Milk of Magnesia. Still there after all these years.

Quietly she made her way back down the stairs. There was a lot of packing to do. It made her tired to think of it. In the kitchen she walked right into a woman. She gasped, the woman screamed.

"Doreen?" Sharon said.

She remembered Doreen as a painfully thin girl with straight, dark blond hair who shook all the time. Sharon remembered looking at her hands once, serving the tea, and wondered if there was something desperately wrong with her.

The Doreen standing in front of her now was still that same girl, but older, still reed thin and wiry, but the dark blond hair had been replaced by a cap of gray springy curls. There were lines around her mouth and the corners of her eyes drooped downward. Her entire visage gave off a weary, sad-mouse look.

"I'm sorry, I didn't see you. Are you okay?" Sharon put her hand on the woman's arm.

She jerked herself away. "I was just coming in to clean up the place a bit for you. I know you might be moving in here. Wanted to get it clean."

"You were upstairs when I drove in?"

Doreen shook her head.

"I thought I saw someone in the window when I arrived."

Doreen backed away, her eyes wide. "That wasn't me." Her voice was a croak. "Oh no, it's started. It's started."

"What's started?"

"God's judgment. God's cruel, cruel judgment."

"It was probably just the light reflecting on the glass, is all."

The woman put her hand to her mouth and stared at Sharon.

TEN

"Two calls," Jeff said when Sharon returned. "Your editor plus that lawyer fellow."

Sharon pulled down one of the thin motel towels from the rack in the bathroom and dried her rain-wet hair. "You would not believe the weirdness of what just happened to me. It was like something out of the *X-Files*. First of all, yes, I did have a nice breakfast with Cos, and then I went to the lawyers, got that straightened out. They're looking for Dean. So then I decide to drop in at Trail's End on my way back here. And so when I drive into the place I swear there is a face in an upstairs window. So, I think it's Doreen, except Doreen isn't there. So I go in, and there I am standing on the sunporch, and I could've sworn, could have absolutely sworn, that there was someone standing behind me. So I turn around real quick, but no one's there. But I see the chair rocking. I swear to you it is really rocking. But when I go over, no, it's not rocking. And then I do see Doreen and she's screaming. And then she's going on about how the judgment of God has started."

"Maybe that's the Alzheimer's." Jeff pushed his glasses up on his nose.

"Maybe that would account for it. Because she was obviously there ahead of me."

"Obviously."

Sharon frowned. "The whole place was kind of creepy."

"Then again, it could've been an epiphany."

"A what?"

"You know how people are always seeing visions of the Virgin Mary on the sides of trees or donut shops."

Sharon grinned. "We could charge admission. Make a fortune."

"More likely it was just your imagination."

"Drat! We could've used the money." She hung the towel on a rod in the bathroom. "What did my editor want?"

"Didn't say. You're supposed to call her. Number's on the dresser."

"I've got it in my book."

She picked up the phone and dialed the number. "I was thinking," she said, looking up from the phone, "on the way home I got to thinking that you and I should move into Trail's End."

"You're kidding, right? You just told me about a ghost in the parlor and an epiphany in the window, and how the whole thing was like an episode from the *X-Files.*"

She put up her hand. "Hello, may I speak with Marge?" She glanced at the note again. "No, I don't mind holding."

She glanced up at Jeff and started humming. "Elevator music. La la de da da. Hello, Marge? This is Sharon. You called?"

"I wanted to give you an update on the TV pilot. They're into production now, but that's no guarantee it will get aired. Still a lot of hurdles to get over, but it's looking good. There are a few people down there who seem to really want this project to move ahead."

"That's great. I still can't believe it! May I ask who they've got playing Summer in the pilot?"

When Marge told her, Sharon said, "Carolyn's not going to be happy."

"Pardon?"

"Never mind."

Next she called Roman Hobbs, who said they had received an answer to one of the ads they had placed.

"You found him already?"

"Ah no, Mrs. Colebrook. What that means is that someone answered the ad. Who that someone is remains to be seen. There are undesirable individuals out there who answer every single ad that comes along."

"Is there any problem with my husband and me moving into Trail's End?"

"It belongs to you. We were, frankly, surprised that you took a motel in the first place."

When she got off the phone she told Jeff they had found her brother.

"Just like that? They found him?"

"Looks that way."

She sat down on the end of the bed and brushed her hair. What would he be like after all these years?

ELEVEN

THE YEAR THEIR MOTHER HAD DIED, Dean had tried to commit suicide for the first time. It was after eleven on a Saturday night when they received the call. Sharon was in the kitchen pouring herself a bowl of cornflakes. Her father was staring into the opened refrigerator, his back to her. He should have been home by now, her father said. His voice was muffled.

Sharon watched the back of him, the way he stood there, quietly, as if meditating on the contents. Yes, I called the pastor and the choir director; they said he left a long time ago. She didn't say anything. He pulled out the container of milk and poured some into a coffee cup. That was their life now, this is what they had come to, not putting things in the right containers. Milk in coffee cups. Tea made in glass tumblers. Water poured into goblets. It would be different if their mother were still alive. Why isn't he home yet? her father asked.

He sat down across from her and she looked away. Maybe he stopped off at a friend's, Sharon offered.

He stared at the milk. Why did I pour this? I don't even want it.

Sharon shrugged, ate a spoonful of cornflakes.

They were like this for several minutes. Then her father said, What does Dean seem like to you now?

Sharon looked at him embarrassed by the earnestness of his question, about the naked pain she saw on his face, the eyes, exposed as if she could see through them to his soul. She stared down at her spoon.

But he kept insisting. What does he seem like? Sharon got up, washed the cornflakes into the sink. She could not look on his nakedness. She stood at the sink, her back to him. I don't know what you mean, she said.

What does he seem like to you?

She wanted to say, he seems sad and scared and afraid and tired and angry and tearful; he seems all of those things. But she didn't. It was God's Perfect Will. Her mother's death on the highway, driving home from a ladies' meeting, hit by a drunk driver, not her fault. All that was somehow a part of God's Perfect Plan. His Timing. Not to be questioned. Never questioned. The church ladies who came by, one by one, to take Sharon shopping for school clothes and then out for ice cream, would look across the table at her and say, "It was ordained in God's Perfect Will that your mother be out on the road on that night. God knew all about it, Sharon. Don't you forget that. He could have stopped it, but he didn't. It was for the best that she be taken." All this said amidst spoonfuls of Neapolitan.

She stood at the sink, washing the bowl, washing, washing.

The phone rang. Sharon stood still, her fingers warmed by the water, the suds. She was washing the counters now, the front of the fridge, the taps, getting them shiny, getting the porcelain sink as white as she could. She could hear her father, Yes, yes, I see.

After he hung up he said, "Do you want to come to the hospital with me? Dean has fallen off a bridge."

"He what?"

"He fell off a bridge."

"He fell off a bridge?"

"He fell off a bridge."

She grabbed her jacket.

"We thought he was diving in for a swim," said the man who found him and drove him to the hospital. "But it was April, the river had just been thawed out now for a couple weeks, and when that thought kicked into my thick skull, I decided the boy might be in trouble there." That's what he was quoted as saying on the front page of the Portland *Times Herald*.

Their father never asked Dean how he happened to fall off a

bridge, how he happened to be in that neighborhood. The mask was back up.

The second time had been only six months later when Dean had swallowed the entire contents of a bottle of aspirin. That didn't kill him either, merely hospitalized him while they pumped out his stomach. Their father told the church that Dean had appendicitis, and the church prayed for him, that he'd be over his appendicitis quickly, and back in Young People's.

Late at night, a week after the aspirin incident, Sharon was walking by Dean's bedroom and heard their father. "And if you ever try anything so stupid like that again you'll live to regret it. Do you know what a bad light that puts me in? Me, a deacon in the church, with a son who tries something like that. Just to get attention."

She had heard Dean's small protest and then her father's loud, "I don't want any more mouthing off, you hear? I've had just about enough."

The third time had been a year later on Dean's sixteenth birthday. He had tried to cut his wrists with razor blades. Sharon found him this time and carefully washed his wrists and bandaged them tightly. But despite the long sleeves Dean wore, their father soon guessed, and punished him by ripping up all his artwork—the comics he had drawn, the intricate characters and scenes he had created. And then their father took all of the ripped up pages out to the backyard and burned them in the incinerator. "This is what's causing it, this ungodly, worldly stuff."

After that, remarkably, Dean had been fine for a time. His grades improved. He worked on the school yearbook committee. He started dating pretty, popular Diane Smith. It was as if he had gotten over that one horrible year. Perhaps that was all it was, grief at the loss of his mother.

Soon after he and Diane ended their relationship, the blackness returned. But by that time Sharon was living on the West Coast.

❦ ❦ ❦

Sharon put her bucket of cleaning supplies inside the front door of Trail's End and tried the light. The power was on. Good. She turned up the thermostats and then while the place heated up, decided to visit Mr. Cosman. She made her way across the rain-pocked beach down toward the Kohler's old place.

This was a beach she remembered. Here is where she and Dean had built sand forts. Over there is where they found those huge horse-shoe crabs, swept north by a hurricane. And here is where Katie sat on the sand, scrunching her cotton dress around her knees and telling them that a troll had murdered a fairy in the night. Over there, behind that rise of land, next to the bushes, is where Dean used to take a pocketful of lead soldiers to play his battles upon the sand.

She passed the tiny Smith cottage where the elderly Smiths sat on their deck all summer in their straw hats, watching the world. Next to it was the small cottage the French Canadian family rented all summer. She could almost hear them now, the mother's foreign words carrying across the sands to her children.

Next to it was the Kohler place, a white clapboard cottage with an enormous wooden deck, larger than the square footage of the place itself. The Kohlers were a family of big noisy boys who came up from Pennsylvania and stayed all summer. When Sharon was young the deck railings were always hung with colored beach towels that flapped in the ocean wind, the deck cluttered with swim rafts and bicycles.

The house was dark as Sharon made her way hesitantly toward it. The rain had started up again, and she swore it was laced with a scattering of wet snow. Chilled, she hugged her arms around herself and knocked on the back door.

TWELVE

HER KNOCK WAS ANSWERED with a raspy "yes?" through the closed door.

"Mr. Cosman, it's me. Sharon Colebrook."

"Oh, my goodness. Would you like to come in?"

"If you're not too busy. Are you okay?"

He opened the door. His large face was red, eyes watery. "I'm afraid I'm down with a cold. But I would love the company, and I'll promise to keep my distance when I sneeze."

Sharon entered. Inside, she heard loud classical music, but the music sounded scratchy and out of focus somehow. The only light was the murky light that came from the far window that overlooked the deck.

He flicked the switch. "I was sitting here in the dark by the window listening to my music. I do that by times." He made his way over to an ancient looking record player and lifted the needle. "I saw you walking down the beach. Not a particularly nice day for a stroll. Is that snow I see out there?"

Sharon laughed. "I think so."

"Can I offer you a cup of tea, perhaps?"

"That would be lovely. But you sit, I can make it if you just tell me where the tea things are."

"That's very kind of you, and I will take you up on your offer. You'll find the tea in that red canister on the counter, the one next to the stove. The kettle is on the stove and the milk is in the icebox. Sugar lumps, if you take sugar, are on the table."

While Sharon filled up the kettle, she told him she was planning to spend the day cleaning up Trail's End, but wanted to stop by and see him first. "I just wanted to thank you for talking so candidly about my aunt to me."

"Oh my, she was quite a lady. Quite a lady." He blew his nose into a large white handkerchief.

"I ran into Doreen at Trail's End yesterday."

"And how was she?"

"Skittish as a spider. She went on about God's judgment. And you don't think there's anything wrong with her?"

He shook his head. "I don't believe she has Alzheimer's, as her brother thinks. Russ is a bit of an overprotective older brother."

A violent wind suddenly shook the walls of Cos's little place.

"Can you believe this is supposed to be spring?" Sharon said. "Are you okay in this house? Is it warm enough? This place is really only a summer cottage, you know."

Cos seemed to look past her when he said, "Spring, yes, this was the time of the year when I met Katie. But not a spring like this. It was a brighter, much younger spring then...."

The kettle began singing and Sharon poured the hot water over a handful of loose tea in the pot. "Are you sure you're warm enough in here in winter?"

"Oh my, yes. I keep the Ben Franklin over there well stoked with firewood. I lay a fire before evening, and then in the morning all I have to do is light it."

"Isn't that a lot of work?"

"I wouldn't...I couldn't live anywhere else. Not now." He paused. "'And may there be no moaning of the bar when I put out to sea.'"

"Pardon me?"

"Never mind."

In the small refrigerator Sharon found a can of evaporated milk. She poured this into a clear glass cream pitcher that was on the counter. Somehow she felt this is what Katie would have done.

She reached for the bowl of sugar on the table and saw leaning against it a yellowed cardboard-backed photo of a young woman. She picked it up and studied it. The woman, who looked no older than a teenager, wore a floor-length white dress with full, ruffled sleeves. She stood behind a small brocade chair, her left hand on the back of it. In her right hand she held a closed fan. The tip of it rested on the seat of the chair. Her long fair hair was loose on her shoulders but held up on the sides with a series of clips. She had a wistful look about her. Sharon turned the picture over. In small script she read:

We walked through the rain
Through the gray half-light
And you wore old shoes
And your eyes were bright
I saw you laugh
I heard you sigh
Your coat was wet
As the drops rushed by
While we walked in the rain.

The poem was unsigned.

"Ah, I see you have found her," said Cos, rising, his handkerchief balled up in his palm.

"This was your wife?"

He rubbed his face with his hand. "Isabella? No, no. That's a picture of Isabella over there, on the mantle."

Sharon glanced toward the shelf above the woodstove. A fairly recent color photo hung there. There was Cos, unmistakably Cos, and beside him a striking silver-haired woman.

"Our fiftieth," he said. "She died a year later. I've been alone for a long time now."

"She's very beautiful."

"Yes."

Sharon was still holding the photograph.

"That is Katie," he said.

"Katie!"

"Yes."

"She gave you this picture?"

"Yes."

"How old was she here, do you know?"

"Eighteen. She was eighteen."

She placed the picture back on the table. "She gave you a picture of herself when she was eighteen?"

He smiled a crooked smile. "I suppose it's a bit odd. But she didn't have anything recent. You remember how she hated to get her picture taken."

"I suppose."

Cos gazed down at the picture, and Sharon took the tea things into the living room beside the window.

"You forgot the cookies," he said. "There is a box of arrowroots on the shelf beside the sink."

She placed a few on a plate and set it on the coffee table beside the teapot. Cos was still looking down at the photo. "I can see my own daughter, Natasha, in Katie here," Sharon said. "The eyes and something about the set of the mouth, although Tash has inherited my mother's bright red hair, but it's long and fluffy, like Katie's here."

"Katie's hair was brown. Like yours."

"I don't look anything like her, though."

He studied her face. "You have more the look of Hilda about you."

"Oh thanks!" She laughed. "I remind you of the evil aunt!"

"The evil aunt?"

"My brother Dean and I called her the evil aunt because she was so strict. We really had to mind our p's and q's around her."

"I'll bet." He looked at her. "I mean no offense. What I mean is that you are a softer version of Hilda. You're how Hilda should have been." He picked up the picture, took off his glasses and held it close to his face. "Look at the picture, Sharon. Look at it and tell me what you see."

"What do you mean?"

"Do you see sadness there or do you see innocence?" He put the picture down, put his glasses back on. "After the sadness came the stories. After the sadness came the fictions." He paused. "She loved the ocean, you know. She refused to leave, to go to the hospital, even at the end. She said to me, 'What do I want to go to the hospital for, Cos? So they can hook me up to machines and keep me alive for a month more? Goodness me, I've lived almost ninety years. I've lived my life. I was born in this house and I plan on dying in this house.'"

"Oh, Cos."

"She loved her house." He picked up his teacup. His hands shook and some slopped into the saucer. "You know why they make saucers don't you? For this very reason—for clumsy ancient people who spill."

"You're not clumsy or ancient."

"I'm nearly ninety. Very few men live to be ninety. Some women do, but very few men. And those who do are usually drooling all over themselves in nursing homes."

"Then you are indeed fortunate."

He put down his teacup. "I'm not so sure about that. I've seen too much." He blew his nose heavily into his handkerchief. "Whenever I get a cold or the flu I wonder if this will be the thing that finally takes me."

Sharon looked at him, said nothing.

"Sometimes thinking about Katie's death cheers me. Does that sound odd? She was so very calm, then. So peaceful. She'd made her peace with God. There was no more to forgive." He paused, took another sip of tea. "Oh my, this is good. So warming. I'm so glad you stopped by."

He leaned his head against the back of the chair, his face suddenly very gray.

"Is there something you need?" Sharon asked. "Can I get you anything?"

He closed his eyes and said nothing.

Sharon rose. "Cos, are you okay?"

He pressed his handkerchief to his forehead. "Fine, fine," he said.

"Can I call somebody for you? Do you have family nearby? Can I make you something to eat?"

He opened his eyes. "My children are in Wisconsin and Minnesota. When Doreen comes to clean, she often makes a meal for me. Sometimes I get those, what do you call it?" He waved his hand. "Meals on Wheels."

"Cos, Jeff and I are moving in to Trail's End in a few days. Why don't you come and live over there with us? There's room."

"Absolutely not. I will stay here. I will not even consider imposing in that way."

"It's not imposing."

"No. My answer must be no. I could never live there. Not now."

THIRTEEN

SHARON PLACED HER BUCKET under the faucet in the tiny upstairs bathroom. Cold. Even though the power was now on, the water hadn't yet warmed; well, at least there was water. She should be thankful for that. She decided to begin her cleaning in the upstairs bedroom. Armed with her soapy bucket, a mop, rags, furniture cleaner, Windex, an armful of huge orange garbage bags, and a portable radio, Sharon entered Katie's bedroom.

At the dressing table, Sharon pulled out the square center drawer and picked up a few pieces of jewelry. Katie was the only aunt who wore jewelry, and she didn't wear much. Hilda never wore any, and the only thing Grandma Pearl wore was a cameo brooch at her neckline. Katie, however, would come downstairs on a Sunday afternoon with numerous strands of multicolored plastic beads draped around her neck and entwined in her hair.

"It's the Sabbath day, Katheryn. How dare you profane it with your outward appearance and broided hair."

"These are pop-beads, Hillie. I'm sure our dear Lord has nothing against pop-beads." And she would wink at Sharon across the table.

Sharon held up the cameo brooch. She pulled out the other items: a few pairs of clip-on earrings, a necklace, a bracelet of green stones. She'd take these back to Victoria. These just might suit Natasha who wore odd combinations of things she picked up at thrift stores: flimsy layers of black, frayed jeans, large earrings, and beaded chokers. And always on her feet, those chunky boots. The effect, however, with her flaming hair was rather stunning. Sharon wiped out the empty drawers with a soapy wet cloth.

Next came the dresser. This held gloves, underwear, stockings, white cotton socks. She held up a slip. She placed some items in a pile for the laundry, some for Goodwill, and some for the garbage. She washed and dried each drawer thoroughly.

The time passed quickly as she sorted through drawer after drawer and listened to a documentary on the environment on the local public radio station. She pulled out jeans and thick sweaters, finding the occasional bit of money and piece of jewelry stashed there. Sharon remembered from her infrequent trips home that Katie always wore blue jeans, sweaters, big straw hats, and brightly colored Keds.

"I will not wear track suits," she had told Sharon. "All old people wear track suits. I will not join their ilk."

Sharon had smiled at this. Her own favorite writing attire was a beat-up pair of sweatpants and an oversize sweatshirt of Jeff's which hung practically to her knees.

From the closet Sharon laid hangers full of dresses on the bed. It seemed that none of the women had thrown a thing out in all the years they had lived here. Pale, flowered, cotton housedresses from the fifties and sixties still hung there, along with the skirts and sweaters Katie wore when she had an occasion to dress up. In the back of the deep closet, Sharon recognized some of their musky Sunday dresses pressed so tightly against each other that they held the imprints of their hangers. Maybe a vintage clothier or costumer would like to buy some of these clothes. She'd show them to Natasha first.

After she had sorted through the clothes, she hauled out suitcases and hat boxes piled in the back of the closet. The environmental interview was over, and now there was an hour of classical music. Sharon found a light-rock station and continued her dusty work.

She found more clothes. Older things in boxes. And hats—what else?—in the hat boxes. Straw ones, old pillbox hats, bonnets. Bonnets? She never remembered anyone wearing bonnets. Some of these things were too delicate to launder. She'd have to find the name of a dry cleaner that specialized in vintage clothing.

At the very back of the deep closet was a large, dusty dress box which she wiped with the damp rag before opening. Inside, wrapped in brittle yellowing tissue paper, was a dress. Carefully she unearthed it from the tissue and held it up. It was a white dress, the bodice beaded and finely embroidered. Inside each puffed sleeve was a wad of tissue paper. More tissue filled out the bodice. Sharon remembered Cos's picture. This was the dress Katie wore in the picture. She laid it across her lap and examined it. The stitching was delicate. The puffed sleeves, the ruffle of lace at the bottom, the lace at the end of each sleeve and around the neckline was exquisite. It looked hand tatted. Sharon held it up in front of her. It looked too small around the waist to fit her, and Sharon was quite petite. It would never fit Natasha.

Before she placed it back in the box, something caught her eye. A tiny square book was caught in the folds of tissue. She picked it up. It measured about four inches by six and was covered with red fabric and edged in gold. Sharon opened it. Each page was written in Katie's careful script. On the first page she read:

> *I have been lost, I have been shorn of power*
> *And even love has not contented me.*
> *But how my soul-face lifted to the shower*
> *Of verse remembered and of words returned.*

And the next:

> *The sun went down in a blaze tonight*
> *Tomorrow is going to be fair*
> *Wind children are chasing old clouds away*
> *And tangling themselves in her hair.*

And the next:

> *How vain is life*
> *A little love*
> *A little strife*
> *A fleeting smile*

A passing sigh
And then good-bye

Some of the words were attributed: Tennyson, Browning. Some were unsigned. On the last page Sharon read a poem attributed to Sara Teasdale:

I ceased to love him long ago
I tell myself so every day
But deep within my heart I know
There is no truth in what I say
And when we meet again by chance
My eyes, that smiled in other years
Can scarcely give him glance for glance
For they are filled with sudden tears
So, sometimes, when the fire is dead
And all the dancing gold is gone,
Above the ashes gray as lead
A faint heat lingers on.

On that last page was a tiny bouquet of petals, red and brown, delicate as rice paper. Sharon picked up a tiny leaf and smoothed it between her fingers. She carefully folded up the dress and put it back in the box. She put the red book in her bag to take back to the motel with her.

On her way home a soft spring snow was falling, settling as a baby blanket of white.

FOURTEEN

Today I have grown taller from walking with the trees
The seven sister poplar who go softly in a line
And I think my heart is whiter for its parley with a star
That tumbled out at nightfall and hung above the pine.

Sharon knelt at her aunt's grave and read from the little red book. Yesterday she had brought the book back to the motel and had read every line, late into the night, saying to her husband, "Do you think she had a secret love? Let me read you this one by Sara Teasdale. *I ceased to love him long ago…."*

He had grinned and reached over for her in the bed. They lay in each other's arms.

"You never know about people," he said.

"This stuff is so romantic. The Katie I knew and loved was eccentric and practical, not this poet person, but there it was, that beautiful white dress and all this poetry in her handwriting like *Sonnets from the Portuguese…."*

"*Sonnets from the Portuguese,* now that is romantic. Read me one."

This morning, she had talked Jeff into going with her to the family grave near Portland. Yesterday's brief snow had quickly turned to rain, and the grass in the cemetery was slick and clumpy. Sharon had brought two bouquets of daisies with her. She placed one on her mother's grave and the other on her aunt's.

"Don't ever put plastic flowers on my grave." Katie had said that to her more than a decade ago as they walked along the sand in front of Trail's End. "Those things," she said, picking up a piece of driftwood, "they call them cemetery saddles. Can you honestly think of a more inane expression? As if one needs to mount it to travel to the hereafter. Promise me, promise me that if you ever come to my grave and someone has placed one of those atrocities on top of me, kindly remove it. You have my permission to place it on the next person's grave."

Sharon had laughed. "I promise. Okay, I promise."

The family plot was on a pleasant, treed sweep of land from which glimpses of ocean were occasionally visible. She'd been here only twice before, when her mother died and then two years later when Grandma Pearl had died. Both times they had stood as a family and sung all four verses of "It Is Well with My Soul," the wind carrying their voices away from them.

She read the inscriptions on the tombstones. *Gerard Boyd Sullivan, February 15, 1890–July 14, 1948. I have worked. I have toiled. God is my reward.* And next to it, *Pearl Esther Goodwright Sullivan, October 31, 1893–March 3, 1972. Gone but not forgotten.* On either side were the two daughters, *Hilda May Sullivan, June 22, 1911–December 25, 1985* and on the other side, *Katheryn Susan Sullivan, May 10, 1912–April 5, 1999.* Next to Hilda's and a grave width away was her mother's, *Rose Florence Fahey Sullivan, beloved wife and mother. You left us too soon, June 5, 1930–April 17, 1970.*

It occurred to Sharon as she knelt there that in life, people require rooms full of furniture, drawers full of socks and shirts, and closets full of clothes. Yet in death they need only one good outfit and a tiny rectangle of space, smaller than a single bed. She hugged her arms around her.

She looked over to where Jeff stood in a small gazebo some distance away, his hands in his pockets, looking down toward the distant sea. Sharon knelt beside Katie's grave and turned a page in the red book to a poem attributed to Tennyson:

> *I hold it true with him who sings*
> *to one clear harp, in diver's tones*
> *That men may raise on stepping stones*
> *of their dead selves, to higher things*

"I never knew you liked poetry, Katie," Sharon said out loud. "You only spoke of trolls and fairies and murders and dark things. Never this."

Sharon thought about her aunt's letters, faithfully one a week for as long as her vision lasted. No poetry in them. None at all. But her aunt's letters were not like other people's letters. They were not filled with the chatter of events and persons and things accomplished. Instead, she wrote long descriptions of the sea, her garden, the cloud formations, the wind. Sometimes her aunt wrote down stories of her own in careful penciled script. Sometimes she mentioned books that Sharon simply must read. Sharon would ask pointed questions in return letters: Tell me, how are you keeping? What are you doing with your days? Do you still tell stories down at the seniors home? How's Doreen? Is she still alive? Remember Old Man Klaus who lived in that shack with all those kids? Is he still there? What are his kids doing now? Are you okay living there by yourself in that old house? But the questions, all of them, remained unanswered by return post.

Even when Sharon visited, Katie never talked of things pertinent. Instead, they would sit companionably together and talk of the tides.

A large droplet of rain plopped on the Tennyson poem, square in the center. The sky was blackening. Sharon closed the book and placed it in the inside pocket of her jacket.

"You okay?" Jeff was kneeling beside her. "I wish I could have met your mother."

Sharon nodded.

"And even your Aunt Hilda. And your grandparents. All those people I never met but are a part of you."

"You're not missing a great deal."

Distant thunder rumbled.

"Where's your other aunt's grave?"

"What?"

"The one they called Little Mary? She should be here, shouldn't she?"

Sharon stared up at him.

"The one everyone called Little Mary?" he said.

"Yes, I know, but…"

"But what?"

Sharon looked around her. "She isn't here. I never realized. I never noticed it before." She bent down and examined the ground with her fingers. "It should be right here, shouldn't it?"

"Maybe she was cremated."

"My family didn't believe in that."

"Maybe she's buried in another section. Maybe there's a main registry or someone we could ask." He turned his collar up against a sudden gust. "What did she die of?"

"Pneumonia. When she was seventeen."

"Nothing more contagious than pneumonia?"

"I don't know. Is that important?"

"From what I understand, if it was something contagious like tuberculosis, she may have been buried elsewhere."

"Really?"

"I think so."

"I guess we could check the death certificate."

A drop of rain landed on his nose. He took her hand. "Let's get out of here before this downpour begins in earnest."

By the time they got back to the main path, the rain was leaving wide rivulets in the gravel road beside the cemetery, and they splashed their way through them toward the main gate.

A groundskeeper was sitting in the small cemetery office, chewing on a toothpick and listening to country music on the radio. He showed Sharon and Jeff the master map of the grave plots. After many checks and rechecks they could find no record of anyone named Mary Sullivan being buried here at all.

"When did she die?" the groundskeeper asked, running his dirt-stained fingers down the map.

"I don't know," Sharon said. "In the early 1940s maybe. I'm guessing."

"These records have only these five Sullivans from this Sullivan family buried here." The toothpick rested on his lower lip when he talked.

"This Sullivan family? Is there another Sullivan family?"

"A little farther over is where Gerard's brothers are buried."

"Could she be there?"

"Doesn't look like it, leastways her name's not here." He scanned the map. "Nothing there, though, not that I can see."

"So, you think we should check those other plots?" Jeff asked. "Just in case?"

"Suit yourself."

Though the rain was coming down in giant, plunky drops, Sharon and Jeff tromped back across the wet ground to the other Sullivan plots. They saw where Gerard's two brothers, Ambrose and Peter, were buried, along with their wives and some of their children.

But no one named Mary.

"You know any of these people, your cousins?" Jeff asked.

"I heard the names sometimes, but never more than that. We rarely socialized with them, if that's what you mean. They were the black sheep of the Sullivan family, who drank and cussed and caroused. They wouldn't have anything to do with my side of the family."

FIFTEEN

"YOU HONESTLY THINK BOTH OF US can fit on this teensy double bed?" Jeff and Sharon were standing in the bedroom Sharon had cleaned the previous day.

"Well, yeah, I thought.... It's nice up here. I like the view."

"Yeah, but the bed. Sweetheart, I'm six foot two. Look," he bounced down on the bed. "See, my feet stick over the edge."

"So we shouldn't move in here?"

"I'm only saying that a regular double bed won't lend itself to a good night's sleep." Jeff paused. "Maybe the motel guy would lend us a queen-size bed, or rent us one."

"Motels do that?"

"I don't know. Maybe he has an extra one. You never know until you ask."

He walked around the small room. "We could fit a queen-size bed in here. But we'd have to put it up against the wall over there, not sticking out in the middle of the room like this one is."

"But you can see out the window from here."

"I know, dear heart, but it won't fit."

"Maybe it would in the other two bedrooms."

"Have you looked at those other rooms? They're even smaller than this one. This is really only a summer cottage, you know."

"My aunts lived here year round."

"It's still the size of a summer cottage."

"It's fully winterized, though."

He began dragging furniture around. "This big dresser could go against the wall. You know, this is really a room for one person."

"But both my grandparents slept in here."

"People must have been smaller then."

"And Katie slept in here and Little Mary."

"You never met Little Mary, did you?"

"Of course not. She died way before I was born, way before I was even thought of."

He pushed his glasses up on his nose.

"What are you thinking?" she asked.

"I'm wondering if there even *was* a Little Mary."

"But I've heard the story about Little Mary and her death all my life."

"But have you ever seen a picture of her?"

"What are you saying?"

"I don't know what I'm saying, I'm just wondering out loud. Thinking thoughts. Maybe Little Mary was one of your aunt's stories."

She sat down at the dressing table's tiny stool. "That seems so impossible. I'm sure my dad talked about her, too."

"And that's another thing that will have to go," he said. "That dressing table. No room for it in here once we get a bigger bed. It could go in the hallway."

"But it's so beautiful. So antique, so unusual." She ran her fingers along the dark wood grain. "Somehow this whole place seemed bigger when I was a kid."

"And that bookshelf will have to go."

"And where will we put the computer?"

"I was thinking down on the dining room table. I can't see us eating in there all that often and it's a nice big table. Or maybe even the sunporch if it wasn't winter."

"It's not winter, it's spring."

He glanced outside. "Could've fooled me. I think I'll head downstairs, see if we can hook the modem up in the dining room."

A sudden gust of wind caused the house to shudder. She stared at her distorted image in the dressing table mirror. Little Mary never existed? Jeff was right—there were no pictures of her. The pictures that had lined the stairway were of Gerard and Pearl and their three children, Hilda, Katie, and Mack. No picture of a Mary.

She got up, stripped the bed, and threw the sheets in a pile in the hallway. She'd get all the sheets and towels washed before they moved in. That done, she began loading books into boxes. Dust balls flew everywhere. The whole thing needed a good cleaning. She dusted each book as she took it from the shelf. There were numerous books of ghost stories: *Ghost Stories along the Coast of Maine, Seafaring Ghosts*, plus a glossy series of books on unexplained phenomena. She picked up *The Riddle of the Sands* by Childers, a series of books on World War II by Winston Churchill, *The Book of Ballads* by Bon Gaultier, and *Letters of Sir Walter Raleigh*, Volumes I and II.

"Sharon?" Jeff was calling her.

She rose, wiped her hands on her knees. At the top of the stairs she called, "Yeah, Jeff?"

"Could you come here a minute, please?" His voice was strained.

She found him on the sunporch staring at something she couldn't see.

"What is it?" she asked quietly.

He pointed. She entered the room and gasped. In the corner, leaning against the plastic-covered door of the sunporch, was the figure of a woman wearing a grimy blue suit, red high heels, and carrying a red purse.

"Mildred!"

"That's Mildred?" Jeff said.

"The scarecrow Mildred, yes."

"Was she here before?"

Sharon shook her head. "No." She walked out onto the sunporch. "How did she get in here?"

"You sure she wasn't here before?"

"No, Jeff. I walked right out onto the sunporch and she wasn't there. I didn't see her in any of the rooms." Sharon looked at the mannequin: at the red mouth which formed the little *O;* the surprised look in those painted eyes; the unkempt bushy doll's hair; the hands, nails chipped, holding the handbag. The years had not been kind to

Mildred. Fine feathered cracks crisscrossed the porcelain of her pink skin. Jeff ran his hand down the mannequin's arm.

"Don't touch her!"

"Why not?"

"I don't know. It's creepy. She looks so weird standing there."

"It's just a mannequin. So, who has a key to this place?"

"Just us and Doreen."

"It had to be Doreen then."

"She's supposed to be cleaning this place; maybe she just moved the mannequin in here."

"So, it would've been Doreen who went through the papers in the dining room?"

"What?"

"In the dining room, papers from the desk are all over the table."

They left Mildred leaning against the sunporch door and made their way into the dining room. The wide dining room table was strewn with papers.

"Most of them look like old utility bills and cancelled checks and grocery receipts." Jeff picked up a handful. "Who saves grocery receipts?"

"When I was here before it wasn't like this. Someone was here," Sharon said.

"Brilliant deduction, Watson. With a mind like that, you should write mysteries. I think I'm going to call the police."

"The police? Don't."

"Why not? Someone broke in here."

Sharon touched his arm. "But you already said it was probably Doreen. Maybe she was working here and didn't finish. I think we should talk to her first."

SIXTEEN

MACK WAS DOZING ON HIS COUCH, a cup of tea on the coffee table in front of him, his meteorology text opened on his lap. His half-awake, half-asleep midday dreams were filled with Rose: He and Rose walking hand-in-hand down a tree-lined street, Rose pointing at something in the distance. Suddenly the two of them are on the beach in front of Trail's End. Rose laughing the way she does. She lets go of his hand then and runs away from him. She takes off her shoes, holds her dress up around her knees, and tiptoes into the surf. She turns and calls for him, urges him to follow her into the water, splashes some on him. It is ice cold. He follows, she backs away from him, laughing; that red hair of hers, masses of it loose, blowing, obscuring her face. Always a little out of reach. He is worried about Hilda, about what she would say if she saw the two of them behaving like children. What if she is watching them, even now? Standing in the upstairs bedroom at Trail's End? "Rose," he calls. "Come back, Rose, you'll get us both in trouble."

Her back is to him, and she is walking away from him, her steps dogged and determined. The waves are bigger now, more menacing. A dark wind had suddenly come up. He calls for her, but his voice is lost to the roar of the sea. And suddenly, just as suddenly, two police officers are standing at his door saying, Sorry, sorry, sorry.

The doorbell rang. Mack woke, terrified. He rubbed his eyes. Was there some plan made that he had forgotten about?

Sharon and Jeff were at the door.

"Hello?" Mack blinked his eyes, to blink away the dream, but he could taste salt water still on his tongue. He ran his tongue over his lips, rubbed a trembling hand over his head.

"Hi, Mack," Jeff said. "Can we come in for a sec?"

He opened the door wide. He was conscious then of the disorder of the place, the television on, the afghan spread haphazardly on the couch, tea things on the coffee table, his jacket over the chair, a box of saltines on the floor, the way the place must smell.

"It seems there have been vandals at Trail's End," Jeff said.

"That's not news. Happens all the time. Tell him, Sharon, how routinely the summer homes are broken into."

"Jeff wants to call the police, but I think it's just Doreen. She put Mildred on the sunporch and went through some of Katie's old papers."

"Someone dug Mildred out?"

"Looks that way," Jeff said.

"From where?"

"Who knows?"

"What exactly was taken?"

"Nothing." Sharon smoothed her hair back into an elastic band. "But that's not the real reason we drove up here."

"We wanted to ask you about Little Mary," Jeff said.

He grunted. "Little Mary?"

Jeff scratched his head. "Did you really have a sister named Little Mary?"

Mack stared at them. "What a ridiculous question."

"First of all," said Jeff, holding up one finger, "her grave is not in the family plot. She's not beside your parents or sisters. There's no record of where she's buried. And then there are no pictures of her, none at all, at Trail's End." Jeff had taken out a little notebook and was tapping it with a pen.

Mack shook his head. "I don't know where she is."

"We were there yesterday, and I put some flowers on Mother's grave and Aunt Katie's. It was Jeff who noticed. Do you remember Aunt Mary?"

"Of course I remember her."

"How did she die?"

"I was a boy when she died. Twelve. It was 1940 when she died.

Yes, she definitely existed. Most definitely did she exist." He was shaking his head.

"But where was she buried? Where did they put her?" Sharon asked.

"I was too young. I didn't go to the funeral."

"But she's not in the family plot. Where is her body?"

"I don't know."

"But she was your sister."

"I was just a boy when she died. I don't remember."

"What did she die of?"

"She was sick."

"With what?" Sharon asked. At the same time Jeff asked, "Was she quarantined?"

"Quarantined?" He stared at them.

"It's an idea."

"Do you have any pictures of her?" Sharon asked. "I don't even know what she looked like."

He wished they would leave—all these questions. "I don't keep many pictures here. You're asking me things I don't know anything about. I was a boy."

"And you were never curious?"

"I accepted what I was told without always trying to argue with my betters."

"What were you told?"

"That God took her. It was as simple as that. That's what I was told and that's what I accepted."

When Sharon and Jeff left, Mack sat down heavily on the couch. It wasn't quite true, what he had told Sharon and Jeff. He didn't accept it, that Little Mary was taken by God. It was Hilda who had shooshed him out of the house that day with her snakelike tongue making all the arrangements for him to go to the uncles'. If he was being sent to the uncles, he knew it was bad. Uncle Ambrose and Uncle Peter weren't saved, and both of them drank amber liquor from flasks they carried around in their pockets. Hilda forbade the uncles and their families to set foot in Trail's End. That prohibition didn't work the other way around, however. If Mack was needed to be "out of the way," the uncles' was where he was sent.

He knew that Mary was sick. He had seen her empty eyes, the way she shuffled around like an old woman, hair uncombed, unwashed, always wrapped up in an old blanket or quilt, sitting for long hours in the parlor, gazing out onto the ocean, not saying anything, just shivering, staring. Staring. When he asked his mother what was wrong with her, she would say, "Just going through a bad patch, Mackie. Just a bit of a bad patch."

He stayed at the uncles' for three days. When his father picked him up in the old black Ford, his face was set and grim, and he told him that Little Mary had died.

Mack had made fists of his hands and pounded them into the seat beside him, screaming, no, no, no, while his father drove the familiar road to Trail's End without flinching.

There was no funeral, was there? If there was, he hadn't gone. That's the assumption he made. He never asked. He sat back down on the couch and tried to get back into his daydream of Rose, the good times with Rose, not when the police came. Not about all that came after. But all he could think about was Little Mary. And Sharon. And Dean. He sank his head into his hands. "Oh God," he prayed. "Oh God, oh God, oh God."

SEVENTEEN

THE CHATTER, THE FRIENDLY BANTER of the initial contact, was gone. Russ Cutcheon stood with his arms folded across his chest and refused to tell them the room number of his sister's motel apartment. Only when Sharon persuaded him that they needed to talk with Doreen about continuing to work for her at Trail's End did he grudgingly point to room 2 right next to the motel office. "That's her place. But don't expect her to be in. She's probably out. She works a lot, you know."

Nevertheless, their knock was quickly answered. Doreen was wearing a faded purple chenille bathrobe that dragged on the floor. She looked at them as if she had never seen them before.

"Doreen?" Jeff said.

Recognition dawned. "You've come about Trail's End. It's not tidy. I try to go there, but I can't. I just can't. Not alone in that place."

"Doreen," said Sharon gently, "the place is fine. We see that you moved Mildred onto the sunporch. That's okay, too."

Doreen put her hand to the side of her face, and for one moment she resembled the mannequin, with the little *O* mouth, the stunned expression, and the bright eyes. "Mildred?" she said.

"Yes," Jeff said. "Mildred was on the sunporch this morning. And you were going through the household bills? Is that something you normally do in the course of your work?"

She shook her head uncomprehendingly, still that little mouth, those wide eyes.

"Can we come in?" asked Jeff, wiping rainwater off his head.

She opened the door wide, which led them into a kitchen that was very clean, but smelled of milk. A small table up against the window was covered in a piece of oilcloth, the pattern long worn off by many wipings. Against the other wall was a small refrigerator and next to it a deep white porcelain sink. On the floor in front of the fridge, on an oval rag rug, curled a carrot-colored cat.

Suddenly Doreen was bustling around them. "Sit down." She pointed to the chairs. "You'll be wanting tea, I suppose."

Jeff and Sharon sat down at the table. In front of Sharon was a china tea service that looked oddly familiar. Doreen noticed Sharon's gaze and said, "Got them pieces of china at a flea market." She placed a large metal kettle uncertainly under the tap and ran the water.

Jeff leaned forward. "Doreen, is there anyone else who has a key to Trail's End?"

Doreen dropped the kettle into the sink, and it clanked hard against the porcelain.

"Oh dear. My kettle. I've like to broke it. This I got at a flea market, too. One near Kittery. For the tourists." She managed to fill the kettle once more and place it on the stove.

Jeff continued, "So, as far as you know, no one else has a key but you?"

"I keep mine hanged on that hook over there. The one by the door. You see it?"

"We're thinking of changing the locks," Jeff said.

Doreen palmed her small hands over the top of her hair, smoothing it back, first with the right hand and then the left, then the right again, the motion hypnotic.

"Doreen, did you move Mildred onto the sunporch?"

Doreen dropped a handful of teaspoons onto the floor. They clanked and the cat startled and ran. Sharon watched as she scooped them up and dropped them several times before she placed them on the table. She put one of the dropped spoons into the sugar bowl.

"Mildred was on the sunporch," Jeff said. "Did you put her there?"

Doreen leaned toward Jeff and said in a conspiratorial whisper, "Mildred must have gotten there of her own accord."

"You didn't put her there?"

Doreen backed away. "I would never touch her. She is a defiled woman."

"Okay, then, we're going to go to the police about this. It's obvious vandals have broken into Trail's End, found Mildred in the attic somewhere and dragged her out onto the sunporch and rifled through the desk looking for money."

"The police won't help." For once, Doreen's voice sounded ordinary and rational. "Mildred walks the place at night, you know."

The teakettle whistled and Doreen jumped up. She counted out five tea bags, dropped them into a small ceramic pot, and poured the water on top.

"That used to be Hilda's pot," Sharon said.

"Oh no. Oh no. I got this one at a flea market. Fifty cents it cost me."

Sharon touched the spout. "But I remember this crack."

"The other day I dropped it. How clumsy of me. Nearly startled David."

"David?" Jeff asked.

"My cat. And I had to sweep up pieces of pottery for days on end. I was worried about pieces getting imbedded into David's little paws."

"No," Sharon said. "That was Hilda's teapot."

Doreen picked it up and looked at it. "Hilda gave me this pot. Yes, I remember now. Hilda let me have this one. Hilda was good to me. After she passed, I had to find other work. But she was good to me."

"You work for people in Beach Haven?"

"Me? Oh yes. I clean for the Klauses, the Amerhands, the Summervilles, the Atlees, all summer people. Right now alls I have is the motel, Mr. Cosman, and the Mudges."

Sharon cupped her hands around her teacup. "You work for Mr. Cosman?"

"Oh yes." She sat down at the table. Her eyes became slits and she whispered to the two of them, "There is a mystery surrounding that man. I told Katie he was up to no good. I told her on more than one occasion."

"What do you mean?"

Doreen leaned toward them. "He was after Hilda's money." She accented each syllable. "I knew that for a fact. I can spot a fortune hunter a mile away, and I told Katie as much. He was probably looking for money at Trail's End. He maybe broke in. I wouldn't put it past him. He doesn't have much of his own, you see." She shook her head, the little gray spirals on her head jumping up and down. "If I were you, I would get the PD to run a background check on him. I watch the mystery shows, *Law and Order.* I watch them all. I know how these things work. You get that background check, then you'll see I'm not taking you for a trip around the mulberry bush. Then you'll see."

"The PD?" Jeff asked.

"Stands for police department."

"Oh." Jeff winked at Sharon across the table.

"I'm sure it wasn't Mr. Cosman," Sharon said. "Doreen, would you like to continue working at Trail's End?"

"Only thing is, I can't work at night. And I can't work when I'd be alone at that place."

"We wouldn't expect you to work at night. And I'll usually be there," Sharon said. "We'll be moving in there."

Her eyes widened. "Oh no, Miss Sullivan, I wouldn't do that."

On the way back their room, Sharon said, "She is one nervous little lady. She's stolen things from Trail's End, accuses Cos of being a fortune hunter…."

"And you hired her? You actually hired her?"

"In kind of a weird way, I feel sorry for her."

EIGHTEEN

Katie's first year of school was spent in the one-room school-house located in the center of Beach Haven's downtown. That year, 1919, the Sullivan family, which included Gerard, Pearl, and their two daughters, eight-year-old Hilda and seven-year-old Katie, lived in Trail's End over the winter. Gerard was ill this year with some sort of a lung ailment, and it was thought by his doctors that the ocean breezes would be healing.

When I was a child, Katie told me about the year their father stayed home. We were out walking, and she said, "Did I ever tell you about The Year Our Father Stayed Home?" That was the way she said it, too, as if it were the title of a chapter in a book.

"None of us wanted him home, least of all your grand-mother. Men just weren't to be underfoot in those days," she told me.

I try to imagine my grandfather, sitting in the chair by the fireplace, a blanket on his knees, crankily barking out orders, or upstairs in his bed, incessantly ringing the bell that later they would use to summon Doreen.

That year was especially hard on Pearl, who by this time had suffered numerous miscarriages. Katie once told me that if all her children had lived, there would have had been nine in all. Three babies, alone, were miscarried between Katie and the "supposed" birth of Little Mary. [Sharon paused in the writing of this, twirled the pen in her fingers.]

All this to say that Katie, who I am really writing about, began her formal schooling in the one-room schoolhouse in Beach Haven. Katie told me all of this on our walk. She and I often walked, and it's on these walks that I learned bits and pieces of the lives of the members of the Sullivan family. Gossip, true stories, fictions, I didn't care. It was all fascinating to me.

Instead of our usual walk down the path to the beach, we were going down the wide street toward town. The school-house was at the end of a wide overgrown driveway. Across the street from it was a small chapel, also overgrown. The school-house stood, disused and run down, its windows broken, white paint peeling.

"This was my school," Katie said. "Hobos sleep here now. Let's go inside."

I kept close to her side as we pushed through the door. I was not entirely sure what a hobo was, but had a feeling it might be related to a troll. We made our way slowly over bits and pieces of old boards and broken glass, nails, and crumpled papers.

The inside was damp and dark and all kinds of insects lived there. There were no desks, no chairs, nothing to indicate that it had once been a school, except for two framed pictures on the wall.

"Still those pictures," said Katie and pointed. "George Washington and Abraham Lincoln. The fathers of our country. Brothers. And the map of the world."

"They weren't brothers." Even I knew that.

I followed her, our feet making crunching noises on the debris.

"This is where I learned my ABCs. One year. One year was all I went here. The Year Our Father Stayed Home."

"Who was your teacher?"

"Miss Bloomsberry, but we called her Miss Bloomers. Oh, we were such naughty children. I was the worst."

"Where are the desks?"

"Gone."

"Where are the hobos?"

"They saw us coming and ran. They might be hiding out near the outhouse." She stood still, her hands on her hips, and looked around her. "Look at that map of the world hanging there. Totally wrong now, all the countries different now. Everything is different."

I am only guessing, but I believe this may have been where the lifelong rivalry between the two sisters began. By the time she was twelve, Hilda had dropped out of school to help with Gerard, who was still recuperating, and her mother, who was pregnant yet again. Katie continued to attend. She would become the creative one while Hilda would be the manager.

This morning I visited the little schoolhouse. It is no longer a falling-down building where the homeless spend the night; it has been completely restored and now houses the Beach Haven Historical Society's Maritime Collection. I walked up the brightly painted steps, remembering the time when Katie held my hand and shown me the ripped and graying pictures of the fathers of our country. There was no sign of them on the far wall now. A white-haired woman in a skirt and sweater insisted I sign the guest book and told me to feel free to look around. I was the only one in the place. My reason for coming was two-fold. First, I wanted to remember the dimensions of Katie's first schoolhouse for the memoirs, and second, Trail's End may be loaded with items that I might wish to donate.

The walls were lined with black-and-white photos of sea captains and their vessels, snapshots of Beach Haven in an earlier era. Glassed display cases were filled with navigational implements, an antique sextant someone had donated, and an old navigational chart of the area, sea monsters around the edges. The far corner was devoted to school mementos. It is there that I went. I craned my eye for a glimpse of Katie or Hilda or the school mistress, Miss Bloomsberry, in the press of children in the browned photos that hung on the wall. They might have been there. I couldn't distinguish.

The woman in the pleated skirt came over and asked me if there was something she could help me with. "My aunts went to this school," I said. "A long time ago."

Sharon put down her pen and massaged her wrist. The only other person in the coffee shop where she sat writing was a woman about her age who was reading what looked like a thick text. It was drizzling outside, and the coffee tasted good. Earlier that morning Roman Hobbs had phoned to say that someone else had come forward claiming to be Dean Sullivan. He was promising to "keep them abreast of the progress in this investigation."

"Would you like any more coffee?" A young man behind the counter held up a coffee pot. "Just brewed a fresh pot."

"No thanks," said Sharon rising. "I've got to be heading back."

The walk back to the motel took twenty minutes. When she opened the door, the phone was ringing. She raced inside to answer it.

"Sharon? Sharon Colebrook?" It was a woman's voice.

"Speaking."

"Hi, Sharon, this is a voice from your past. Diane Petrescu. Do you remember me? I used to be Diane Smith a long time ago. My father told me you were in the area, and since we never seem to be in the same place at the same time, I thought to myself, I must call Sharon Sullivan."

"Hi, Diane." She pushed back her hair.

"The first thing I have to say is how proud we are of you. Both Ron and I just adore your books! I tell everyone, I used to be friends with her. Can you imagine? My mom loves your mysteries, too." She chuckled. "But I have to admit I haven't been able to get my dad to read any. If it doesn't flicker on a screen in front of him and you can't change it with a remote, he's just not interested."

Sharon stared out the window. "It's nice to hear from you."

"We're in Portland for the summer and probably into the fall. Our son Matthew is headed for his first year of college, and we have to get him settled in before we head back to Taiwan. We may not go back until the spring. Anyway, I was telling Ron that I'd love to see you and your husband, and he suggested we invite the two of you up for a meal. How does Saturday sound to you?"

Sharon put her hand to her forehead. Saturday was in two days. "I'm not sure we'll still be here then. As soon as the business is taken care of, we'll be leaving."

"Oh, yes, I forgot. Maybe earlier then?"

"I just don't know. We're planning to move into Trail's End tomorrow."

"Trail's End. I remember that place. I remember once we even had a Sunday school picnic there."

"I don't remember that."

"Oh, you must, Sharon, you *must*. We were all around eleven or twelve. And your aunts were there, along with your grandmother. And Pastor Harley, bless his dear little soul, trying to bring order to the confusion. But I think the commotion of all the kids running through was too much for your aunts. I don't remember us ever going back. Ever even being *invited* back. Your Aunt Hilda kept pressing her forehead with a white handkerchief and saying, 'Oh dear, oh dear.'"

Despite herself, Sharon laughed. "Sounds like Hilda. Both of my aunts concurred with W. C. Fields on that one: 'Anyone who hates children and dogs can't be all bad.' What ever happened to Pastor Harley, anyway?"

"Oh, he went to be with the Lord a long time ago now. Can't even remember. Ron and I may have already been in Taiwan for our first term. He lived for a long time in a nursing home, from what I understand. Had that disease they call Lou Gehrig's disease."

"I didn't know that."

"But I imagine he kept that hair of his right up until the end."

Sharon burst out laughing. "His hair."

"The ultimate in combovers. So, can you make it on Saturday?"

"Sure. Sure, we can. Yes. That would be nice."

By the time Sharon got directions and hung up, Jeff was walking in the door, all smiles, waving papers.

NINETEEN

"WHAT YOU WERE TOLD IS RIGHT. She did die of pneumonia. I checked with Portland city records, who phoned Augusta, who faxed a copy of the death certificate, and I got a photocopy." He removed it from a manila envelope and handed it to Sharon.

She read: Mary Anne Sullivan, born, February 17, 1923, died March 18, 1940. The cause of death—pneumonia—was scrawled on the line, barely legible. The certificate also included the name of the attending physician. A Dr. George Peter Koch, Portland, Maine.

"Furthermore," Jeff said, "I looked up the name George Peter Koch in their registry. The good doctor Koch died in 1941. So, it turns out that Little Mary did exist and did die of pneumonia, just like you said. But," he shifted his weight from foot to foot, "it gets a bit curiouser. Dr. Koch was not the coroner for the city of Portland. He was the private physician for the Sullivan family."

"Is that so odd? To have a family doctor sign the certificate?"

"Well, it wouldn't be so odd if George Koch was listed anywhere as a doctor."

"So, he might not have been a doctor, is that what you're saying?"

"I don't know what I'm saying. I just think this whole thing deserves a bit more checking. Plus, the place of burial still remains a mystery."

Sharon smiled up at him, "I do believe you are enjoying this, Mr. Newspaperman."

He sat down and spread his hands on the desk and grinned. "Yeah, I guess. It's like the old days, when I actually got out there and did some investigative reporting, not sitting behind a desk putting out fires, talking to reporters about misquoting the mayor, or the way my new, young reporters feel that the story should fall into their laps without any legwork. Sometimes what is needed to get a story is nothing but old-fashioned legwork. I don't think they teach that in journalism school. That sometimes you just got to get out there. So what've you been up to?"

"Gathering some of our stuff together so we can move over to Trail's End, writing down some Katie memories, and—oh, and guess where we're going for supper on Saturday."

"I give up."

"Diane and Ron Petrescu's."

"Who are Diane and Ron Petrescu?"

"Diane is Fred Smith's daughter. Home from Taiwan. She called and invited us, and I said yes."

He squinted at her. "I thought you wouldn't go over there in your dreams."

"She was so friendly over the phone."

He grinned his crooked grin. "That's just a ploy by these religious people."

"Well."

"So, tell me, what was this friend of yours like?"

"She wasn't exactly a close friend of mine. She was more Dean's friend. She and Dean were a year younger than me. But she was beautiful."

He raised his eyebrows.

"You have to promise to keep your eyes off her. Back in high school Diane was one of those beautiful girls that we all wished we looked like. She had these cheerleader looks with this long, straight blond hair. The kind of hair everybody wanted back then."

"Oh, I bet she wasn't as pretty as you."

Sharon snorted. "You didn't know me then. I had this straight, thin brown hair and my ears used to stick out of it at the sides. And I had to wear these thick glasses back then. I was definitely the studious one, and she was this outgoing, popular cheerleader."

"You know I have eyes only for you," he said, getting down on one knee.

TWENTY

RUSS CUTCHEON, HIS ARMS FOLDED across his chest, scowling, warned them that Trail's End would be cold, damp, and unfit for human habitation.

"My aunts lived there summer and winter," Sharon said. "It's fully winterized."

"The place needs work now, though." He grabbed the MasterCard out of Jeff's hand, jammed it into an old-fashioned credit card machine, and scraped it roughly across the slip. "Just don't come to me later saying I didn't warn you fellas."

"We'll be fine," said Jeff, attempting a smile. Russ thrust the flimsy piece of paper forward for Jeff to sign.

Sharon said, "We'll be sure to come back for some of your wonderful coffee and those pies."

He shook his head. "Sorry, the café is only for paying guests."

Sharon looked at Jeff and raised her eyebrows.

"Just don't say I didn't warn you."

"The furnace works fine," said Jeff, smiling. "My wife and I thank you for your concern."

"It's not concern I'm talking about," Mr. Cutcheon said under his breath. "I don't want to be telling tales about that place."

"What tales?" Sharon asked.

"About what people are saying about it."

"What are people saying about it?"

"I can't say now, I can't say."

"Fine, then," Jeff said. "If you can't say, we'll be on our way."

"He was sure strange," Sharon said in the car on the way out. "It's like he took it personally, our leaving."

"Lost revenue, my dear."

"It seemed more than merely lost revenue, and it's not like we didn't give him notice." Sharon settled back into her seat. "Well I, for one, will be glad to get into our own place."

It was raining when they arrived at Trail's End and began unpacking. Upstairs, they made the double bed with the sheets and blankets they washed earlier at the Laundromat. Despite the smallness of the bed—and Jeff's loud complaints that he would have to look for a queen-size the next day, the very next day—both fell immediately to sleep.

A few hours later Sharon awoke to a far-off tinkling sound. A bell buoy out on the ocean? A ship's bell? She could hear the pattering of rain through the window they had left open a crack. Fully awake now, she turned onto her back and listened.

It was the music box. She was sure of it, the tinny tune she remembered from childhood. She could almost see it, the pink ballerina going round and round.

The sound faded. Gone. It was her imagination. It was a bell buoy far out in the channel, a warning to sailors. That was all.

When Sharon awoke the second time, gray light was filtering in around the edges of the window shade, which was flapping against the window. Jeff was gone. Jogging along the beach in the rain, she supposed. She hadn't heard him get up.

She grabbed her robe and headed downstairs. He had made a pot of coffee, and she helped herself to a mugful. She took it into the parlor. Above the mantel the ballerina looked much the same. Had it been moved? She couldn't tell. She touched the edge of it with one finger. It tinkled slightly and she backed away. The chime clock was still stopped at 4:15.

Out on the sunporch she grabbed a blanket from the daybed and wrapped herself in it. Through a tear in the plastic she could see the gray sea. She looked up and down the beach but couldn't see Jeff. She loved the smell of him when he came in from his morning jogs, legs glistening with sweat, his long fingers combing through his sweat-damp hair. He always backed away, laughing, "Oh, you don't want to hug me now, I'm wet with sweat." But it wasn't merely the smell of him she adored, it was his energy, his smile. He smiled all the time.

She didn't see him, so she contented herself by looking out at the line where the sea met the sky. The sun would soon rise. She waited for it.

"I get up before the sun," Katie had told her once. It had been a warm afternoon when the two of them sat in this sunporch, the plastic removed, the windows wide open. In front of them children chased a kite across the sand. Sharon pressed a glass of iced tea against her knee.

"But I have not yet seen the light. To be able to see it, that is a gift given to only a few."

"What light?"

"I will see it one day. Of that I can be guaranteed." The old woman smiled then, and Sharon could see beyond the wrinkles, the deep clefts of aged skin, the wisps of hair, the arthritic fingers, knuckles twice their size, and saw there the delighted child, bright with discovery. "The Amadon Light," Katie said. "I will see it one day." She bent her head. Sharon could see her pink scalp behind the tufts of hair. "There is a small green flash when the sun sets. Did you know that? That is commonly seen. But," her eyes flashed, "the early morning flash is rarely seen." She pointed a bent finger toward the sea. "That is the Amadon Light."

The day was whitening, the ocean now light and frothy like boiled-over milk. Sharon liked it here. She could understand why her aunt stayed all these years.

Now, sitting wrapped in blankets, she waited for Jeff. Bookshelves loaded with *National Geographic*s and *Reader's Digest*s lined the walls underneath the windows. On the top lay a few paperbacks, contemporary mysteries and horror. Sharon leafed through a few she hadn't read. At the far end of the shelf was a soft, blue leather book. She got up, reached for it, and was surprised to see that it was a Bible. She took it back to the daybed and sat with it on her lap.

Back in Young People's they had to read the Bible for points. At the end of every week, they filled out a sheet of paper on how many days they had had a "quiet time," what verses they had read, how many minutes they had spent in prayer, and how many people they had witnessed to. It was an honor system, the pastor explained. "Only between you and God." But they were cautioned not to lie to the Holy Spirit, warned by the story of Ananias and Sapphira who fell dead, right there on the very spot, because they had lied about this very thing, Pastor Harley said. This very thing.

She opened the front cover of the Bible that now lay on her lap.

Beloved Katie,
I cherish our time together, and we shall be together always in God's kingdom.
Cos, 1990

Flipping through, she saw her aunt had underlined passage after passage, and had penciled little notes in the margins in her tight, tiny script. Sharon turned to the first chapter of Genesis and read through the account of creation, while ahead of her the ocean surged against the cold sands.

"And God said, 'Let the water teem with living creatures, and let birds fly above the earth across the expanse of the sky.' So God created the great creatures of the sea and every living and moving thing with which the water teems...."

"What's this blasted thing doing in here!" It was Jeff's voice booming from the back hall.

Sharon placed the Bible back on the bookshelf and walked down the hall toward the kitchen. Ahead of her, in his jogging trunks and tee-shirt, Jeff was holding Mildred out in front of him.

"Where'd she come from?" Sharon asked.

"That's what I'd like to know. I come in from the outside, I go into the downstairs bathroom to grab a towel, and there she is, standing in the shower. Thought it was you at first. Scared me half to death.

That day we found her on the sunporch, I wrapped her up in a tarp and put her under the house. And you didn't put her here? As a joke or anything?"

Sharon shook her head. "No, I would never do that. Jeff, last night I woke up and thought I heard the music box. I thought I was just imagining things, so I went back to sleep."

He walked into the parlor and she followed. He grabbed the music box, wound it up, and placed it back on the mantel. The ballerina danced around.

"Is this the tune you heard?"

"Yes." Sharon suddenly felt ice cold.

"I'm calling the police."

TWENTY-ONE

THE POLICE CAME AND WALKED through the place and said one word: kids.

"When we arrived," Jeff said, "this mannequin was on the sunporch leaning up against the wall. And it looked as though the desk in the dining room had been gone through."

"Was anything taken?" asked a female officer, a tiny woman with very short hair.

"We don't know."

"Why didn't you call us then?" asked the other officer, a young burly man who looked like a bodybuilder.

"We thought maybe it was the cleaning lady who put Mildred there and that maybe she had gone through the papers for some reason," Sharon said.

"Whole lot of these summer places get broken into. It's something we deal with every single spring."

"This one wasn't a summer home. It was inhabited until a few months ago, when the owner passed away."

The officer was scratching his neck. "This is a prank. Kids, pure and simple. Finding and dressing up an old mannequin—where they found her is beyond me—dressing her up and setting her in the parlor. Classic."

"The mannequin belonged here," Sharon said.

"You owned it?"

"It was used as a scarecrow. Will you be taking fingerprints?"

"Don't need to. We know who these kids are, and if it'll make you folks feel any better, I'll bring them in myself and read the riot act to them. Now, if you find anything missing, well, that's a different kettle of fish altogether. Then we're dealing with theft. This, this is kid's stuff. Especially since they never took that portable computer of yours, which was sitting right there in full view."

And that was it. They left. Jeff went to take his shower at long last, and Sharon walked over to the stove and poured herself more coffee.

Once in Victoria, she and Jeff had been broken into. Some jewelry, plus their VCR and stereo, were taken. She knew well that feeling of violation. This wasn't that. This was something else. Something she couldn't explain. It wasn't exactly fear, although there was some of that. Apprehension? She shook her head. Dread? It was all of those things in small measure, plus the sound of the music box in the middle of the night, the face in the window, Mildred showing up at will, Doreen's nervousness, Russ's veiled warnings.

She turned on the radio and filled the sink with hot sudsy water. Into the garbage went the sponge that was in the sink, along with a fuzzy pink scrubber stuck to the counter behind the sink. From the drawer beside the stove she grabbed a clean washcloth and began unloading the dishes from the cupboards. The Sullivan women were small, like she was, and one of those little kitchen step stools was underneath the table. Sharon made good use of it to reach the top shelves of the cupboard. This was the kitchen she remembered, with its faded linoleum on the floor and Hilda making bread, ten loaves at a time, her hands working the dough in harsh rhythm.

I can see clearly now the rain is gone. Sharon hummed along with the radio. Six songs in a row about rain. Well, that seemed appropriate. She threw out tiny smeared bottles of spices, chocolate chips so old they were completely white, and a loaf of plastic-wrapped bread, blue and greasy with mold. She held it by its edge and dropped it into a garbage bag.

Hours passed in this way, contented hours, she in the kitchen, Jeff on the computer. This was good, safe work. This was daylight. She could understand Doreen's fear of this place at night. She washed the old white dishes with the red flowers. She washed the newer set of green and white Corelle. She washed the wheat-colored stoneware. In the dining room were the good dishes that were taken out on Sundays when Pastor Harley and his small, round wife and their huge brood of stair-step children came for dinner. Even though she didn't admit it, the children made Hilda nervous. Children should be seen and not heard, Hilda would say after they left. For a long time Sharon thought that phrase was one Hilda made up herself.

The kitchen finished, Sharon turned her energies to the papers in the dining room. Jeff was on the phone talking to one of his editors in Victoria. He had shoved all of the papers aside, and Sharon scooped them up and began going through them. Mostly they were bills: power bills, bank statements, a bill from a local grocery store, along with grocery receipts. It looked as though Katie ordered her groceries and had them delivered by this little corner grocery. An overdue reminder from *Ellery Queen* magazine. And files and files of income tax receipts and papers.

A church bulletin cover caught her eye, and she picked it up. It was the bulletin for Katie's funeral, held at the white chapel across from the school. She opened it and read. Names of pallbearers she didn't know. Hymn titles, "A Mighty Fortress," "Amazing Grace," "Fairest Lord Jesus." She turned it over and read the old shoes poem that was on the back of Katie's picture at Cos's house.

"Look Jeff. This poem."

He had hung up the phone. "What about it?"

"This was on the back of Katie's picture at Cos's house."

"Who wrote it?"

"It says anonymous."

"Good old anonymous. He or she writes a lot of poems." Jeff yawned. "I think we should get the locks changed. Maybe I'll head into Portland and check that out. You want to come?"

"I think I'll stay," she said, placing the bulletin on the table. "I'm on a roll here with this cleaning."

"I can see that."

"I want to get those upstairs bedrooms cleaned."

"What are you going to have Doreen do? I mean, you did hire the lady."

"I'm thinking of the little room off the kitchen, the one that was hers. It's piled high with junk. A lot of it would be hers, I think, anyway."

An hour later, Jeff was still gone. Papers Sharon had retrieved from a very damp box in the closet were spread out to dry on the pink chenille bedspread on the bed in the upstairs back bedroom. There was a leak in the ceiling above the closet, and a slithery liquid snake was worming its way down the back wall. Sharon was reluctant to throw anything out without thoroughly examining it. Also in the box were the black-and-white photographs, still in their frames, that had hung on the stairwell wall: Gerard and Pearl and their two daughters; their two daughters; a family photo with Gerard, Pearl, their two daughters, grown now, and her father, baby Mack, on Pearl's lap. None of Little Mary.

Jeff had been gone maybe an hour and a half when Sharon heard the noises. She sat still on the bed, a mildewed school scribbler in her hands. A fluttering sound, footsteps downstairs. Jeff? But he wasn't back yet. The driveway was empty. Just the rain, she thought. The rain on this crazy place.

A soft footfall on the floor below. *Mildred walks the place at night, you know. Mildred must have gotten there of her own accord.* Sharon couldn't move.

Soft footfalls on the stairs? A voice calling? *Last night a troll came right up the stairs, one at a time.*

She was sitting on the bed staring at the opened door. She waited, watched, unable to move. More sounds of footsteps. Not Jeff's. She recognized his. Finally, around the corner, a woman peered in at her. She was a tall, very thin young woman with straight black hair that fell to her shoulders, a small brown bowler cap on her head. She had pale skin and wore blue-black lipstick. It was no one she recognized.

"Mom?"

Sharon dropped the binder. "Natasha?"

"Hi, Mom. I was calling and calling, didn't think anyone was in here."

"Natasha?" She said it quieter this time.

"At the motel they told me you and dad were here, so I took a cab over. Boy, that motel guy was strange. Didn't want to tell me where you guys were. Quit looking at me like that."

"Your hair."

"Hi to you, too. I'm fine, Mother, thanks for asking."

"Well, it's such a radical change. Of course it was the first thing I'd see. I didn't even recognize you."

"Let's just say I got tired of being called carrottop."

"But black, Tash? And so straight." Sharon got up and walked toward her.

"I had to shed my Anne of Green Gables look."

"Your face. It's so white."

"Do you like this makeup? I got it in England. It's supposed to get rid of freckles. Well, make them lighter anyway."

"It's made your whole face lighter. It's so white."

"Is it really awful? Do you absolutely hate it?"

"Oh Tash, I'm sorry. Come here, let me hug you. Just so much has been going on. Strange things. We've had two break-ins in this place, and strange noises at night. And then you show up looking like a ghost, and it's been so long since we've seen you. And the police were here earlier. Everything's a little on edge."

Natasha was taller than her mother, and when she hugged her, Sharon could feel her daughter's tiny waist, the bony feel of her shoulders. Sharon backed away, held her daughter at arm's length.

"You came home! You're actually here!"

"Yeah."

"The last postcard said that you and Jordan were going to stay and work in Ireland."

Natasha looked away. "Slight change of plans, shall we say."

"Is everything all right?"

"Not really. Can I stay here? Can I stay here with you?"

"Of course, Tash. Of course. Where's Jordan? He with you?"

"I have absolutely no idea where Jordan is, nor do I particularly care." She was looking at her fingernails, which were painted a dark shade of blue.

"How did you know we were in Maine?"

"I called home about a hundred times from Ireland, and finally I clued in, so I called your friend Carolyn Borthwick. She told me where you guys were. She even knew the motel. So I decided to fly over here instead of home, so I get to the motel and find you've left and are here." She took off the little bowler cap and spun it in her fingers.

"Oh, Dad will be so pleased that you're here. You can stay in this bedroom if you want. I'm just in the process of cleaning it."

"This room smells."

"The smell is these papers. There's a leak in the roof above the closet."

"Can I sleep on the sunporch?"

"If you want. But it's awfully cold down there and there are no curtains on any of those big windows."

"I think I would like it there."

"Do you have much stuff?"

"Not really. Just my backpack. And a small bag."

"Natasha?" She looked at her very thin daughter. "Are you okay?"

"You mean apart from jet lag and no job, fine, just fine."

"Are you giving some thought to school now?"

"School, Mother? I'm not in the house five minutes and you're nagging me about school?"

TWENTY-TWO

NATASHA MADE FISTS OF HER HANDS, clenching and unclenching them, until she could feel her blue fingernails digging in to her palms. Coming home. Maybe not such a good idea. Too many questions, too many things she just didn't want to talk about. She hadn't told her mother—she couldn't—that she had seen Jordan with that Irish girl one too many times, until finally, she had given him the ultimatum: me or her. So he'd said in that little way of his, "I think we should start seeing other people."

That's when she had started phoning home. Where else could she go? Well, she supposed there were places. Long-ago girlfriends from Vic High she could look up, crash at their places for a week or two until she got her feet underneath her again. It felt so strange not to be with Jordan; the two had been together for three years. Lots of people aren't even married that long. To do things without Jordan, not to ask his advice on things, not to have him make those little jokes he always did.

And now her mother's first question was school. Well, what did she expect? Her mother even used to bug Jordan about it. "So, Jordan, given any thought to your future?" Translated: "When are you going to quit lazing around?"

It was raining against the window of the sunporch as she unpacked her belongings. Thing was, she knew plenty of people who had spent their wad and more on an education, come out with these majorly enormous student loans, and then were working at McDonald's or Wendy's. And look at her. She didn't have some huge student loan, just a few thou on MasterCard, and a few more on Visa. That was nothing compared to some people she knew. And she bet she could walk into any McDonald's in the country and get a job. Without a college degree, Mother.

She caught a reflection of herself in the window. She had to admit she was still stopped by her black hair. The hairdresser in London had run her fingers through Natasha's thick mane of red hair and said, "You sure you want to do this, dearie?"

"Yes."

"It's a bit severe, lovey."

"I don't care. It's what I want."

She was leaving Jordan. He was in Ireland with little Laureena, and here she was in London getting a whole new look. Already it was growing out a bit, and the hair coming in along the roots was spirally and strawberry. She figured she could do it at home now, touch up the roots with a box of hair coloring. That wouldn't take much doing, and when it got too curly again, she'd buy one of those home straighteners. It had cost a fortune in London to get it done, and she'd put it on her Visa. After her hair was done, she had stopped at a cosmetic counter and purchased the pale makeup, guaranteed to gradually remove freckles.

In a corner of the sunporch she piled her dirty clothes. Her mother said they didn't have a washer and dryer here. She'd have to hitch a ride to town to get them clean. If she still had her bicycle she could ride into town, but she'd sold it in Ireland to buy a plane ticket home.

Tonight her parents were driving up to Portland to have dinner with some old school friends of her mom. "If we'd known you were coming…"

"That's all right."

"Do you want to come along?" Her mother said, her brow furrowed.

"No thanks. I've got a major case of jet lag. I'm going to crash as soon as I'm unpacked."

"I'll call Diane. I'm sure if she heard you were in town, she'd insist that you come."

"Who is this Diane person anyway?"

"An old school friend. From Portland."

She pushed her hair out of her face and tucked it up under a flowered denim cap. She could glimpse the ocean clearly through a rip in the plastic. It was comforting in an odd sort of way, to be so close to the elements, yet safe and inside at the same time.

"People go by here regularly," her mother told her earlier. "Joggers and beachcombers. I don't think you'll want to sleep here, Natasha."

"I don't care."

Jordan was a beachcomber. He'd walk for hours dragging her along the Irish beaches kicking at stones, picking up odd bits of things, strange shaped rocks and shells. She pressed her fists into her eyes to try to erase the images of him. It wasn't supposed to hurt like this. It wasn't supposed to make her whole body start shaking and her throat close up. It wasn't supposed to make it so she couldn't eat, that every little thing she tried to swallow stuck in her throat like wadded-up chewing gum. She was supposed to move on. That's what the lady at the salon in London had told her.

"You're young and beautiful, love. You'll find someone else straightaway."

At the bottom of her backpack were her birth control pills. She threw the little blue plastic container against the far wall. The case cracked open and the tiny pink pills spattered over the floor, sounding like little pellets of sleet. She wouldn't be needing those things anymore. Stupid, stupid Jordan! How could you be so stupid? She was choking back sobs, and her mother chose this moment to walk in.

"Well, sunshine, you haven't had a nap yet."

Natasha spun around. Her mother was carrying what looked like an armload of papers.

"Are you all right, Tash?"

"Yeah, Mom, caught some bug in England, I think. Makes me get into these coughing fits."

"There's Kleenex on the table over there. Do you want to see a doctor?"

"No, I'm fine. Does the shower in the downstairs bathroom work?"

"Works fine. There's one upstairs, too. Take your pick."

"Is there any tea?"

"There's coffee and even some hot chocolate, I think. Come with me to the kitchen, I'll show you where things are."

Natasha surveyed her pile of dirty laundry. "Can I use the car to drive into Beach Haven and do this laundry? There a Laundromat there?"

"Dad's out with the car, but I'm sure we can work something out. Are you sure you're okay?"

"I'm fine, Mom. I just have to blow my nose all the time with this cold."

"Would you like something to eat? I could fix you a sandwich."

"Not hungry."

"You're so thin, Tash."

"I told you, I'm not hungry. I couldn't eat a bite, even if I tried. I'm just going to have a shower and maybe a cup of tea, and then I'm going to go to bed."

"Well, okay then." Her mother looked at her tentatively. "I'll be in the dining room working through your Great-aunt Katie's stuff if you need me."

"I remember her. She was an old, old lady who sat in a chair, right?"

TWENTY-THREE

NATASHA WAS HERE. Sharon was still trying to get her mind around the fact that the daughter she hadn't seen in almost two years showed up all of a sudden with dyed hair. The last time she had seen her daughter it was to watch her and Jordan race across the tarmac to catch the plane on their grand adventure. Jeff was not back yet. Would he be surprised!

On the bed were hangers full of clothes, old things of Grandma Pearl's, short, wide dresses of flimsy material that fit her squat body. Sharon pulled out a brown square wool coat with a nubby fake fur collar. Grandma Pearl again.

Natasha hadn't talked much, and Sharon decided it was jet lag and exhaustion. She had followed Natasha onto the sunporch, telling her where the sheets and towels were, offering to make her lunch, asking about her flight, about the food on her flight. Did you have enough to eat? Was there much turbulence? But not asking about Jordan, not taking her into her motherly arms and stroking her hair and saying, It's okay. Tell me, I'll try to understand. Nothing like that. She and Natasha talked around the surfaces of things. Sharon had pestered her with little questions until Natasha turned to her and said, "Mom, I'm like totally wiped."

Okay, maybe that was it.

The closet emptied, Sharon tackled it with a wet, sudsy rag. She had taken some of the more threadbare towels and torn them into cleaning rags. The bed and floor were strewn with hat boxes, pieces of luggage, and boxes of jigsaw puzzles, their corners held together with yellowing adhesive tape. Sharon opened an old train case. It was filled with bits and pieces of jewelry, clip-on earrings, another brooch that Grandma Pearl had worn, more hat pins, pieces of lace, and loose pearls. Sharon dug through with her fingers. Junk. Still, Natasha might have fun going through this stuff. When she was young, she used to love to play dress up with Sharon's jewelry and shoes. She gathered these things, plus the musty papers she was trying to dry, and carried them downstairs.

On the dining room table, Sharon picked through the papers. Most of them were stiff with age and many clung together. Sharon had already ripped a few of the pages trying to separate them. She picked up a black school scribbler and opened it at the beginning. Across the top of the first page was Katheryn Sullivan, June 4, 1927. Sharon read:

> *Opera. An Opera is a musical where the parts are sung. There are two forms of opera. Grand Opera where there is no speech, and Light Opera where parts are both sung and spoken.*

School notes. Kept high in a box in Katie's childhood bedroom. Sharon continued reading:

> *German Opera's greatest composer was Richard Wagner 1813–1883. Characteristics of a Wagner Opera...*

Sharon did a quick calculation. Katie would have been fifteen when she wrote this.

> *II. The Symphony orchestra*
>   *A. Founded*
>   *1. Vienna, Austria*
>   *2. Early in 18th century*
>   *3. Franz Joseph Haydn*
>   *B. Four sections or choirs...*

And on and on Sharon read about the orchestra, the opera, the difference between light opera and grand opera; German opera, Italian opera. Near the end was a long list of names: Rachel Anna, Jane Alexandria, Sarah Marie… Were these real people Katie knew or lists of favorite names? When Sharon was a girl, she made lists of names she wished her parents had named her instead of Sharon: Angela, Melinda, Celia, Heather. She placed this scribbler on the rolltop desk. She might find some use for it in her Katie book.

Sharon also riffled through school reports. One from Portland Grammar School, dated June 1922, read:

Katheryn will be promoted to Sixth Grade. It will be necessary for her to work very hard next term if she wishes to keep up with her sums and tables. Katheryn will also have to pay more attention to her work in this regard and less attention to day-dreaming.
   Helen Polk, teacher

An old, old lady who sat in a chair. That's how Natasha had described Katie, yet here she was entering sixth grade and needing to pay more attention to her sums, a storyteller and a dreamer who even then caught up her skirt in her hands and ran across the beach.

Maybe that's what we all become eventually, Sharon thought, old people who sit in chairs. We who have lived full lives—loved and done things and written stories and rocked children on our laps and traveled—we all end up being described by our youngers as Old People Who Sit in Chairs.

The other pieces of paper in the box were mostly old grocery receipts, lists of names, and bills. At the bottom she found a guest book for Trail's End, a faded pink book which began in 1930. She read through a few of the names at the beginning, but none were familiar. The guest book ended in 1959. Sharon put it on top of the black scribbler. She heard the car and went to the door.

"You are not going to believe this!" Jeff said before she could speak. "George Peter Koch was not a doctor."

"I have news, too, Jeff…"

"Let me go first, this is just so amazing. I found out that the one who signed the death certificate for your Aunt Mary was not a doctor." Jeff was waving papers. "He was a druggist."

"And that's making you smile?"

"It shows there were some definite shenanigans going on back then."

"Maybe a pharmacist is allowed to sign a death certificate."

"Not a chance. Plus he signed it 'doctor.'"

"Maybe he was a doctor."

"Wrong again. I visited his daughter."

"You did?"

"She's in a nursing home. Fairly coherent but very excitable. The nurses were concerned that I not get her agitated. So I don't know how much of what was said was true, but she seemed to be coherent. Her name is Marina Makepeace. She's seventy-seven, about the same age Little Mary would have been. They were school friends. 'Chums' was her word. They also went to the same church. Your grandfather practically ran that church. That's the impression I got from Marina. That Gerard would snap his fingers and everyone, including the minister, would come to attention. I don't think Marina particularly liked Gerard. She kept going on about how she wasn't allowed to visit Little Mary when she was sick. I think she may have tried to visit her friend, because she kept going on about Pearl, how Pearl would stop her at the door. She kept saying, 'She stopped me at the door, right at the door. May God have mercy on her soul.' I don't know whose soul she was referring to, Pearl's or Little Mary's. I think I want to look into this some more. So many of the people who knew anything are dead. That's the part that makes it tough. Oh, and I also stopped by to see your dad. He wasn't there so I went to that restaurant he goes to. I wanted to see if the name George Peter Koch meant anything."

"Hi, Dad." Natasha stood in the doorway. "Could I have the car to go do some laundry?"

He spun around. "Natasha!"

"That's what I wanted to tell you," Sharon said meekly. "Natasha is home."

He was staring at her.

"I know I look different, but it's me. Plain old me."

He enveloped her in a hug. "It is so great to see you! Man, so great! Jordan here, too?"

"Nope."

"We've got to sit down and talk. You've got to tell us about your travels."

The three of them moved into the kitchen. Natasha told them all about Europe, about traveling through Ireland, about the castles they visited, about the music they heard, about kissing the Blarney Stone, about the little Irish pubs where people sat around, whole families of them, out for Friday evenings. And the music and the dancing. She told them about renting bicycles and touring the countryside, then about purchasing their own bikes. "It was so much cheaper," she said.

She told them about working, how they would do odd jobs for people, working for a shepherd at one place, and then in a little craft store. And about moving on and meeting people, about the pubs in the big city and the night life.

"It's a very beautiful place," Natasha said. "And I love the ocean and the hillsides."

"You would have fit right in with your red hair."

She ran her fingers through her hair. "Yeah. It was red then."

"And you know you have Irish blood in you. Your grandmother was Irish," Sharon said.

"Yeah."

"It sounds nice," said Jeff, leaning back, his hands behind his head. "I take it you want to go back."

"I never want to go back." Natasha stood up. "Can I borrow the car to do my laundry?"

"Sure. I'll give you some of ours, if you don't mind," Sharon said. "Some sheets and towels from the cupboards. But we need the car back by about six. Dad and I are going in to Portland then."

TWENTY-FOUR

WHAT WAS ALL THE SUDDEN INTEREST in Little Mary? Mack wondered. Why was Sharon's husband suddenly so interested in figuring this out? Jeff had found him in his corner booth at Mona's. When Jeff had walked in, Mona was sitting across from him, wiping her hands on her apron and telling him about one of her grandchildren.

"She comes to me. She says to me, Nana, I need a job. So I say, all right, Amanda, but you have to work hard, this is hard work. Kids these days, they don't know what hard work is, ah?" And Mack had nodded in a halfhearted way. "So, Mandy, she comes to me halfway through her shift, says, 'Nana, my feet hurt, I need to sit down. I need to rub my feet. Nana, my head hurts. Nana, I'm tired.' I say to her, 'Mandy, I'm on my feet all day from five-thirty. I'm seventy-three years old. Do you see me sitting down?' No. I tell you, Mack, kids these days don't know work. Don't know the meaning of the word."

Mack continued nodding and drinking his coffee. His meteorology text lay on the table, bookmarked to the chapter he was reading, a plate of Mona's cabbage rolls beside it.

"So then her mother, my daughter, comes to see me. 'Mother,' she says, 'Mandy says you been embarrassing her in front of the other waitresses.' 'Marie,' I say, 'I got a business to run. I treat Mandy no different.' So then Marie leaves, all in tears. Now, I'll have to go over there. Apologize. Tell me, Mack, why's it always me? Always me apologizes. Kids." She shook her head. "Don't know the meaning of the word."

It was at this point that Jeff had walked in, towering in the doorway, his beige trench coat billowing around him, his glasses reflecting the light from an overhead lamp.

"Ach me," said Mona, rising. "More customers."

Mack could hear the exchange.

"You like a seat? You like to see a menu, ah?"

"No, I'm looking for my father-in-law, Mack Sullivan. Ah, I see him."

"Your father-in-law?"

"Yes."

"You want coffee, no?"

"Yes, please. Coffee would be very nice."

And then he sat down right across from Mack, not asking Mack if he wanted any company, just sitting there. Mona was right. Kids these days. Mack dug his fork into his cabbage rolls.

"I'm doing some checking," said Jeff as he shook himself out of his trench coat. "Did you know that your sister, the one everyone called Little Mary, her death certificate was not signed by a doctor or a medical examiner, but by a pharmacist?"

Mack looked at him.

"I've been on this merry goose chase since the other day when we couldn't find Mary Sullivan in the family plot. Does the name Marina Makepeace ring a bell?"

Mack grunted and said, "No, should it?"

"Her father was George Peter Koch." Jeff was wiping the rain off his glasses with a napkin from the dispenser. "It was George Peter Koch who signed the death certificate as Doctor George Peter Koch. Trouble is, George Peter Koch was no doctor. He was a druggist. His daughter, the one I talked to, she and Little Mary were good friends. Marina told me Little Mary wasn't allowed any visitors before her death. There are a whole lot of things that are fishy. One," Jeff held up his forefinger, "there was no funeral. Nothing that I could find." He held up two fingers. "Two, she is not buried with the rest of the Sullivans. Three, even the circumstances of her death are suspect. She was so sick, so sick that she died, but she was never admitted to a hospital, plus friends weren't allowed to see her. Does that make sense, Mack?"

Mona came with Jeff's coffee and eyed Mack in a knowing way before she left.

"It's my opinion," Jeff said, "that Mary may not be dead at all. Or that she didn't die then, in any case. Do you remember, Mack, do you remember anything about the circumstances of her death?"

"I was twelve."

"I know, but do you remember anything about that time? Was she sick? Do you know the story?"

Mack shook his head. "She was sick. She was sick all right. She had medicine. Castor oil. I was sent away to my uncles' the day she died. When I came back, she was already dead."

Jeff leaned forward. "But did you see her? Did you actually see the body?"

Mack scowled at him and shook his head.

"What was your father like?" Jeff asked when Mack didn't answer right away.

"What?"

"What was your father like? Was he very autocratic?"

"Are you blaming my father for something here?"

"Oh no, nothing like that. I didn't mean to say that."

"What then?"

"I just want to know what he was like."

"He provided for us. We never went without. He was stern, but he had to be. He did what a father's got to do. To make his children respect him."

Jeff took a gulp of his coffee. "Hey. Hot, good. I can see why you like it here."

"What a father should *not* do," Mack continued, "is what fathers all across this country are doing these days, even fathers who proclaim to be saved—not working hard enough, making their wives go out and work. That's not what's in the Bible." Mack pointed with his fork. "My father worked hard, and never once, never once did my mother have to go out and earn her own way. Neither did my sisters, although they never married. God rest them. He provided for their welfare. That's what a father's got to do. That's what a husband's got to do. And I don't see a lot of fathers doing this. I see women working all over the place, even women in our churches nowadays, bringing shame to the name of God." He said this between chews of his cabbage rolls.

Jeff took a long sip of his coffee. "Your friend Mona here, she works pretty hard."

"That's different. That's a different story."

Jeff finished his coffee and flipped open his wallet. Mack was taking a few dollars out of his billfold, but Jeff flashed his MasterCard. "My treat, Mack."

Mack scowled. As if he couldn't afford it, as if he were some poor street person who had to have his rich son-in-law pay for his every need. That was the trouble these days.

In the corner by the cash register, Mona rolled her eyes at him. He smiled back.

When Jeff left, Mack helped himself to more coffee from Mona's urn and then got out his textbook. But he wasn't concentrating on the text. He was thinking about his sister, about Little Mary, and about that day so long ago.

TWENTY-FIVE

"DIDN'T WE TELL NATASHA WHAT TIME we needed the car?" Jeff was leaning against the fireplace, his trench coat draped over his arm, ringing the little bell. Sharon, meanwhile, was pacing.

"How long does it take to do laundry? She's been gone three hours. Quit ringing that bell, Jeff, it's making me crazy."

"We told her we needed it by six, didn't we?"

Sharon smoothed her hair back into a ponytail. "I'm pretty sure we did. Do you think something may have happened to her?"

"What I'm wondering is, is she insured for that rental? Did we check that out before we merrily allowed her to take the car? Was there an age stipulation or anything on the rental form?"

Sharon dropped her hands to her side. "Oh great. Another thing to worry about. How come we didn't think of any of this before she left? What if she doesn't get back in time? We're supposed to be there in half an hour. I'm nervous enough as it is, without this."

"If she doesn't come, then we just get a cab or something."

"A cab all the way to Portland?"

"A bus then. We'll work something out. We'll rent another car."

"How you can be so calm about this is beyond me. As you can see, Natasha is still Natasha without a thought for anyone else on the planet but herself. Honestly. That girl."

"Speaking of that girl, I think I hear the car now."

Natasha came slamming in the back door, humming, dragging with her two bags of clean laundry.

"Hi," she said. "Got all your towels done, Mom."

Sharon could not keep her voice steady. "Natasha! Where have you been? We were worried sick."

Natasha stopped. "Laundry. You knew that."

"It took you three hours to do laundry? Dad and I have to be in

Portland in about twenty minutes. Or did you forget?"

"I remembered. I'm back in time, right?"

"You had us worried."

She shrugged.

"It took three hours to do laundry?"

"Mother, yes, it took three hours to do laundry."

"Does laundry take that long?" Jeff said.

Natasha threw her backpack in the corner. "I don't know how long it's supposed to take, but I know how long it did take. It took three hours. The machines were busy. I had to wait behind this mother with these three absolutely impossible kids who were dripping their ice-cream cones all over everything. And it was raining so they couldn't go outside. Plus, the machines didn't look all that clean in the first place. And I had all your extra stuff to do. I needed about five machines, so yes, it took that long."

Natasha flopped down on the couch.

"Do you want to come with us?" Sharon said. "I talked to Diane. You're invited, you know. We could wait."

"We're late already. We better get a move on," Jeff said.

"I'll stay here," Natasha said. "I wish there was a TV, though."

"There are books in absolutely every room of the house, even the bathroom. I'm sure you'll find something to your liking," Sharon said.

"Maybe I'll walk into town and catch a movie or something."

"Town's pretty far. And the weather's bad."

"I don't care about getting wet."

It took forty-five minutes to get to Portland. Normally the trip took twenty, but an accident on the highway forced the slowdown. When they got to Portland, Jeff was sure he knew the way. He promptly got lost, and they nattered at each other until Sharon managed to find the directions Diane had given to her over the phone. By the time they parked in front of the Petrescus' front porch, they were forty minutes late for dinner, and they apologized profusely.

"It happens," said Ron, taking their coats. The Petrescus lived in an old house in a fairly rundown neighborhood. Inside, though, it was cheery and nicely decorated and had the warm aroma of a home-cooked meal.

Diane greeted Sharon with a hug. The long, blond cheerleader hair had been replaced by a short style, frosted on the top. She still had that long and lean, freckled healthy look about her, though. Ron was several inches shorter than his wife. Several children of adult proportions stood behind them in various corners of the living room.

"Sharon! Oh my goodness, it's been so long!"

"I've heard a lot about you," Jeff said. "Both of you. My wife talks of you."

"What about this weather we're having?" Ron said.

Diane was gesturing with her hands. "Come here, Matthew, Heather, Jonathan, come meet an old friend of mine from a long time ago. Back when I was your age I knew this person."

The three children moved out of the shadows and shyly shook hands.

"And you didn't bring Natasha?" Diane said. "How disappointing. We were looking forward to meeting her. The kids were, too."

"She flew in yesterday from Europe," Jeff said. "She's still catching up on her sleep."

"We can relate," Diane said.

"Been there, done that," said her husband.

The meal was an old-fashioned supper of roast beef, potatoes, and peas, the kind of Sunday dinners Sharon remembered at Trail's End. They talked about their respective careers, their respective children, their respective lives. Sharon learned that Ron was the administrator of the overseas mission board, and Diane was the nurse at the school for missionary children. Matthew was heading off to college in the fall. That was about all Jeff got out of Matthew, whose sentences tended to be one syllables. Heather was in her last year in high school and wanted to be a veterinarian. She had a lot of friends in Taiwan and couldn't wait to get back. She said all of this through long strands of yellow hair that fell forward, covering her eyes. She had at least two pierced earrings on each ear. Jonathan, the youngest, was fourteen, talkative, and interested in sports.

"What kind of sports?" Jeff asked.

"Any kind. Soccer, especially."

"He's quite a star," Ron said. The boy beamed.

"Soccer. Now, you need to come to Victoria for that."

They talked about mutual interests in movies and books.

"You get to see movies in Taiwan?" Sharon asked.

"Pretty much," Heather said. "But not right away. We didn't get to see *Titanic* until about a year later."

"Plus, they have Chinese subtitles underneath," Jonathan said. "But you get used to it."

"So you aren't out in the boonies?" Sharon said.

"No, we're pretty much in the city."

Sharon shook her head. "No straw huts."

"The world is fairly well industrialized now," said Ron smiling. "That's a common misconception, that we're out there with the uncivilized natives. Some missionaries are, but we aren't. We come back to Portland and feel like we're in a small town."

"Your books are even there, Sharon. In a huge English bookstore, one that we go to a lot. I get the manager to bring them in."

By now, Heather and Matthew were clearing the table while Jonathan talked on and on about Taiwan. Heather brought out an apple pie and a carton of ice cream.

"You even baked a pie!" Sharon said.

Diane laughed. "Not exactly. This comes from the Portland Public Market. To tell you the truth, there's a little baker there who bakes better than I could even attempt."

After dessert was finished, the children left, the oldest one to go out with friends and the two younger ones to some church activity. "You have very obedient children," Sharon said, "clearing the table and all."

"They were under strict orders. We've had our share of problems. Matthew? The oldest? He wants nothing to do with church now. Nothing whatsoever. Well, he's eighteen, so what can you do? We can't make him go to church with us anymore. It's a real worry for us, especially when we'll be heading back to Taiwan in the fall, and we leave him in a University of Maine dormitory up in Orono."

"Be happy that your son wants to go to college," Jeff said. "Our Natasha thinks education is a waste of time. Ask her what she wants to do and she'll say travel."

"More coffee?" Diane rose. When she returned with the coffeepot, she said, "I'm so glad you're here, because I've wanted to tell you how much I enjoy your books. Ron can tell you that after a particularly wearying day, they are so delightful, such a needed escape sometimes."

"She's great, isn't she?" Jeff said.

Ron said, "My wife is always telling people, 'I used to know her. We used to be friends.'"

"Oh my," Sharon said.

"My mom likes your books, too," Diane said. She turned to Jeff. "You didn't know her in school, but everyone envied Sharon Sullivan. She was the smart one. Straight A's. In the honor society."

"Oh come on, Diane, no one envied me; I was the nerd. Pastor Harley ran when he saw me coming because he knew I'd have some question he couldn't answer."

"You remember Bud Harley?" asked Diane quietly.

"Oh, of course. The fat one."

"He's in jail."

Sharon put her hands flat on the table. "You're kidding!"

"Drug dealing."

"I can't believe it. He was the spiritual one. Always carried his Bible on top of his books. Always arguing Creation in science class."

Diane shook her head. "He really went off the deep end when he graduated. No one knows what happened. The other kids are doing okay, I think. You remember the littlest girl, Karen?"

"The crybaby. We would have them out to dinner at Trail's End, and Karen would sit on a chair and whine and whine and whine."

"Yeah, the crybaby. Well, she's a teacher now at a private school in Rhode Island."

"Unbelievable."

"Time passes."

"And here we are."

As the two women shared remembrances, Ron and Jeff went to the living room and talked computers. Ron was in charge of upgrading the computers in the mission office and was looking for anyone who would give him advice.

"How is Dean?" Diane asked it quietly, stirring a spoonful of sugar into her second cup of coffee.

Sharon looked down at the pattern in the lace tablecloth. "Diane, you're not going to believe this, but I haven't seen Dean since I left. He and my father had a falling out. I don't even know what it was about. The next thing I know, he's gone. The lawyers are trying to find him; he's inherited Trail's End along with me." Sharon paused. "I don't even know if he's dead or alive."

Diane looked at her sadly. "I didn't know."

"The lawyers keep calling with updates. First, they thought they'd found him, then it wasn't him, now they've found someone else. They might hire a detective."

"When I knew him, he was troubled," Diane said. "Maybe that's why we finally broke up. I got to the place where I couldn't take his grimness anymore. I was too much into having fun at the time. He would tell me I wasn't serious enough, and I would tell him he was a stick in the mud. He was always running off to every faith healer that came through."

"Faith healers? Really?"

"He didn't want your father to know, or anybody in the church for that matter. So I promised."

"What did he need healing from?"

"Demons, he said."

"Demons?"

"Yeah, demons."

"But he was so much better when he was with you. He even worked on the yearbook, did those illustrations and cartoons. He was so good at that."

Diane sighed. "I don't think he was really better. Even then. I think it was the death of your mother. He became fascinated, obsessed, with death. He wrote a paper in his senior year about famous people who'd committed suicide. He let me read it. He got an A on it. When I went away to Bible school we lost touch."

Sharon shook her head. "I haven't kept in touch with anyone here really. Except for my aunt."

Diane touched her arm. "There is so much to catch up on, and God is so good, isn't he?"

Sharon blinked at her, said nothing.

"Knowing about Dean now, I will pray for him. There was a time when I prayed for him every day of my life. Sometimes that's the only thing you can do."

"Go ahead, pray, if you think it will help."

Diane looked across at her.

"There's a lot you don't know about me, either," Sharon said. "Probably the last time I prayed about anything in my life was more than twenty-five years ago."

Diane looked at her through wide blue eyes. Sharon could see the Diane she knew in high school, the Diane that was Dean's friend.

"Sharon, I didn't know. I'm so sorry."

TWENTY-SIX

As soon as her parents left, Natasha made herself a cup of Irish Breakfast tea. It hadn't taken quite three hours to do her laundry, as she had said. She'd spent about half an hour at a tea and coffee shop across from the Laundromat. She'd developed a taste for tea in the past year and even though her finances were dwindling, she'd counted out her money for the laundry and then had enough to pick up a packet of tea bags. But she'd have to get to a bank soon to change her British pounds to American dollars.

She filled the kettle with water and leaned against the sink. She liked this kitchen. It was old-fashioned, with high ceilings and open cupboard shelves that held thick dishes and crack-lined teacups and bottles and jars of odd smelling and exotic foods—things her mother never bought, such as RyCrisp crackers and shortbread cookies. She had been here a few times when she was younger. When she was six, her Great-aunt Hilda had died, and they'd all flown back for the funeral. "I'm only doing this for Katie's sake," her mother kept saying to her father. "Only for Katie's sake."

"So happy to meet you, Natasha," Great-aunt Katie had said. She had extended her hand and Natasha shook it importantly. Great-aunt Katie didn't talk to her like a child, didn't ruffle her hair, telling her what wonderful red hair she had. And oh, weren't the freckles darling. She liked it that she didn't.

When she was eleven, she and her parents had driven out here to visit her grandfather and her great-aunt. She had stayed overnight in the tiny third bedroom upstairs, from where she could hear Great-aunt Katie snoring and her parents talking. All night long she heard noises, thumps and groans and scrapings. In the morning, Katie told her it was the sound of the furnace and the wind.

"I think it's a ghost," Natasha had said.

Katie looked up from the chair she always sat in and said, "Oh, my dear, no ghosts here."

The tea ready now, she carried it, along with a broom, back to the sunporch. She set the tea down on the bookshelf and swept the floor. She unloaded her clean clothes and placed them in piles along the wall: jeans in one stack, shirts in another, underwear and socks in yet another. Part of the plastic on the window was already ripped, so she pulled the piece off entirely and immediately felt a rush of cold air. Still, it was nice to be able to see out clearly.

Her cleaning done, she huddled into a gray woolen blanket and stared out at the ocean. A lot about this coast reminded her of Ireland. The gray rain, the mist. If she closed her eyes and listened to the breakers, she could pretend she was back there and Jordan was with her and things were the way they used to be.

She reached for an old *National Geographic* and began leafing through it. So intent was she in a story about volcanoes, that at first the noise didn't register. A few minutes later, however, she looked up. That *was* a sound. Someone knocking? Or just the sound of the wind and furnace? No, there was someone at the back door. Reluctantly, she put down her magazine, the blanket still wrapped around her, and made her way through the parlor and down the hall to the back door.

"Who is it?" she yelled through the door.

"My name is Cos, Harold Cosman. I've come to see Sharon Sullivan Colebrook."

He had a dignified, upper-class New England accent. He also sounded old.

"She's not here," Natasha yelled. "I'll give her a message."

"I have some more information about Katie."

"You mean my great-aunt?"

"And you would be the daughter?"

"I would be the daughter, yes." She paused. "You can pass the information to me when I open the door. I'll make sure she gets it."

She opened the door a crack. "Actually," he said in crisp English, "it's nothing that's written. I just wished to speak with her."

She opened the door an inch wider. "Well, she's not here." He looked like a harmless old man, water splatting off his wide-brimmed white safari hat.

"Oh my, you are the daughter?" Water was dripping off his nose.

"I'm Natasha, yes, the daughter."

"Well, oh my, you look nothing like your mother, and I can't say if you look anything like your father either. Not even Katie." He was rubbing his chin, as if the enigma of who she looked like were of some vital importance.

"Actually, I'm adopted."

"Oh me." He put his hand to his chest. "I meant no offense."

She laughed out loud. "I'm not really adopted."

"But the black hair. Neither Katie nor Hilda had black hair."

"Actually, mine is red."

He peered at her as if his eyes were failing, took off his glasses, wiped them on the sleeve of his jacket, and put them on again.

He looked so serious, so cute, standing there, that Natasha said, "Would you like to come in for a minute? At least to dry off. I could get a piece of paper and jot down the information you want to tell my mother."

"Oh my, thank you, indeed." He shook off his raincoat, hung it on a hook by the door, and then placed his hat on top of it. His scalp was very pink, and he seemed about half her size.

She scrabbled in various drawers looking for paper and a pen, but found nothing.

"Oh, my dear," he said, "you needn't take notes. I'll come back at a more convenient time. If I could just dry off and then I'll be on my way. The rain has begun in earnest, I see."

"Where do you live?"

"Just down the beach a little. Not far." He extended his hand. "My name is Harold Cosman, but please call me Cos."

"I'm Natasha." She shook his hand. "The daughter."

He winked at her. She couldn't tell if it was a real wink or just something caught in his eye.

He looked around him. "Could I possibly trouble you for a cup of tea?"

"Tea? You want tea?"

"If it would be no trouble."

"Well, I don't know. I suppose. I just had some, I suppose I could make more."

"I see you have a packet of Irish Breakfast on the counter there."

"Got it at that coffee store on the corner across from the Irving."

"Good choice, my dear."

She kept her eyes on this strange little pink man while she filled the kettle with water.

"That isn't, by any chance, loose tea, is it?"

"No. Sorry."

"Katie always used loose tea. So much better."

She spun around. "Do you want this tea or not?"

"Oh, my dear, I meant no offense. I seem to be saying all the wrong things. Yes, you are like your mother. No doubt about that now, even with the black hair. Also a bit like Katie, too. If you must know."

Natasha poured boiling water over two tea bags in a round, ceramic pot. She brought two teacups down from the cupboard.

"That would be most delightful. To share a cup of tea with the grand-niece of a friend." He looked around him. "It is indeed so strange to come back here and have Katie gone. So strange, indeed." He shook his head. "And so sad."

"I only met Katie twice. She was very old."

His pale eyes gleamed. "Age, my dear young person, is not a characteristic. It's not like blond hair or blue eyes. Everyone will have a time of being old. You, although you feel that you are immortal now, will have your time of being old. Just as I had a time of being young.

Like you." He poured himself a cup of tea. "And would you have milk with this?"

"I don't know if there is any. I drink it plain."

"One cannot drink tea without milk; that would be sacrilege."

She got up, found a carton of milk, and placed it on the table. "Is this okay, or should I pour it in a little cream pitcher over there?"

"A cream pitcher would be very nice."

She poured the milk into a pitcher, put the carton in the fridge, and set the pitcher down on the table. "There. Milk in a pitcher. Irish Breakfast tea. Anything else?"

"No, dear, this will be fine."

"Well, that's good." She sat down.

"Thank you."

"No prob."

"Tell me, Natasha, are you staying here long?"

She shrugged. "I don't know. I needed a place to come to. Had a, um, *situation* in Ireland. Had to leave. Couldn't take it. Had to have a place to go to."

"Ah yes." He nodded.

"It wasn't my fault. It was the fault of that stupid Laureena. It's like I didn't exist anymore. And what were the past three years for anyway? Didn't they mean anything?" She held her hands around her teacup, surprised she was talking like this to a complete stranger.

"Ah, Ireland," he said. "The land of romance."

"I've never heard it called the land of romance. It certainly wasn't the land of romance for me. I will never think of Ireland as the land of romance."

"But all those songs, 'Danny Boy'…" He hummed a few bars. "So hard when love dies."

"Tell me about it."

"It's as though your little part of the world has ended. Even the simple pleasures of a nice cup of tea are marred by love's ending."

"Yeah." She looked down at her fingernails. Some of the blue was chipping off. She'd have to redo them.

"And one begins to wonder about the end of life and what it all means."

She looked over at him.

"It's too bad you never met Katie," he said. "You two would have a lot in common."

"I told you I did meet her."

He shook his head. "But to talk with her. To know her as a young person. You would have understood. It would be so interesting if we all could be for a few moments, a day, maybe, the same age."

"I suppose."

"We shall be, in the great hereafter. Ah me, the rain has let up. I should make a run for it before it begins again."

He rose and carefully put on his coat and hat, taking the time to do up all the buttons and fasten his hat under his chin. "Thank you for the tea, my dear, and please tell your mother I have more information about the murder."

TWENTY-SEVEN

THE KITCHEN WAS THOROUGHLY CLEANED. The back upstairs bedroom was cleaned. The mushy cardboard box had been folded up and placed outside beside the garbage can and the papers that seemed of no value had been bagged up and placed beside it. Today Sharon was going to tackle the remaining books in their bedroom, all five bookshelves full of them. She'd dust them off, box them up, and then figure out what to do with them. A used bookstore? She wasn't sure but she couldn't bear to throw out books of any description. All of those old *National Geographics* and *Reader's Digests* out on the sunporch, she was sure they were worth something. Yet she knew when it came down to it, she wouldn't be able to part with them either.

Last night when they arrived home from Portland, Sharon had noticed two teacups and her aunt's cream pitcher in the sink along with the teapot. She'd have to talk to Natasha about cleaning up her things and only using one cup per evening. And certainly milk poured directly from the carton would be good enough.

As she began with the books, she thought about the previous evening. It had been pleasant, despite her earlier misgivings. Before they left, Diane hugged her and said they ought to get together again. Ron added that if she and Jeff wanted, they could come out and see about that ghost.

"You're a missionary, right?" Jeff said. "That's sort of like a minister?"

"Sort of. Not exactly. I'm not ordained or anything."

"Maybe you can come out and perform an exorcism."

"I wasn't thinking of that. I was thinking more of trying to figure out what's causing the phenomenon."

Neither she nor Jeff had heard the ghost the previous night, but when they came downstairs for breakfast, the ballerina dancer was facing the wall and the chime clock stood at 8:30.

With the radio tuned in low, she began dusting books and placing them in the boxes. At first she read the title of each book and skimmed through it. After a while she realized that if she continued to do that, this job would take all day.

She heard talking downstairs and figured Natasha was up, but Sharon continued dusting and packing. There was so much dust that it wadded together like dryer lint, and she could pick it up by handfuls.

Inside the pages of an old encyclopedia she saw a small manila envelope, gray with dust and age. She pulled it out, blew it off. It contained church bulletins, black-and-white snapshots, and tiny yellowed news clippings. She swept aside a T-shirt and Jeff's jogging clothes and dumped the contents onto the bed.

She picked up one of the photographs and stared down at it. Gerard, Pearl, and their two daughters, Hilda and Katie, one year apart, dressed identically in those sailor dresses with big collars and white ribbons in their hair. But on Grandma Pearl's lap was a baby, a white ribbon in her hair. Little Mary? It was a studio photo taken at the same time as the photos on the stairwell. But she had never seen this one hanging there. She picked it up and examined it. The edges were marked and scraped, as if it had once been in a frame. She compared it to the framed photos she had found in the box in the bedroom closet. The same size, yet removed from the frame and taken down from the wall. Why?

There were several more pictures of Little Mary: Little Mary sitting in a wooden wagon; Little Mary on a sleigh and dressed in mufflers and standing between her older sisters. The four of them, Hilda, Katie, Little Mary, and Mack. She lined up the photos in rows and columns across the bed covers. She was engaged in this odd game of solitaire when another photo caught her eye. Katie and a young man. She was wearing the same white dress that she wore in Cos's picture, the same white dress that lay even now in the dress box in her closet.

In this picture Katie was seated on the brocade chair. In one hand she held the fan and standing behind her was a solemn young man with pale, wild-looking hair. His hand was on her shoulder. Neither was smiling, but there was a serenity about the two of them. Sharon turned the photo over. Nothing was written on the back.

She put the photos in a pile and skimmed through the bulletins. All of them were from the church in Portland, the church she grew up in, the church her grandparents went to, the church that no longer existed. She read of choral selections, prelude music, guest speakers, missionary conferences. Tucked into one of the bulletins was a small, slim baby book. A tiny photo of a chubby baby's face and a lock of blonde hair were pasted onto the first page. She ran her fingers over the soft, pale curl. It was for a baby named David Thomas. She puzzled over this for a moment, until she remembered that for a little while her aunts had taken in a local orphan boy by that name.

After the first couple of pages, the baby book was blank, as if whoever was responsible for keeping it up had lost interest. At the back of the baby book was a small card. It was a pencil sketch of the shoreline in front of Trail's End, with driftwood and dunes and the path going down through the shrubbery to the beach. She read:

Inscribed for Mildred,
In appreciation of our friendship which I will never forget and the sharing of thought. That is the sort of friendship one cherishes. Most sincerely and with love, D.

She gathered up her finds to take downstairs. She'd add them to the Katie file.

Natasha, just coming out of the shower, was combing through her hair with her fingers and said, "Oh hi, Mom. You're supposed to call that man, Cos or Gus or whoever he is. He says he knows who did it."

TWENTY-EIGHT

SHARON ARRIVED AT COS'S HOUSE, and Doreen answered the door, a mop in her roughened hands. Cos was out, she told her.

"Do you know when he'll be back?"

The little round woman shook her head vigorously, her mop of gray curls springing back and forth like a slinky. "I don't know when he's back. He didn't tell me when he's back. He went out for a walk."

"A walk?" said Sharon looking skyward. "In this?"

"He don't mind so much about the weather, Cos don't."

"So you think he'll be back soon?"

"Most likely."

"Can I wait for him inside?"

Doreen opened the door and Sharon entered. All of the furniture in the tiny place was shoved up to the end of the room, and Doreen had a mop bucket in the center of the floor.

"No place to sit here. I do this on occasion. Give her a good cleaning."

"Looks like you're doing a great job," Sharon said.

"Sometimes there's no other way around it. You got to clean right down to the bones. Sometimes that's all a place needs."

"Yes."

"But sometimes no matter how hard a body cleans a place, there's that smidgen of dirt that nothin' will get out. Nothin' at all. Ya scrub and ya scrub at that place, it just don't get clean. Still smells like the dickens."

"It smells very clean in here, Doreen, very lemony."

"I try and I try and I try," she said without looking up. "I try and I try, but nothin' gets clean. Nothin' ever."

"But it looks just fine."

She peered up at Sharon then, as if seeing her for the first time. "What do you want Cos for, anyhow?"

"He came to see me, said he had some information that he wanted to pass on to me."

She placed her hand on top of the mop handle. "What kind of information?"

"Just something I'm working on."

"Well, I'm sure Cos has no information for you, that I can be sure of. He ain't been here long enough to collect much information about anything. If I were you I'd head on home. When he comes back from his walk he'll be in no mood to talk, that I can say for sure. He'll be tired and wanting his tea, and then a nap. That's all." Her fingers curled and uncurled over the top of the mop handle while she talked.

"Maybe I'll just wait."

"You'd be just getting in my way here, when I got all this work to do. I'd head on home now, and I'll be sure to tell him you were here and that you stopped by and for what reason. You'd be in my way here, what with the furniture I got to move and the likes of everything I'm doing here."

"Well."

"There, you go now, and I'll make sure he knows you were here. I have work to do here and have to be at the Mudges' after this. They're expecting me at one."

Doreen shooed at her with both hands, like one would a stray dog or an errant child. Sharon walked gingerly toward the door. Doreen turned back to her loud, sloppy mopping of Cos's floor.

From Sharon's earliest memories Doreen had always been there, answering the tinny bell when Hilda rang it. When Sharon was a little girl, Doreen was a tiny, skinny, nervous, mousy teenager whose brown hair fell forward, hiding her face most of the time. Doreen was not an old woman, yet she had the aura of someone old: the steel gray hair, the callused hands, the lines around the eyes, month permanently turned down into a frown.

It was always Hilda that Doreen deferred to. Sharon remembered that when Grandma Pearl would ring for Doreen to do this or that, Doreen would look to Hilda, it seemed, for permission. Can I? May I fetch this cup of tea for Grandma Pearl? And then Hilda would give an imperceptible nod of her head and Doreen would proceed with the task.

Sharon stood by the door, swinging her keys. "I guess it's difficult for you now. With Hilda gone."

Doreen didn't move, kept her pace with the mop, but did Sharon see an involuntary tensing?

"Doreen?"

"I have to be to the Mudges' by one," she said without turning around.

"I was just wondering about my Aunt Hilda."

"There's nothing to wonder about."

"You must miss her."

Doreen turned. "She provided me a home, all those years I lived at Trail's End. All those years. And then Hilda's body wasn't cold, and Katie kicked me out into the streets, she did. Had no place to live. Hilda never would've done that; no, she wouldn't have. Not to me. She understood."

"You went to live in your brother's motel."

She made a noise that was something between a grunt and a snort. "Mighty good thing that place opened up."

"You kept working for Katie, though, didn't you?"

"She needed help, didn't she? And I knew that place better than anyone, being in service there for so long."

"Did she really kick you out? I can't imagine that."

Doreen put her hand to her heart. "I couldn't live there, not with them stories she used to tell. Making up things about me. Herself going on and on, scaring people." She looked nervously around her. "Now, you go, you hear? You get on back to Trail's End, and I'll be sure to tell Mr. Cosman you was by."

Sharon left, with more questions about this strange woman than answers.

TWENTY-NINE

GOD TOOK HER. Mack's father had told him that many times. God took Little Mary; he had no choice. She was a cancer that had to be plucked out. His father had said those very words. Or were those Hilda's words? So much of the past he had trouble remembering. He was walking to Mona's Café now through a drizzle that was more mist than rain, slowly walking and thinking. To Mack, God had become a God who took things. His sister, his wife, his son.

When Mack returned to Trail's End after staying with the uncles, all traces of Little Mary were gone. It was as though she had never existed. He had raced up the stairs to her bedroom, stood in the doorway and stared, just stared. Her bed was made up with a white chenille bedspread he had never seen before. Mack tore it off the bed and it landed in a heap on the floor, but no, her pink one with the embroidered roses was gone. Even the sheets were not the ones she used. Her medicines were gone, the big bottle of castor oil that she took for her illness was not there. Even her frilly curtains were gone, replaced by something stark and blue and all wrong for this room. He had raced down to the kitchen to where his mother was leaning her belly against the sink peeling potatoes. "Where are Little Mary's clothes? Her bedspread? The doll in the window? What did you do with them?" His hands were shaking. His voice, he could not control. Tears sputtered from his eyes and rapidly, he blinked them back.

"Ah, Mackie." His mother wiped her hands on her apron. "I don't expect you to understand. Someday you will. She defiled this house, and God took her. It's better this way." She turned back to the sink, but he watched her reach up and wipe her eyes with the corner of her apron.

Defiled? What was defiled? He walked into the parlor where his father was sitting in the rocking chair, hands folded on his lap. The look on his father's face caused Mack to back away. There would be no more questions about Little Mary to his father.

Outside, Katie was sitting quietly on the sand. Underneath her was Little Mary's pink bedspread with the roses.

"That's Little Mary's blanket," he said.

"I needed to keep something."

She wasn't looking at him, but was gazing ahead of her, out toward the sea. The breeze was blowing her soft brown hair across her face.

"What happened to her?" he asked. "What did she do to the house?"

"Hilda arranged it," Katie said, picking up a handful of sand and running it through her fingers. "You were sent to the uncles'; I was sent to Marina's. If I'd have been here, maybe things would have turned out differently. They said they were getting help for her." She was breaking a small shell into pieces and throwing them into the waves. Ahead of them the pale sea groaned.

More than thirty years later Mack knew what defiling a house meant. Dean had done just that.

It was misting harder now, and Mack felt the dampness seep through his tweed wool cap. Since the day Dean left, Mack's constant prayer had been that God would help him to forget about his son.

I followed what the Bible commands, I put him out. Yet, why can't I stop thinking about him, stop worrying about him? I shouldn't even pray for him. Yet, here I am praying for him. Again.

He entered the warm atmosphere of Mona's, and she raised her hand to greet him from behind the counter. He grabbed a newspaper from the rack Mona provided for regulars, took his customary booth by the window, and read the headlines. Maybe some overseas war would help him get his mind off his own morbid thoughts.

Mona's granddaughter, Mandy, brought over coffee and a menu.

"I don't need a menu," he said. "Tell your grandmother I'll have my usual."

"Okay, Mr. Sullivan."

He opened the paper and read through the weather report, always the first thing he turned to. But even that couldn't hold his interest. His coffee came. He stirred in sugar and cream. He was remembering something, and he wondered if it was important. It wasn't until after Little Mary died that Katie started telling stories, started making things up that would shock the family and startle the neighbors. Did she tell stories before then? He wasn't sure, but he didn't think so. That day on Little Mary's blanket, Katie talked about the evil trolls who lived just beneath the surface of things.

"You mean right underneath us? Below the sand?"

Katie had whooped out loud and clapped her hands in that way she did.

"That's exactly it, Mackie. Exactly it. Right underneath Trail's End with all its good deeds and helping the poor. They're building tunnels under the sand, even as we sit here. And there's no way we can stop them."

"There isn't?"

"Absolutely none."

Mack's long-ago memories were interrupted by a man with grizzled hair and wind-roughened skin who slid into the booth across from him.

"You Mack Sullivan?"

"Yes?" He folded his paper, looked up.

"Name's Joe, Joe Lazur." He reached his hand across the table. Mack shook it.

"You don't know me." The man's voice had a gruff edge to it. "But I understand that you are the local expert on weather."

Mack raised his eyebrows.

"Thing is…" The man reached into a jacket pocket and brought out a crumpled weather fax. He unfolded it and spread it on the table. "I'm a sailor. Want to head south along the coast. Thing is, the weather maps you get from the weather office, you may as well use them for kindling."

Mack studied the weather fax, tracing his fingers across its markings. They made sense to him.

"What I want is an opinion, nothing else. On this weather system we're wallowing in currently." He rubbed thick, stained fingers across the page. "Alls this says, far as I can read it, is no end in sight. Meanwhile I'm stuck here. What I'm looking for is a window. Just a window. Eight hours oughtta do it."

Mack bent over the map, adjusting his bifocals, and then abandoned them altogether and took out the magnifying glass he always carried. "The old eyes aren't what they used to be," he said.

The man chuckled. "Know what you mean there, pal. What do you see? Any chance of a window?"

"As soon as this low pressure system lifts, you can be guaranteed wind, that I can tell you."

"That's what I'm asking. Any knowledge of when it will lift."

Mack leaned back in the booth, studied the map, then got up and went outside. He stood there for several minutes, testing the air, facing this way and that. He didn't know. He couldn't be sure. It was a feeling, as if the air were sweeping down like layers of cloth, one rough, one smooth. He could reach out his hand and feel the difference. Back inside he said, "It will clear tomorrow. Briefly. And you'll have wind."

"That's not what the weather office says."

"You said you wanted an opinion; I'm giving an opinion. Opinions are free. Take it or leave it."

The man clapped Mack on the shoulder before he left. "Thanks, pal."

When Mack sat down, he felt good. It was a strange feeling, but he felt good, puzzled but exhilarated all at once. At the cash register Mona winked at him.

THIRTY

EVEN THOUGH SHARON NEVER WENT TO CHURCH anymore, she had talked to numerous ministers, had been given many tours of churches, had read many religious pamphlets and books in her Summer Whitney research. But no matter how many times she told herself that this was research, that this time was just like all those other times, driving now into the church parking lot felt different. This time it felt personal. This was the church Katie and Cos went to. This was the church that held Katie's funeral.

The church was an L-shaped building, and the older part, the sanctuary, faced forward, and along the back a rectangular newer addition had been built. There were two other cars in the lot, and Sharon parked beside a brown Buick. The door that led into the newer part of the church was unlocked. She opened it slowly and stepped into a carpeted foyer, like dozens of other church foyers she had been in. This one had the requisite coatrack along one wall, a lone sweater hanging crookedly in the corner. On the top were a few stray hats, a pile of loose Sunday school papers, and a bunch of Bibles. There were posters on the walls advertising children's summer camp, Third World relief, and vacation Bible school. An umbrella in a round bin stood beside the door, with a pair of black shoe rubbers next to it. The whole place had that quiet, reverent smell of old hymnbooks and choir gowns.

From a hallway to her right a figure emerged. He wore a casual gray sweater vest and wire-rimmed glasses.

"Hello there," he said. "Need help with anything?"

"I'm not sure. My name's Sharon Colebrook. Katheryn Sullivan was my aunt. Did you know her?"

"Katie!" His face brightened. "She was a wonderful woman, our Katie was. And you're Sharon, the writer. She often spoke of you."

"I hope good stuff."

"Only the good stuff." He had a ready smile. "My name's Barry," he said as he stuck out his hand. He took hers and shook it vigorously. "Barry Brannin, the minister here."

"Nice to meet you. I'm sorry I missed her funeral."

"Katie was quite a sweetheart. She used to tell stories—"

"Oh, I know all about her stories."

"—to the seniors. They all loved her. She could take a Bible story and act it out, and her audience would become completely mesmerized. Everyone loved her."

"No stories of trolls and fairies?"

"Trolls and fairies?"

"When I was little it was stories of trolls and fairies."

He grinned. "Oh, I don't remember trolls and fairies. She and Cos were quite an addition to our little group here." His face momentarily clouded. "I'm a little afraid for Cos now. He seems so lost without her. Do you know him? I haven't seen him at the services since Katie died. I've been up to see him a few times, and I should go again."

"I've visited with him."

"That's good."

She looked around her. "So this was Katie's church?"

He followed her gaze. "This was Katie's church."

"It's nice."

"It's on the historical register. We're right across from the museum so we get a lot of tourist traffic in the summer. It's quite an old building, as you can see. Built in the early 1800s. This new addition," he pointed to the right, "was added, oh, a dozen years or so ago, just before I got here. We've got a gym now, and classrooms, and a well-needed couple of offices."

She pointed to a set of large decorative oak doors to the left. "That's the sanctuary over there?"

"Yes, it is. It's a very beautiful one, with stained-glass windows done by one of the foremost artisans in New England."

"May I go in there?"

"By all means. Feel free. The sanctuary is always open. Unlike many Protestant churches, which have taken to locking their doors, we leave this one open, even at night."

"You don't worry about vandalism?"

"We've never had a problem with it. And if the occasional homeless person or traveler wants to seek refuge within its walls—well, isn't that what the church is all about anyway? We leave the doors unlocked for prayer and meditation. Would you like a tour?"

"Yes, thank you." Sharon got out her notebook.

"You taking notes?"

"I'm writing up something about my aunt."

"Oh, that's a wonderful idea."

She followed him across the thick carpet to the office area.

"Let's start with the newer addition, shall we? Save the best for last."

A perky, chubby secretary said hello with a strong Boston accent. Barry introduced her to Lucy, and they shook hands. Barry showed her the classrooms and the gym, talking nonstop while they walked.

"Nice," Sharon said.

On their way back to his office, he snapped his fingers. "Hey, I bet you'd like to see the bulletin for Katie's funeral. I think we've got a few of them kicking around. Lucy saves bulletins, keeps them right in order. She tells me it's so we don't repeat hymns too often."

"I already have one. There was one at the house."

She followed him into the office, where Barry told Lucy, "She's writing a biography of Katie."

"A book?" Lucy asked.

"Well, I don't know what form it will take. I don't know if it will be a book. Maybe only short pieces."

"Why don't you have a seat?" Barry said. "We could talk for hours about Katie, couldn't we, Lucy?"

Lucy nodded.

Sharon took notes while the two of them talked. Everyone loved

Katie, that's basically what she learned.

Sharon tapped her pen on her notebook. "Did my aunt ever talk about a murder? A body on the beach?"

Barry winked at Lucy. "You know, of course, that this is Sharon Sullivan Colebrook, the mystery writer."

Lucy's eyes widened.

Sharon doodled on her page. "A lot of Katie's stories concerned a murder."

"As far as I know she only told Bible stories," Lucy said. "That's all I ever remember. I don't remember anything about a murder."

Barry's hands were on his knees, but he, too, was shaking his head. "Only Bible stories. You should have seen her tell the story of David and Goliath. She'd get right into the parts."

"My favorite was Daniel and the lion's den," Lucy said.

"Shame she didn't share them with the children, though," Barry said. "She told stories to seniors, to groups of adults, even to the young adult's clubs, but never to children's groups. I would say, Katie, can we put you down for the children's story this week? Can we drive you out to the children's camp? But she always said no."

Sharon shrugged. "She wasn't good with children."

He shook his head. "I'm not so sure it wasn't something else."

"What do you think it was?" Sharon asked.

"I can't put my finger on it."

The phone rang. It was for Barry, and he said he would take it in his office. He waved to Sharon. "Sorry we didn't get to complete that tour, but by all means, you go into the sanctuary. Have a look around. When I'm finished with this call, I'll join you. Point out some of the features."

Sharon shoved open one of the large ornate doors and entered the quiet. She stood for several seconds in the back of the sanctuary. Barry was right. The stained-glass windows were exquisite. She sat in a back pew to admire them. The scenes were the same—Jesus' baptism, the ascension, the Last Supper—yet there seemed to be more light to these windows, more shades of yellow, more brightness. The sanctuary itself seemed brighter, lighter, more cheerful, more joyful than some she had toured.

She was not alone in the sanctuary. From the front she heard noises, a faint whimpering. Her first thought was that a stray dog or kitten had somehow gotten inside. She made her way down the aisle and stopped. Ahead of her a woman was kneeling at the altar, her head bent into her hands. She wore an apron around her tiny body, and her shoulders were shaking.

Sharon backed away.

Doreen was weeping, her little shoulders shaking, crying bitterly.

Sharon left without waiting for Barry to return.

THIRTY-ONE

A WHILE LATER SHARON WAS KNOCKING at Cos's back door.

"Oh, how pleasant," he said when he opened the door. "I was just about to have tea. How nice to have someone drop by. Doreen was to come by. I don't know where she has gotten to."

"I saw her."

Sharon took off her jacket and placed it on the back of a kitchen chair. "I went to the church you and Katie went to, and she was there. Meditating in the church. She didn't see me. The minister said you and Katie were well liked there. That's a beautiful church, Cos."

"It is at that, isn't it? Wonderful old building."

"I hear you came by last night?"

"Ah yes, a lovely daughter you have there. She invited me in and we had tea together."

"You had tea with Natasha?"

"A lovely chat we had, too."

"She didn't tell me that."

"I expect not."

"She said you had information about the murder."

"There's time for that. Let's get the tea made first, and then we shall chat." While the kettle boiled, Cos talked about small things, walks on the beach, the color of the sea, the grayness of the sky. His talk reminded Sharon of visits with her aunt. Yes, she could imagine these two sitting down to tea and happily chatting away for hours about nothing in particular. When the tea was ready and the arrowroot cookies on a tray, only then did Cos bring up the subject of the murder.

"What I have is not a lot," he said. "Merely an impression. I'm sure it had something to do with two things. Firstly, the light."

"The light."

"The morning light. The Amadon Light." He poured milk into his tea. "Katie was a firm believer in symbols. If this happened, then that would happen, and so forth."

"But what could that possibly have to do with the murder?"

"Did you notice that the story always included a bright light, a green flash of light?"

"But I don't know if that means anything."

"I'm not sure." He shook his head. "But it is curious, don't you think?"

"You said there were two things."

Cos nodded. "Yes. The second would be Doreen."

"Doreen?"

"I believe she may know something about this. Recently I asked her if there was any truth to Katie's story, and she began babbling about the judgment of God."

"I told you I saw her this morning, meditating. That's not quite true. She was crying. She seems so troubled. But when I try to be nice to her, she jumps all over me, points fingers, and yells."

"Katie's exact predicament. She tried so hard with that girl, but all she got was rebuttal."

"Doreen told me that Katie kicked her out of the house after Hilda died."

"Nonsense!" His large nose sniffed at the air. "She did nothing of the sort. Katie would have gladly let her stay. My goodness, there was room in that place, and it would have been a help to Katie. No, when Hilda died, Doreen moved out almost immediately of her own accord."

Sharon shook her head. "That's not what Doreen says."

"On more than one occasion Katie said she had approached Doreen to stay, but to no avail. Her brother was opening up a motel and needed her help. She would come back to Katie's to clean twice a week. But that was all. Those were her terms. But you know," he leaned forward, "I always got the sense that there was a tension between Doreen and Katie. It almost seemed to me as if Doreen was afraid of her." Cos leaned back, looked at the ceiling. "I expect the only person who really understood Doreen was Hilda. You must remember, Doreen's been in that house for a long time, a very long time, longer than most anyone else who is still alive."

"So if there really was a murder, Doreen may have heard something, seen something?"

He nodded, pursed his lips. "That is a distinct possibility. And it may account for her strange behavior toward Katie."

"If she knows something, why won't she talk?"

He shook his head, rubbed his nose. "I don't know. Fear?"

"But everybody is dead."

He nodded, took a cookie. "So true, so true."

"Where did Doreen come from anyway?"

"Now, my dear, I thought you would know the answer to that question."

"I thought Katie might have told you."

"Katie and I seldom discussed Doreen's antecedents. The fact that Doreen didn't trust her I could see was a great disappointment to her, but there was nothing she could do. When I visited, I would see Doreen about, dusting here and there, and Katie was always the pillar of grace with her. But Doreen cowered under her. I merely thought that was her nature."

"The only thing I knew about her was that she was taken in by Hilda, that she'd had a bad life and some sort of nervous breakdown." Sharon reached into her pocket. "I found some old photos. I was wondering if you might know any of these people."

They looked first at the one of Katie and Hilda and Little Mary. He picked it up and brought it close to his eyes. "Yes, Little Mary."

"Did Katie tell you much about Little Mary?"

"The beloved sister who died in her teens. A bit, only a bit. It seemed a painful memory for her. I never asked why."

"Jeff is on a wild goose chase to find out where Little Mary is buried. Seems she's not in the sacred family plot."

Next, Sharon passed to Cos the picture of Katie and the young man. His fingers seemed to quiver as he gazed down at it.

"Do you know who that young man is?" she asked.

"No." Cos reached into his pocket for a handkerchief and wiped his forehead.

"Are you okay?"

He laid the picture down on the coffee table between them. "She told me the story of this once. She told me about this young man."

Sharon studied his face.

"They were in love with each other. I guess he was not the sort of young man her father would have her marry. The Sullivans had high hopes for their daughters. There was quite a fuss about her betrothal in the church and in the community. From what she told me, this young man's father was a common laborer."

"Oh, perish the thought."

"In those days that sort of thing mattered. The Sullivans were quite a prestigious, God-fearing, well-respected family. They couldn't have their name besmirched by having their daughter marry a common laborer."

"Why didn't the two of them just run away and get married?"

He sighed. "Times were different then. One didn't do that sort of thing. Oh, maybe some people did it, but not churchgoers. I know it was this experience that made her who she was—different, outrageous, a teller of tales." He paused, picked up the photo again. "Katie and I shared a lot during our ten years together. Both of us making peace with the past. She making peace with hers. Me with my own."

"She never told you his name?"

He looked past her, out the window toward the sea. "'The sea never changes and its works, for all the talk of men, are wrapped in mystery.'"

There was silence for a few moments. Sharon drank her tea. Cos stared out to the sea. Finally Sharon said, "You know I'm working on these memoirs of Katie. She never kept a journal, so I don't know what was going on in her mind at certain times of her life. She only wrote stories. I have scribblers filled with them, but to get inside of her head, that's what I'm having difficulty with. You knew her. You were her last best friend. Maybe her best friend, ever. I guess I'm trying to get a handle on Katie, the person she was, what made her like she was. I remember her as this outrageous, eccentric aunt that I envied. In an age when everyone was conforming to the norm, she was different."

"A true nonconformist."

"I want to know what made her so."

"How do we ever know what makes a person the way she is?"

Sharon shook her head. "My job would be so much easier if I could just uncover a long-lost journal of hers."

"There will be no such book."

"Instead I have snippets of notes, old bulletins, stray photos that I have to make sense of."

"Tell me, Sharon, do you keep a journal?"

She shook her head, smiled up at him. "No. Never. I write stories."

"You are much like her, then."

THIRTY-TWO

When Katie was eighteen she fell in love with the wrong person. I have found only one picture of him, a studio photo tucked away in a dusty manila envelope hidden between pages 3152 and 3153 of the 1922 edition of *The World Book Encyclopedia, Volume V, From Gumarabic to Kumquat*.

The cardboard-backed photo measures four inches by six, and in it an eighteen-year-old Katie is seated on a brocade chair, her white dress full around her. In one hand she holds a closed fan. Standing behind her, with a hand protectively on her shoulder, is a fair-haired young man wearing a dark suit with a bow tie and vest. He is clean shaven except for a pale brush of a mustache across his upper lip. Both look solemn enough, yet there is a hint of smile on the two of them, as if they found the whole procedure of posing outrageously funny. If you were to come upon them a moment after the photographer had finished, they would have burst into gales of laughter.

He looks well dressed. He looks upper class. He doesn't look the common laborer. But I am told that he was not suited to marry Katie. His family lacked the connections of the Sullivans. The marriage never happened.

I think of the Teasdale poem, the one Katie wrote out in full in her cloth book.

> *I ceased to love him long ago*
> *I tell myself so every day*
> *But deep within my heart I know*
> *There is no truth in what I say...*

And I wonder. Was this young man, this man with the rather wild-looking pale hair and jaunty smile, is he the one she is thinking about as she copied these words into her book? I try to imagine the day he was driven away. I think about it, envision it, calling up the conversation that must have occurred between the unyielding Gerard and the willful, yet still compliant Katie. Were Katie and the young man allowed, at least, one last walk along the beach? Did they share a lingering kiss? What became of that young man? Do we know his name?

Katie never married. Neither did Hilda. Neither, also, did Little Mary. None of the Sullivan daughters had the privilege of marrying well, it seems.

Why didn't they just run away? My modern, liberated twenty-first century mind demands an answer to that question. What was stopping them? If Katie were here, if I were allowed one last chance to talk to her, I would ask her. But I can almost hear her sigh, look past me, and tell me that times were different then. It's different now, she would say, placing her hands on the thighs of her blue jeans. You young people can make up your own minds, you can judge things for yourself. You can make your own decisions. I could not. It was just the times, Sharon, just the times.

I wonder, is this when Katie concocted the story of the murder and the fireplace poker? Is this when she looked at those implements and began to imagine to what purposes they might be put?

The telephone rang, startling Sharon out of her reverie. It was the lawyer, who cleared his throat before he said, "I'm just calling to, ah, bring you up to date on the search for your brother."

"You've found him?"

"No, not yet. Which is why I'm calling."

"Yes?"

"So far, using the channels that we've come up with, we have not located him. That man who came forward a few days ago was not Dean. We have checked with the death records, and none of the records of the Dean Sullivans who have, ah, passed away match the date of birth we have for Dean Sullivan, your brother. And none of the classified ads have yielded the results we had hoped for."

"So now what?"

"We would like your permission to hire a private investigator to locate your brother. That's the final step."

"Fine."

"He may not be in California now. He may have moved. He may be living in another country."

"Okay."

"I just wanted to let you know."

"Fine. Keep me posted."

"It may cost a bit."

"That's okay."

THIRTY-THREE

IN THE NIGHT SHARON WOKE to a loud thump against the side of the house. The sound had occurred in that thin line between waking and sleeping, where dream sound is easily mistaken for real sound. She turned and lay on her back so she could listen with both ears. Nothing. The only sound was the breakers against far-off sand.

She turned onto her side to go back to sleep and heard it again. This time the sound of something scraping. Something being dragged? She leaned over and put her hand on Jeff's shoulder, shaking him awake.

"Wha...what?" he said loudly.

"Shh. There's someone downstairs. I hear something."

He rubbed his eyes. "What did you say?"

"There's a noise downstairs. I hear something. This time I'm not imagining it."

"You mean besides Natasha?"

She stared at him in the darkness. It had been just the two of them for so long that she had forgotten what it was like to have someone else in the house. It was just Natasha coming home. Of course, how silly of her! She went back to sleep.

Early in the morning, before it was light, Sharon rose and tiptoed downstairs. She longed to go out onto the sunporch, maybe grab Katie's old blue Bible and sit out there on the daybed and look through it. At the parlor doorway, she stood for a second. Out on the sunporch her daughter lay sleeping, her head barely visible above the mound of blankets. She didn't stir when Sharon made her way through the murky dark room, stepping over piles of Natasha's clothes, to the bookshelf.

Sharon searched the shelves for the Bible, her eyes adjusting to the dim light. *National Geographics* lay in haphazard piles all over the floor.

Maybe this is what she heard last night, Natasha, unable to sleep, rifling through the magazines for something interesting to read.

The Bible was in a far corner next to the plastic-taped door. Part of it was shoved up against the cold outside wall. Gingerly, she moved it from its place. She glanced over at her daughter. Still no sound. She lifted the leather Bible out with two fingers, and it slipped from her grasp and dropped heavily onto the floor. Sharon bent down to retrieve it and discovered a couple of tiny pink pills on the floor. She picked them up and put them on the bookshelf. Natasha slept on.

Back in the dining room, she sat by the window and paged through the book, this time beginning from the back. It was full of Katie's penciled notes in the margins. The entire book of Revelation was marked up with pencil scrawls, arrows, and drawings.

When Sharon was a girl, their church had annual prophecy conferences in which visiting ministers explained in great detail the long timelines of history. All around the walls of the church were chart after chart. When this happens, then that will happen, then this will happen, followed by that. She leafed through the book. Between the pages was a tiny drawing on card stock. "Revelation 4" was written across the top in green ink. It was an ornate drawing of a massive throne done in colored pencils, a green rainbow circling the entire thing. Along the bottom she read: *To Katie, from D. This is my favorite because the rainbow is green. The awesomeness of Jesus: This is what we forget about.*

The awesomeness of Jesus? When the timelines were explained by those traveling evangelists, no one ever talked about any awesomeness of Jesus. It was all about fears and plagues and water turning to blood, and how we needed to get out there and witness even more because if we didn't and someone went to hell, his blood would be on our hands, and this was something we'd have to deal with for all eternity. Nothing was mentioned of the awesomeness of Jesus when they were given all those timelines to copy into their Bibles.

Sharon put the drawing back into the Bible and read the passage in the fourth chapter of Revelation. In the margin, Katie had written: *The glory of God, his love, his power, the slain Lamb. You are right, D, we forget these things.*

"Natasha still asleep?" Jeff was standing in the doorway, his jogging clothes on.

Sharon closed the Bible. "You're up early. I tried not to disturb you."

"You didn't. I didn't even hear you get up."

"You going running then?"

"Maybe after I've had my coffee. It's pouring outside."

"Lazy bones."

He grinned at her.

"Natasha's sound asleep," she said. "I went in to get Katie's Bible and she didn't even move."

"Must be jet lag still. I'll get coffee going." She followed him into the kitchen.

They were sitting at the kitchen table when Natasha walked in through the back door, dressed for the outdoors in a rain-spattered jacket, her backpack flung over her shoulder. She stared at them. "I didn't think you guys would be up yet."

Sharon looked at her curiously. "You went out for a walk just now? I didn't hear you leave."

Natasha took off her jacket and hung her backpack on the end of a chair. "I was hoping to get into bed before you guys got up."

"I must have been really absorbed in my book. I didn't even see you walk past me."

"We heard you come in last night," Jeff said.

Natasha rubbed her eyes. "Oh, these contacts are absolutely killing my eyes. I've got to take them out. I think I've had them in for twenty-four hours at least. What I need is a shower. And to get to bed."

Sharon looked over at her daughter. "Natasha?"

Natasha turned. "Yeah?"

"You were here last night."

"No, Mom. And I'm so sorry. I should've called." She ran her hand through her hair. Sharon noticed that her fingernails were a slightly darker shade of blue. "I'm so used to being on my own."

"I heard you come in in the middle of the night," Sharon said. "We both did. When I came down this morning, I saw you sleeping on the sunporch."

"I was in Portsmouth all night. I'm sorry, I should've called." Natasha unlaced her hiking books.

"You were in your room not more than thirty minutes ago."

"Thirty minutes ago I was driving up the interstate from New Hampshire."

Sharon put a hand to her mouth.

"You're saying that you were out all night?" Jeff said.

"By the time I realized I should call, it was like one o'clock and I didn't want to wake you."

"What were you doing in Portsmouth all night?" Jeff asked.

"Just sort of hanging around. Went to a few clubs."

"How did you get there?"

"Cos loaned me his car."

"Cos loaned you his car?" Jeff said.

"Yep."

Sharon held up her hand. "Jeff, wait. Natasha. That's not important. This is serious. I'm not imagining this. I saw you sleeping in your bed this morning. I saw a bunch of hair at the top of the blankets. If you are not out in the daybed, then someone else is."

"Maybe it was my blankets piled up."

"No, there was the shape of a person. I saw the dark hair."

Natasha started for the sunporch. "Wait!" Jeff said. He led the way and the two women followed. There was someone in the daybed. Someone with dark hair.

Jeff moved forward cautiously. "You guys go back to the kitchen."

They didn't.

Carefully, slowly, standing as far back as he could, he pulled back the blankets. The hair was dark and wild, the blue eyes wide open, the little red mouth formed in an *O*. Natasha screamed. Sharon gasped.

"I put this stupid mannequin under the house," Jeff said. "I wrapped her up in an old tarp and put her under the house."

"It's the ghost!" Natasha said.

He dropped the blankets back onto the mannequin and walked past them. "I'm calling the police. Again."

THIRTY-FOUR

NATASHA WAS DEAD TIRED. First, there was the little matter that she was still suffering jet lag. Second, she'd been up all night as it was, and now she had to sit here at the kitchen table while the police grilled them all and tromped around the inside of the house, tromped around the outside of the house, took fingerprints from everywhere, and talked to her parents in serious tones, while her mother stood there, furrowed face, hands on her hips.

Natasha combed two fingers through her hair. Ugh! It felt greasier than ever. She blinked her eyes and rubbed her face. She had taken out her contact lenses before the police came, so now everything was a blur. She refused to wear her glasses. Even though she couldn't see clearly, she could tell that the young police officer sitting across from her was eyeing her. He kept asking her questions, too. Where was she from? Victoria, same as her parents. Where was she last night? Portsmouth. Doing what? Visiting a friend. What's this friend's name? Can't remember.

When they finally left, they took Mildred with them, carrying her out like a sack of flour, her little face with the round red mouth gazing after them, as if to say, "Where are you taking me? What are you going to do with me?"

The first time Natasha had visited Trail's End, Mildred was out in the garden leaning up against a fence post. She remembered being quite frightened of the "lady" until Great-aunt Katie told her it was a scaregull.

"A what?"

"She means scarecrow," her mother said.

"No, Sharry, it's a scaregull." Then Katie lifted up her hands and clapped three times. "It's scares the gulls away from my garden."

"My name for it is a scarepeople," Natasha had said.

Katie had laughed and clapped her hands again.

"Natasha," her mother said after Natasha had come out of the shower, "you're not going to want to sleep on the sunporch anymore. I've made up the bed upstairs with clean sheets."

"The sunporch is fine. I like it out there."

"But it's a disaster area. At least sleep upstairs for today and let me clean off all the fingerprint stuff. The police really left a mess for us."

"I'll do it. Before I go to sleep."

Her mother sighed. "Oh well, Natasha, do what you want. I want to talk to you after you've had some sleep, and remember that tonight your grandfather is coming to dinner. So don't make any plans, okay. I'm sure he'll want to see you."

"Yeah, he always wants to see me. I'm the delight of his life."

It took Natasha about half an hour to clean up the sunporch before she felt comfortable enough to go to sleep. She stripped the bed to get the smell of Mildred out of it, and placed clean sheets on it from the upstairs hall closet.

She thought she would crash the minute she laid her head on the pillow, but that didn't happen. She was tired but restless. Her thoughts kept spinning from Jordan to Ireland to the Irish girl she wanted to squash like a bug, to driving around Portsmouth last night with nothing particular to do.

Last evening, while her parents were upstairs, Natasha had roamed around the quiet house, turned the radio on then off again, redone her fingernails. Then she had dumped the contents of a jigsaw puzzle on the card table in the parlor. After becoming bored with that, she decided that despite the downpour, she'd go for a walk. When she got to the beach, she turned right and walked on the wet sand letting the rain wash down her hair and run off her face.

She had been walking maybe fifteen minutes when she heard her name called. Startled, she saw someone frantically waving at her from a doorway. This was the old man she had had tea with the previous night. Maybe he needed some help. She turned and walked up through the sand toward the small beach house. She climbed up the long wooden stairway to the large deck. He opened the door and ushered her in.

"Are you okay?" she asked. "Did you want me for something?"

"You need to get out of the cold and rain. Here, come in. Come in."

Natasha gave him a curious look. "You're not in trouble or anything?"

"I was about to ask you the same question. Why does a person walk so slowly across the beach when it's raining down like cats and dogs?"

"I don't mind the rain. I'm washable."

He hobbled toward the bathroom and returned with a fluffy yellow towel and handed it to her. "Here, that rain is nasty. And sit, sit while I make us a nice hot cup of tea."

From the small kitchenette he talked while he filled the kettle. "I have purchased the kind of tea you enjoy. Although mine is loose, and now I want you to tell me which you prefer. We shall turn this into a contest."

Despite herself Natasha giggled. The house, though small and meant to be only a summer place, was comfortable and warm. She listened to a fire crackling in a small black woodstove in the corner.

"Do you have a TV?" she asked. It had been almost two years since she had seen American television.

"No, I'm afraid not. When my wife passed on, I gave ours to one of our children, Blake. His picture is there on the wall above the woodstove. He's the one on the far left. His wife Angela and their young ones."

"They look nice and happy." She rubbed her hair with the towel.

"That was taken a number of years ago now. One of the youngsters is married with children of her own. And one of those children has children. That makes me a great-great-grandfather. But I can't remember how many children they have. Isn't that something, to forget such obvious facts?"

"I'd probably forget, too." Natasha felt herself relax. "Is that your wife over there?" She pointed to the picture of the two of them on the mantle.

"That is she, yes. Isabella. Taken on our fiftieth. A lovely woman, so patient with all of my foibles and faux pas. Everyone should be so lucky to have loved."

"Not everyone is lucky."

He brought over their tea and a plate of arrowroot cookies, and for several minutes the two of them sat in companionable silence, enjoying the tea, listening to the fire, watching the rain. Then Natasha felt a tear slide down her cheek. She didn't know why the sadness came, so sudden. She wiped it away with the sleeve of her sweatshirt. "Don't know why." She laughed. "Think I'm just tired. So tired."

For a long time Cos didn't say anything. Then he got up, and after a moment returned with a small, thick brown book with a tattered cover. "Would you like me to read you some of my favorite poems?"

"What?"

"I used to read to Katie. Long hours we would sit here, much like this, and I would read. If you would indulge me, I'd like to read out loud again. It's been so long. I would be appreciative of the opportunity."

"Go ahead."

For the next hour she drank tea and listened. The entire pot of tea had been consumed, the ceramic pot cold to the touch, and still Cos read on. She was hypnotized, soothed, cheered by the sound of his voice, the words that spoke of love and loss and death and God.

Death is the end of life; ah why
Should life all labor be?
Let us alone. Time driveth onward fast.
And in a little while our lips are dumb.

Let us alone. What is it that will last?...
...And tho' from out our bourne of Time and Place
The flood may bear me far
I hope to see my Pilot face to face
When I have crost the bar...

But when he started to recite, *A plenteous place is Ireland for hospitable cheer,* Natasha sat upright. "Don't read that one."

He rubbed his palms together and turned the page. About an hour later he closed the book, placed it on the coffee table between them, and patted the top of it gently. Natasha looked at his hands as they lay there, large-knuckled, road-mapped with veins.

She said, "If you had been my English teacher I might have stayed in school." She picked up the book, her knees tucked underneath her, and flipped through it. "We had to read poetry at school, but when you read it, it makes sense. It's not like studying it."

"Poetry should be read aloud. That's the secret. That's the key."

"Can you tell me about the different poets? The ones you read tonight?"

"Tennyson, Elizabeth Barrett Browning, Sara Teasdale. You would like a lesson on poetry?"

"A lesson?"

"A lesson."

"Okay, sure. A lesson."

They made another pot of tea, and Cos, his features animated, explained poets and poetry to Natasha.

Finally he sighed, put his large hands on his knees and rose slowly. "It's time for this old man to get himself to bed. But you, Natasha, you can stay. Read, if you want. I've no end of reading material. You may borrow that book if you like. Take it with you."

"Thank you." She held the book close to her.

"Shall you head back or shall you stay?"

"I was thinking of going into New Hampshire. I'm having trouble sleeping at normal times." She pushed her hair out of her face. "Jet lag."

"How shall you get there?"

She shrugged. "I don't know. Hitchhike. Maybe there's a bus."

He shook his head. "Please take my car. I don't drive it much anymore, just to town and back. Don't trust myself on the highway."

"I couldn't do that."

He was fishing through a glass dish on the kitchen table. "Nonsense." He handed her the keys.

"Really, I'm fine. I'm real used to getting around by myself."

He pressed the keys into her palm. His hand felt dry and cold. "I insist."

"Are you sure?"

"Absolutely."

"Well, okay then."

"I have just one requirement: that you refrain from driving while impaired."

She had driven into Portsmouth. Downtown, she found a noisy bar, sat down at a booth by herself, and sipped on a Coke while she read through the poetry. Cos's requirement kept her from ordering even one beer. If her parents had said the same thing, she would have rolled her eyes and done what she wanted.

She walked for a while, until the cold and rain got to her. She stopped at another bar where she danced with a tall, skinny young man with short, spiky orange hair. He bought her a beer, which she didn't drink. They talked for a while. When he asked her back to his place, she excused herself and went to the ladies' room. She left by the back door and drove around some more. Eventually, she went to another bar, where a local band was playing, and sat at a table with a bunch of kids her age. They talked. She talked. When they found out she was Canadian they wanted to know all about her. She thought them boring. After the female member of the band did a bad rendition of "Who Will Save Your Soul?" she left. She drove. She parked.

She listened to the rain. At predawn, she drove back to Trail's End. And now, finally, sleep came.

THIRTY-FIVE

THE SKY WAS LIGHTENING. Not just lightening, but brightening, the sun actually blinking now and again through the clouds, knife glints of yellow through the layers of gray. Sharon was seated at the dining room table, the computer opened up in front of her. Yes, the weather had finally broken. When the police were here it had been pouring rain. But now it was clearing and even the sounds were brighter, the gulls' calls cheerier. The breakers had a different sound when the sun was out, less mournful somehow. They spoke of expectancy this morning and not of sorrow. This was a surprise to even the weather forecasters, apparently. Good drying conditions, she heard on the radio; take advantage of that breeze. "You want to get those blankets aired out, now's the time!" the radio announcer said.

After some straining and shoving, Sharon managed to get the dining room window open. A warm spring breeze she could almost taste moved the lace curtains in slow motion. A walk along the beach would be nice, but just her luck, she'd get out there and the police would call. Or the people from Hollywood who wanted to do that TV series. And then, of course, she had work to do. She could write about Katie all she wanted, but it was a Summer Whitney book that came attached to a deadline. And that deadline was a scant three months away. She thought of a bumper sticker she had seen, Warning: dates on this calendar are closer than they appear. She pressed her fingers into her temples.

Jeff would be gone most of the morning. He was driving up to Augusta to further check on the whereabouts of Little Mary's bones. He was becoming obsessed by "the mystery" as he called it, and was tackling the project with Woodward and Bernstein enthusiasm. At noon Doreen would be here to sort through the junk in the small bedroom off the kitchen, the room that had been her home for so many years.

And then, at some point today, Sharon was going to have to figure out what she was going to make for supper. Her father would be here by six. And if that weren't enough, there was the little matter of Natasha being out all night. In Cos's car, no less. Sharon put her chin in her hands and stared at the computer screen. She could picture Natasha, as cheeky as ever, knocking on Cos's door, waking him up, most likely, asking if she could borrow his car. What could he say but yes? If Natasha wanted to come back home, there would have to be rules. And she had crossed the line on this one.

Before the police had left, the older of the two officers told them not to mention the break-in to too many people. "There's this feeling among the locals that this place is, well, haunted. We don't want to add fuel to the fire. We'll do everything we can to try and find out what really happened here."

"That's ridiculous," Sharon said. "This house has been inhabited until just recently."

"Yeah," said the younger officer, the one that Sharon noticed had been eyeing Natasha earlier. "But you know how people talk around here."

Sharon typed one sentence, the first sentence of a new Summer Whitney book:

I tend to avoid beaches. The whole bikini, sunscreen, salt water in the iced tea, sand in the hoagies deal...

She pressed her hands against her temples; her headache was worsening. When the phone rang, she jumped to answer it. It took a few moments before she said, "Hello, Marge."

"Don't sound so disappointed."

"No, it's not that. We've had a couple of break-ins. So, I'm kind of on edge."

"Oh dear. I hope they find the perps." Marge, the mystery editor.

"Yeah."

Sharon learned that the latest Summer Whitney was getting great reviews and it looked as if this whole television thing was coming together, and how was the next Summer Whitney coming along?

"It's off to a good start," said Sharon, looking at the sentence she had just written.

"I know we're jumping ahead of things here, but do you think you could have it completed in, say, a month?"

Sharon nearly dropped the phone. "I don't know. I don't think so. Uh, there's this break-in plus these pressing family matters to take care of here."

"Sorry to be so un-understanding. I know your aunt was special to you."

Sharon paused. "Marge, I may have this other idea. For a book. Maybe."

"Other idea?"

"Let me run it past you. My aunt was quite a character. She was the true storyteller. I'm just a poor imitation. If she had written books, she would've made you a millionaire. Actually—and this is true—I have sort of based my whole character of Summer Whitney on her." Sharon paused.

"I'm listening."

"I'm thinking of a memoir, a biography of sorts."

"A biography of someone nobody knows?"

"She was quite eccentric and wonderful."

"Sharon, big name authors can write anything and have it sell. You are not that well known. You, my dear, still have to work for a living."

"Thanks, Marge."

"But after this television thing, things may turn around. Well, I can say definitely they will turn around for you. Writing novels is like entering the lottery, you've heard me say that before. Some writers make it big, most don't. But we've got a good chance at winning the lottery with this television thing."

"Marge, getting back to this other idea. My Aunt Katie used to tell stories. She had this elaborate tale of trolls and fairies—"

"We don't publish children's fantasy, Sharon. We publish some of the finest genre mystery in North America."

Sharon made a face. "I know, and I'm not talking about children's fantasy. She also used to talk about a murder. I'm trying my darnedest while I'm here to figure out if this murder had any basis in reality. I mean she would absolutely shock the family with this tale—"

"And you're thinking of fictionalizing this, and bringing Summer into it? Well, that could work."

"Well."

"Okay, send me what you have. I'll have a look. Just make sure you include Summer. The TV people want as many Summer Whitneys as you can come up with."

After she said goodbye to Marge she wrote:

I tend to avoid beaches. The whole bikini, sunscreen, salt water in the thermos, sand in the hoagies is not my cup of iced tea. When it's hot, I'd rather be sitting in my cool basement apartment reading the latest true crime. I hate the beach, hate the sun, hate the sunburn that accompanies the sun. So what am I doing, then, tripping over bikini-clad sun worshipers on Old Orchard Beach, Maine, on the hottest day in the middle of the hottest month of the hottest year on record, looking for a ghost? Right now I could do with a bit of that ice-cold air they say accompanies a spirit from beyond.

I don't even own a bathing suit. When it's time for me to go on vacation, if I ever do find the time to take one, I'm more likely to pack up my camping gear and hike up mountains than lie like a turkey basting in the heat. Besides, I've been given the kind of skin that burns rather than tans. So I avoid the sun. Right now I've got on my jeans and the jacket I own with all the pockets. I'm a private investigator and carry around with me a tiny tape recorder, a notebook, a miniature camera, and a flashlight. There are not a whole lot of places to conceal these tools of my trade in a bikini.

It had been against my better judgment to come here in the first place. Come to investigate a ghost? I don't want to burst anyone's bubble, but usually ghosts, in my experience, have some basis in reality. So when the cousin of a client I had done some insurance work for called, and since I had no pressing deadlines and my bank balance was dwindling awfully close to the zero mark, I said, "Maybe."

This cousin of a client owned a beachfront clothing store, the kind that specializes in those T-shirts that say, "My mommy and daddy went to Old Orchard Beach and all they got me was this T-shirt." You know the kind. At first I said no. Maine is too far away. But he made an offer I couldn't refuse. All expenses, and I'd be staying in their beach house right on the water. Maybe I could learn to be like other people and sit on towels in the sun. Besides, Maine is pretty northerly, how hot could it get?

Hot hot is what I discovered.

The case involved a mysterious mannequin named Mildred that kept appearing and disappearing at will. She would show up in corner cafés, sitting there in a booth, a teacup in her mannequinly hands. Or on the beach, clad in a bikini, lying on her stomach catching a few rays.

"You don't need me. Sounds like you got a practical joker on your hands."

"That's what we thought until the bodies started appearing."

"Bodies?"

"Whenever Mildred comes out of hiding another local person is murdered."

"What do the police say?"

"They're about to arrest me."

"You?"

"It's my mannequin."

Sharon got up and closed the window. The rain had come back. She rubbed her eyes, pulled her hair back into a ponytail, wandered into the kitchen, took out some hamburger meat. She'd make meat loaf. Meat, potatoes, a cooked vegetable, maybe a lettuce salad, and an apple pie, and her father would be satisfied. Nothing casseroled together, cooked in one pot. No sauces for him, except maybe brown gravy. She did a bit of cleaning, washed up a few dishes. Doreen would be here in an hour. Back in the dining room, she sat down at her computer again.

She heard rustling from the front of the house; it was Natasha walking by on her way to the bathroom.

"Natasha," she called, "when you've finished your shower I'd like to have a word with you."

She opened a new word processing file and labeled it THINGS THAT COULD HAPPEN, and began making a sort-of outline of things that could happen in this new book. People were always surprised when she told them she seldom wrote from an outline, and that she often began a book with no clue as to whodunit and why. She came up with a few ideas, got bored, then opened another file. Her Katie file. Could she mix the two? Katie and Summer? The true story of Katie with the fantastic superwoman crime sleuthing of Summer? It was a strange thought, but did she want Summer Whitney invading her own territory? "I'm like Dr. Frankenstein," she said out loud. "I have created a monster."

"What did you say, Mom?" Natasha stood in the doorway, fresh from her shower.

"Oh nothing. I was talking to myself as usual, trying to write. My editor wants a new mystery in a month, and I'm pulling my hair out."

"Oh, you'll do it, Mom. You always do."

"Thanks for the vote of confidence."

"You said you wanted to see me?"

Sharon looked over at her daughter.

"If this is about last night, I told you, by the time I thought to call you it was too late. And I didn't want to wake you guys up. I'm really sorry."

"It's not that. It's the little matter of Cos's car."

"You don't have to worry. I returned it to him in perfectly good shape. He asked me not to drink and drive, and I didn't. Not even one beer. Nothing."

Sharon made a sound somewhere between a sigh and a grunt. "That's not it. It's the very fact that you went over there and asked to borrow it. Natasha, he's a kindly old man. Of course he's going to say yes. You shouldn't have taken advantage of him."

"Mom, it wasn't like that. He told me I could have it. I wasn't going to, and he practically shoved the keys in my hand."

"I find that hard to believe. You went over, knocked on his door, and all of a sudden he's pressing his keys into your hand?"

"No, that wasn't it either. It was after we talked for a while."

"You need to be more respectful of people."

"I am, Mom. He offered his car to me. You can even ask him. Go ahead, ask him. He's teaching me poetry."

"He's what?"

"Teaching me poetry."

Natasha turned then, and walked toward the sunporch.

THIRTY-SIX

MACK HAD FELT LIGHT-HEADED and happy all day. It was the weather. Well, not so much the actual weather, but that he had accurately predicted its break. Even sitting here at the kitchen table in Trail's End with Sharon and Jeff wasn't defusing his mood. Even Jeff commented on it.

"You must be feeling much better, Mack."

"Oh just fine, just fine."

"Well, that's good, isn't it, Sharon?"

She nodded.

The last time Mack had been here in Trail's End it had been to arrange Katie's funeral with Harold Cosman. Cos had called him when Katie was dying.

"She has something she wants to tell you," Cos had said.

"What?"

"That I don't know."

Mona's granddaughter drove Mack, but they arrived too late. Katie had died half an hour before he arrived. In the kitchen, with the body of his dead sister in the adjoining room, the two men made plans for the funeral, while Mona's granddaughter sat in the sunporch reading through old *National Geographics*.

"She wasn't in the church," Mack said, "so I don't think a funeral is appropriate."

Cos glared at him then, his large fleshy face red and damp with crying. "She was most assuredly in the church, my dear man, most assuredly."

The funeral was held in the small white church in Beach Haven, the one Mack's father had dismissed as being too liberal. The service was attended by hundreds of people, another surprise to Mack.

And now he was back here, sitting at the table while Sharon, Jeff, and Natasha busied themselves around him. His granddaughter was helping to set the table in the dining room, and every once in a while she would yell in, Do we use the blue glasses or the red? Do you want the good silverware? He told them they didn't have to fuss, that the kitchen was just fine, but Sharon said the kitchen table was too small, besides, sitting in the dining room you didn't have to see all the mounds of dirty dishes. They were having meat loaf, Sharon said. And when he offered to help, Sharon said no, everything was under control.

Something Hilda would say. As he watched his daughter move, briskly, efficiently, across the linoleum, the brown hair combed back and severe off her scalp, he could see the barbed edges of his eldest sister, hands on her hips, the thinness of her frame, the thorny points of her shoulders and elbows. He rubbed his knees and forced himself to say, "Smells good."

She looked at him, spatula in hand, thin lips pursed. "Well, I hope it's good. It's been a real circus here today. Did Jeff tell you about Mildred?"

"No, I didn't," said Jeff, aproned and spooning mashed potatoes from a metal pot into a bowl. "Didn't think we needed to alarm him."

"What happened?" he asked.

"Oh, just a few vandals thought it quite funny to scare us half to death, is all. Had the police here most of the morning."

Natasha had entered. Mack still couldn't get used to the look of her. He hadn't remembered her hair being so dark. In the pictures of her that Sharon sent each year, pictures he faithfully framed and placed on his bedroom dresser, her hair was lighter, strawberry like Rosie's, and she was freckled. When had her hair turned so dark? And her skin that ghastly white color? Was she ill?

Natasha, a load of plates in the crook of her arm, said, "Someone broke into the house in the middle of the night, found Mildred, and put her in my bed when I wasn't there. And the night before, someone decided that Mildred needed a shower."

"A shower?"

"They put her in the downstairs bathtub."

"The police've been all over the house," Sharon said.

"The funny thing is," said Jeff, straining the gravy, "they didn't take anything, even though our computer was sitting right out on the dining room table, plain as day. The police found that odd, too."

"The police told us this place is haunted. What do you think, Grandpa?"

"Natasha, the police didn't say it was haunted. They said some people think it's haunted," Sharon said.

"Well, it could be," Natasha said. "Someone died here, remember?"

"If every house where someone died was haunted, there'd be very few houses that weren't," Jeff said.

"Yes, but Mother, she died under mysterious circumstances."

"No, she didn't. She died of old age. She was nearly ninety. Her heart gave out."

"My heart would too if I had to live in a haunted house."

Sharon rolled her eyes. Jeff laughed out loud. Mack just stared at them.

"I think dinner is ready," said Jeff, opening the oven.

The four of them sat down in the dining room, and Mack was surprised when Jeff asked him to say the blessing. He mumbled something into his folded hands. Mack was glad the food was home cooked. Home-cooked food was much better than restaurant, that's what he always said. Much better than that place Sharon and Jeff had taken him to last week. That was one of the reasons he liked Mona's so much; hers was home cooked. Nothing but home cooked.

"I'm getting closer to figuring out what happened to Little Mary," Jeff said between mouthfuls. "I was in Augusta all day chasing down leads. Her death certificate was not signed by a medical doctor or a coroner, but by a druggist, a pharmacist, and in those days, druggists actually prepared the pills and vials of medications, mixing this and that until they came up with medicines. And here's what I think: I think Little Mary didn't die at all—well, not then anyway." He gestured with his fork. "I believe she had some sort of a nervous breakdown or maybe a form of mental illness. And that druggist friend, George Koch, was trying to come up with a sort of prescription for her because having a mental illness was a great embarrassment to the family." He turned to Mack. "I know you were just a boy at the time, Mack, but how did she seem to you?"

Mack grunted. "I was young. She was sick. That I remember. It's cold in here, don't you think? I feel a cold draft right on the small of my back. It's always been damp in this room, that's why we never ate in here."

"We always ate in here," Sharon said.

"No, I don't remember that."

"Only about every Sunday of my childhood."

"And it was cold then, too. The north wind. I remember those Sundays."

"Natasha, turn up the heat, please," Sharon said.

Natasha rose, rolled her eyes, and flicked up the thermostat.

Jeff leaned forward. "Mack, did she seem distraught? Depressed to you in any way?"

"Who?"

"Little Mary. Your sister."

"Why are you asking me all these questions? These things are long past."

"I'm just trying to figure this out."

"Dad," Sharon said, "we just want to find out what happened. Can't you humor Jeff? Why does it always have to end up like this?"

"End up like what?" Mack said quietly. He put down his roll, store-bought he could see, and said, "She was sick. That's what I remember. She had these dark circles under her eyes, and no one would tell me what was wrong with her. She wouldn't talk to anyone. Not me, not anyone. She was inside for weeks on end, just sitting on the sunporch, not even going to church. We were here at the time.

Here at Trail's End. It was summer."

Jeff beamed, dropped his fork into his peas. "I knew my theory was correct! That death certificate was a phony. Little Mary was really taken to a hospital of some sort, probably what they called insane asylums in those days."

"Oh, heavy," Natasha said.

"She probably died there some years later, but the family was so concerned about protecting their name that they concocted the whole story about her death being caused by pneumonia. In those days mental illness was thought to be caused by evil spirits. Demons."

Natasha raised her fingers like claws and hissed like a cat. Mack noticed for the first time that her fingernails were blue. He stared at them, wondering if this was something intentional or if she had gotten them all caught in a door.

"Natasha," Sharon said.

"There are ghosts in this place," she said. "Evil spirits. I was just trying to call them up."

Jeff continued. "I talked to a minister today."

Sharon nearly choked on her glass of water. "You talked to a what?"

"A minister. Of a church. And he told me that mental illness was not recognized for what it was."

"Where'd you come across a minister? You just drive up to a church and walk in?"

"Not quite. Well almost. I went to the church you went to, the white one across from the museum building. The one that had Katie's funeral."

"My dad, the religious fanatic."

"I met Reverend Barry Brannin. You said you met him, so I thought I might as well, too. We had lunch."

"You had lunch?"

"We had lunch. Nice guy. Talkative. But I guess it helps to be talkative in that profession. He told me a lot about evil spirits and demons and mental illness. It was quite enlightening. I'm more convinced than ever that Mary was mentally ill. In the afternoon I called a lot of the mental hospitals that would have been around in 1940, but there was no record of a Mary Sullivan being admitted, and so many of those records are private. If she checked in under a different name, which she probably did, there will probably be no way to trace her. A few places are checking for me. Sad thing is that in a number of them the records are destroyed."

"Why are you doing this?" Mack asked. He felt awfully hot now and wondered if he should say something.

"I don't know. I don't really know. I just am."

"Mountain climbers climb mountains because they're there," Natasha said. "My dad noses around in other people's business because it's there."

"Natasha," Sharon said, "this is not other people's business, this is family business, and we're allowed to find out what happened to family. Would you please go and see if the coffee's finished percolating?"

Natasha rose, cleared some of the plates off the table, and retreated into the kitchen. While she was gone, Sharon reached for an envelope on the sideboard. "Dad, I found some pictures I want you to look at and see if you can tell me who these people are."

Mack wiped his forehead with his napkin and looked down at the picture of Katie and the young man.

"Katie," he said.

"I know, but who's the boy?"

He put on his glasses. "I don't know."

"No idea?"

"Katie was sixteen by the time I was even born. My sisters were always more like aunts to me than sisters. When this picture was taken I was probably around three. I have no idea who he was."

"No one talked about a boyfriend that Katie had?"

"No. Katie never married."

"Could it be a cousin or something?"

"Maybe. I don't know."

"You guys reminisce," said Jeff rising. "Natasha and I will clear the table and bring out the pie."

Mack looked up. "We can look at these pictures later, Sharon."

Jeff put his hand on Mack's shoulder. "No, Mack, you two talk. Not often enough that father and daughter get to visit. Natasha and I are fine."

Mack took off his glasses, placed them on the table, and ran his napkin over his damp face. It was wrong in the order of things, it just was, men clearing and serving meals. He looked down at the picture again. Katie had never talked about a boyfriend. Neither had Hilda. And, no, he had no idea why there were no pictures of Little Mary around. He always figured they just hadn't gotten around to taking any.

The apple pie was good. "Did you make this, Sharon?" he asked.

"No, I got it in a little bakery in the Portland Public Market."

Mack grunted. "Used to be women made their own pies—rolled out the dough, cut up the apples. Times have changed, I guess."

"Yes, they have," Sharon said.

"My mom never bakes anything," Natasha said. "She believes that if God had intended us to bake, he wouldn't have invented bakeries."

Mack looked at her.

Sharon said, "Natasha."

Jeff started talking about the weather, and it came to Mack as he sat there that this was his family. This was all he had, a backslidden daughter, his only son gone, living who knows where and doing who knows what, one granddaughter who mouthed off continually with no reprimand at all from her parents. No family devotions. No wife to grow old with, to pray with. It was different for Fred and Sylvia, he knew; their large family all Christians, all serving God. His own quiver was indeed empty.

As soon as was polite, he said his good-byes. "I like to be in bed by nine-thirty," he said.

"We'll have to do this again, Dad," said Sharon, but her voice was thin.

He was sure all of them would breathe a sigh of relief as soon as he left.

Before he went to sleep, he took Rose's picture from the mantle and talked to her for a few moments. And in his bedside prayers he knelt and asked God why he had taken her. Why he thought it in his great wisdom to take the only thing that meant anything to him in the entire world?

THIRTY-SEVEN

SHARON WONDERED HOW BIOGRAPHERS WORKED. The clutter, the piles of things. They would be continually stepping over mountains of papers, photos, mementos, bulletins, newspaper articles, address books, date books, guest books, receipts, certificates, shoe boxes full of birthday cards, get-well cards, anniversary cards, sympathy cards. And then they would have to somehow find an order there, a pattern emerging from chaos.

What had begun as a handful of letters and an idea to immortalize her aunt was now turning into something that had taken over the dining room. She had already added the third leaf to the table, yet the stacks of papers and notes was growing higher.

Last evening, after her father had left, Sharon had forced herself to work on the Summer Whitney story. "I don't want to do this," she told her husband. "Not this one, not the one with Mildred."

"Why not? Having Summer come to Maine, investigate Mildred. That's a stroke of genius."

She groaned. "It's weird, but I'm afraid if I do this novel, I'll somehow miss the real story. Does that make sense? I don't know."

Now, this morning, she couldn't face Summer, but instead was trying to make order from the piles of Katie's things. Across from her, Jeff was going through his own notes.

"This is going to be a good article. Going to make for interesting reading."

"What?" asked Sharon.

"Mental illness. How it was perceived only a few years ago. I've got the go-ahead from *MacLean's*. Editor is a fellow I met at a convention a few years back. It's not like this is a subject that hasn't been written about before, but what I've got is a new angle."

"Oh yeah?"

"The whole demon possession thing. Look at the facts. All the photos of Little Mary were destroyed or at least taken down. Plus, she wasn't even buried with the rest of the family. The fact that this house is perceived to be haunted. Even if we don't find out exactly what happened to Little Mary, this whole thing will make for interesting reading. I'll be heading into Portland this morning, see what I can dig up at the library and the newspaper office about demonism, insane asylums, and mental illness in general."

"Have fun."

He left and Sharon went back to her sorting. Summer Whitney was hanging over her head, but Katie's mementos and school notes were far more interesting.

A little while later Natasha called from the sunporch. "Dad left?"

"Yep."

"Oh, darn. I was hoping for a ride into Portland."

"You should've gotten up earlier."

She walked into the dining room yawning and stretching. "I think I'm finally over my jet lag."

"Well, that's good. That means no more all night trips to Portsmouth. What're you up to today, then?"

"I don't know. Maybe I'll go for a walk. Go sit in that coffee shop and check out the locals."

"Have you gone through that box of jewelry and old clothes I showed you?"

Natasha shook her head. "Nope. Not interested."

Sharon went back to her computer.

"So what're you doing, Mom?"

"Oh, just this idea for a book. Sometimes I think I'm making myself crazy with all of this."

"I wish we had a TV."

"I know. You've said that."

"There's nothing to do. Not a thing. And this rain has been like going on forever."

"Are you giving any thought, Natasha, about your future?" Sharon said it carefully.

"My future?"

"Your future."

Natasha shrugged her shoulders. "I don't know. Go back to Victoria with you guys. Get a job."

"What kind of a job?"

"I was thinking about maybe being a travel agent."

Sharon smiled. "Well, that's wonderful! You'd be a great travel agent. I think there must be a community college in Victoria, or in Vancouver at least, that offers a program in tourism and travel. You could set up your own business. I've heard people are quite successful in that line of work. Plus, it would allow you to travel, something I know you enjoy. You really are the regular globe-trotter, you know."

"I was also thinking about applying with the RCMP, help them meet their quota for females."

"A police officer?" Sharon looked doubtful. "If you want my opinion, I think you'd make a better travel agent than a police officer."

"Maybe I'll be a private eye like Summer Whitney. She didn't go to school anywhere. I know, I've read the books."

Sharon frowned. "Summer Whitney is a fictionalized hero. Summer Whitney does not live in the real world. You do."

"Just kidding, Mom." Natasha flopped down in the chair beside the window. "It's no different now than it was in your Aunt Katie's day." She hung her legs over the chair arms. "I read your stuff, Mom. After you guys went to bed, I read the stuff you printed on marrying well, and how you would love to ask Katie some questions about why she didn't run away. And all about her parents being so concerned with their daughters' marrying well. It's exactly the same now."

Sharon shook her head. "Natasha, I don't care who you marry, when you marry, if you marry. That's your choice. Did I ever, ever make a negative comment about Jordan, all the time you were with him? Absolutely, I did not. Neither did your father. We may have had our doubts, but we said nothing."

"Yeah, you're such a new millennium Mom." Natasha paused, then said, "Back then, parents wanted their daughters to marry well. Now, they just want to see them in careers. Successful careers are the most important thing now, and how many degrees you have, can't forget that. 'Hello, my name is Sharon Sullivan Colebrook, I am a very successful mystery writer, and meet my husband Jeff, he's the managing editor of the famous *Times-Colonist*. And our daughter, why our daughter, well she has her very own successful business as a travel agent. Or our daughter? She's working on her Ph.D. in microbiology.' You'd love to be able to say that, wouldn't you? Whereas in the olden days, they'd say, 'Our daughter, well, she married into that very influential Sullivan family.'" Natasha had picked up the old guest book and was waving it around to make her point.

"But your dad and I are concerned about your future."

Natasha was leafing through the guest book now. "What is this book, anyway?"

"An old guest book. I'm using it in my memoirs of your great-aunt."

"The who's who of 1928. All of these people who probably don't even exist anymore. All dead."

"Probably."

Natasha read a few names out loud. "Phyllis and Arnie Schwab wrote, 'Wonderful hospitality.' Owen and Betty Corso write, 'Thank you for the spinach.'" Natasha guffawed. "Thank you for the spinach? Someone actually gave away spinach to departing guests? Here, have some spinach for your trip home. A bunch for the road."

"They grew spinach in the garden here. That wouldn't have been so strange."

"Vera Mountain wrote, 'A lovely time.' What kind of a name is Mountain? Did you know any of these people, Mom?"

"Nope."

"Well, you got to be sure to include them in the book. Merle and Olive Huddisfield. Who names their baby Olive? You might as well call your baby Fig or Date. Fig Colebrook. How come you didn't name me Fig Colebrook?"

"Maybe I should have. You want me to start calling you Fig? I will if you want."

"Then I would've gotten to sign this guest book. Look at all these people, Mom. All these people and their only claim to fame is that they signed this guest book and probably took home spinach, and I bet some of them put the spinach in their fridges, if they had fridges back then, and let it sit there until it rotted and got slimy, never intending to cook it in the first place, because who in their right mind eats spinach, anyway? And then they'd say to each other, 'We better not go to the Sullivans anymore, they make you take a bagful of their awful spinach home with you.'" She closed the book. "You live your whole life wanting something better—a good family for your daughter to marry into, a good career for your daughters—and what do you end up with? A bagful of spinach."

Sharon looked over at her. "What do you want, Natasha? What do you really want?"

"To be happy." She folded her long legs underneath her in that way only the young can manage. Sharon noticed that even her toenails were dark blue.

"That's nice and idealistic, Natasha, but in the real world people have to have jobs and work for a living. And granted, it's best if you can enjoy what you do. I love writing, and your dad loves his work. He's so excited about a new article he's writing. And we've worked hard. We're both fairly successful because we have worked hard."

"Successful. That's the most important thing, right?"

"Being successful at something you enjoy. That's what's important. That's why your dad and I are so concerned that you get a good education, so you can do something that makes you happy and provides you with a living."

"Lots of people I know are up to their ears in student loan debts. They got this wonderful degree and they still can't find all these wonderful jobs you say are out there." Natasha's head was bent over the guest book again. "He liked poetry. He read lots to me. Some of the *Sonnets from the Portuguese*. Do you know them?"

Sharon looked up from the computer. "Who did? Jordan?"

"Jordan couldn't read his own name. I'm talking about Mr. Cosman. When I was over there, he read me poetry."

"He did?"

"His name's here, that's all." She slammed the book shut.

"Whose name's where?"

"Mr. Cosman is in the guest book." She opened it again. "'Harold Cosman: A delightful visit, Hilda and Katie, June 21, 1930.' I wonder if they gave him spinach?"

Sharon grabbed the guest book. "Show me where it says Harold Cosman?"

Natasha did.

Sharon looked at the entry. "Cos," she said. "Harold Cosman was here. I can't believe Cos was here. Cos knew her then. Why didn't he tell me?"

"Mom, what's so weird about that?"

"I'm going over there. Right now."

"Can I come?"

"Fine, but I'm not waiting for you to have a shower."

Fifteen minutes later, the two of them were standing at Cos's back door.

"You were there," said Sharon bursting in on him. "You were there, and you didn't tell me." She laid the guest book down on the kitchen table, pointing to the page. "You visited them. You signed their guest book."

Cos pressed his hands together. "Yes, I guess I did sign the registry. I hadn't realized. I hadn't remembered."

"But you said you only met Katie ten years ago."

"I don't recall saying it exactly that way."

"Why didn't you say something?"

His eyes flickered and he looked away. "I may have hedged the truth a bit there."

"Hedged the truth? You led me to believe you only met Katie ten years ago."

He shrugged, rubbed his nose.

"That means you must have known who that young man was, the one with Katie in the picture."

"Ah, yes." He clasped his hands together.

Sharon stared hard at him. "That's you in the picture, isn't it? You were the boyfriend that Gerard drove away. That poem about the old shoes…"

He nodded. "I wrote that one. I wrote it on the back of the photograph, the one I kept of her. All those years. She copied it down in her book. Not terribly good, though."

"I think it's beautiful," Natasha said.

"Thank you, Natasha."

"Gerard drove you away?" Sharon asked. "You were the one he drove away?"

"What happened, Mr. Cosman?"

He sighed, a long sound of air blown out of his cheeks. "Let's sit down. Come, come into the living room, why don't we?" They sat. "I met Hilda at the bank where Gerard worked. I began calling on her. My mother thought it would be a splendid match."

"Hilda?" Sharon asked.

He nodded. "Hilda. It was in the summer, so the family was at Trail's End. The first time I came calling on Hilda I met Katie, or rather Katie served us tea in the parlor. I took one look at her and completely forgot about the elder sister, who I really didn't like so much anyway. From then on, it was Katie I was interested in. And she in me. Katie was impish, a clown. Always pulling practical jokes, telling stories. One never knew whether she was serious or pulling your leg. That's how she was.

"We were going to be married. The wedding date was set. You have to remember the times. It was 1930. The Depression had just begun. It didn't affect the Sullivans, of course, but my father lost everything. He owned a small clothing store in Portland. I had to go out and work as a laborer, my father's health not being robust enough for that kind of employment. This was during the time Katie and I were courting.

"Our plans had to be canceled. It was my father. You see, he owed most of his money to Katie's father's bank, and so the marriage would be deemed unsuitable. Her father wouldn't allow it."

"That's all? Just because your father's business went under?"

He sighed. "There was more to it than that. There was Hilda to think about. She hated me for turning to Katie. Plus it wouldn't be right for the younger to marry ahead of the elder, that's what Gerard said to my father. Plus there was the fact that Hilda…Hilda…" He pressed his big hands together, his cheeks were pouches of pink.

"Hilda what?"

"May I be so bold as to say that Hilda was in love with me."

Sharon smiled. The only picture that came into her mind was a rigid, thin-lipped woman who was her aunt.

"Oh, Mr. Cosman," Natasha said.

"I moved to Pennsylvania and married a lovely woman named Isabella. We had four children, and I think now," he counted on his fingers, "I have seven grandchildren and, let me see, three great-granddaughters and even a few great-great-grandchildren."

"But Katie was your first love," Natasha said. "You said people never get over their first loves. That's what you told me."

He shut his pale eyes and folded his hands on his lap. "Sometimes not. Isabella was a wonderful wife, and I loved her dearly. But after my Isy died I came back here."

"I could live here myself. It's a beautiful place," Natasha said.

Sharon stood and went to the window. "So that's why you could say that I reminded you of Hilda. I didn't clue in as to how you could know that."

He nodded. "I said you reminded me of Hilda, of her looks a bit, only a bit because, mind you, she never smiled, and you smile freely."

"What about the dress?" Sharon said. "And the studio photographs?"

He smiled; his ears wiggled. "Do you like the dress? My mother made it for Katie. My mother was a dear, dear lady. She lived to be eighty-seven. She made it for Katie, and her brother, my uncle, was the photographer. My mother gave Katie a bouquet of flowers the day we had those pictures taken. We had a number taken with the flowers. And then some taken with the fan, a prop my uncle kept on hand. But when we showed them to Gerard and Pearl, Gerard tore them out of our hands and ripped them up. Fortunately, we had saved two, the one of Katie and the one of Katie and me. That's all that remained. That was the day I left."

"Oh, that is so sad," said Natasha, placing her hands across her chest.

THIRTY-EIGHT

At one-thirty in the morning the phone rang. Her parents had long since gone to bed, but Natasha couldn't sleep. She was in the kitchen, scrounging up something to eat. There was a very old-looking box of RyKrisp that she found behind the blue Morton salt container. She took a bite of one. Stale. She put them back in the cupboard.

Then the phone had jarred her with its ring. Her first thought was that it was Jordan, that somehow he had found out where she was and was trying to call her. He was furious and hurt that she had left without saying good-bye. Where was she? Didn't she know he had been frantic with worry? She picked it up after the first ring. A dial tone. She replaced the phone on the cradle.

It rang a second time. Again, a dial tone.

The fourth time it rang, she took the phone off the hook and covered it with a blanket.

But what if it *was* Jordan and there was some glitch on the line that kept him from getting through? She hung up the phone again. A few minutes later it rang again.

"Jordan!" she screamed into the receiver. "If that's you, quit playing these stupid games!"

Her voice was met by the sound of a dial tone.

When it rang again, she grabbed it from the receiver and put the blanket over it the second time. Her hands were shaking. He was playing a game with her. He and Laureena right now, right this minute, were whooping it up, thinking, isn't this fun? Natasha could picture her, she with the light hair that cascaded down her shoulders. That was the word Jordan used to describe it—it cascades, he said, like a waterfall. Natasha rolled her eyes. Laureena seemed devoid of color and substance, a waif, a wisp with ashen hair, pale eyebrows, and eyes so colorless it seemed you could look through them. She would waft away like dandelion fluff if you blew too hard. Maybe that was why Natasha had straightened her hair and dyed it black, to be as different from Laureena as she possibly could, to be dark where Laureena was pale. The stale RyCrisp she had eaten earlier was settling oddly in her stomach, and she wondered if it would make her sick.

For a brief, hasty moment yesterday Natasha had thought of telling her mother about Jordan. She had gone into the dining room to do just that. But her mother-with-the-successful-life had jumped right into schooling and careers, as if that were the only important thing in the entire world.

She had done her part, she felt, by coming out here. She could have gone straight to Victoria or not come home at all. It was odd that Cos, a total stranger, and someone so old and so solitary and so completely different than she was seemed to understand her in a way her parents didn't even attempt to. But Cos was so old that he had become young again. She thought about that. He had passed through the middle-aged-striving-for-success state of her parents, had gone through the crotchety-old-man stage of her grandfather, and was almost childlike again. Innocent. Wide-eyed. Yearning for life. It was as if he were getting ready for the childhood of the hereafter. If there were such a thing.

Through the window she saw a sliver of moon. She pulled on her boots and put on her jacket and a woolen hat. Outside, a cold wind hit her face like needles, and she made her way down the path by feel. Ahead of her the dark Atlantic surged. At night the ocean and sky were one, a dark, endless abyss. She liked the beach at night. She snugged her wool cap down on her head and shoved her hands into her pockets. Cos's house, ahead of her on the right, was dark. The air smelled faintly of wood smoke, and she thought of Cos keeping warm on a night like this. In Ireland peat fires had kept them warm. She remembered a warmer, softer aroma to the Irish fires, not the pungent smell of wood.

Another half hour and she turned back. The cold was seeping

through her jacket, chilling her from the inside out. She should have grabbed Jordan's thick woolen sweater. Maybe that's what he was calling about. I don't care if you left, but please send me back my expensive sweater. He had paid good money for it, gotten it, in fact, from Laureena's shop before they knew her, before Jordan became so charmed by her.

Before she left, Natasha had casually taken it from his backpack and just as casually put it in her own. She hadn't been able to bring herself to wear it yet, but sometimes at night she slept with it. It still had his smell embedded in its fibers.

She stood at the edge of the black sea, her boot tips grazing the foam, and said, "O Jordan," but her voice was swallowed up by the sound of the wind and the sea. She backed away as an incoming surge of tide erased her boot prints, erased where she had been. It came to her then that she was invisible. She could walk across the sand, her voice making no sound, her feet leaving no prints.

When she rounded the curve and headed back, Trail's End was lit up like a jack-o'-lantern. Every light on. Quietly, she opened the back door and let herself in. Her mother's back was to her and she was talking on the phone, one hand on her hip.

"Yes, noises," her mother was saying. "No, nothing definite. Right. No, no sign of her. Yes. Nothing's been stolen. No, we found the chime clock on the rocking chair, and puzzle pieces on the floor. Yes. The ballerina was smashed. That's what initially woke us up. No, nothing else looks harmed. At least as far as we can see. Jeff is looking for her outside. Thank you. Yes, we'll wait."

Her mother hung up, turned and saw her daughter, and gasped. "Natasha! We were worried sick. You weren't in your room."

"I went for a walk."

"At this time of night?"

"At this time of night."

"We heard noises."

"Maybe that was me getting something to eat."

"And when we came downstairs the music box was smashed and you were gone."

Her mother put her hand to her head, and she suddenly looked old to Natasha. She could see in her mother now the old woman she would become. Her mother was shaking her head, almost crying.

"That music box has been in this house for so long. Why would someone do something like that? And then, when you were gone, I was just beside myself. I had these crazy thoughts. Like you'd been kidnapped."

"I'm fine." Natasha hung her damp jacket on a hook.

"You're shivering."

"I'm okay."

"Why is someone doing this to us?"

"Maybe it really is a ghost, Mom. Such things do exist. Maybe it's just that lame ghost that everyone around here is *getting sick of!*" She shouted out the last of her sentence into the hallway.

Her mother hugged her arms around her. "And the phone was off the hook, too. And a blanket on it. So no one could reach us."

"Oh. Mom, that was me. It kept ringing and ringing and no one was there so I put a blanket on it. Where's Dad?"

"Outside, taking a look around."

"Mom, now *you're* shivering."

"I'm scared. At first it was just a nuisance thing. But now for the first time I'm scared."

Jeff walked in at that moment, carrying a flashlight and wearing sweatpants and an oversized hockey shirt.

"Where have you been, young lady?"

"She was out walking," Sharon said.

"Natasha, you shouldn't go out walking. Especially with what's been happening around here lately."

Natasha shrugged and ran her fingers through her hair.

"The police are on their way," said Sharon, looking up at Jeff. "They should be here any minute."

"They're really becoming regulars," Natasha said. "Maybe we should keep some donuts on hand. Should I stay here or go to bed?"

"Maybe you better stay up. They might have questions for you. They'll want to know about the phone calls."

"This might be a good time to call up that minister friend of yours," Natasha said. "Find out if he does exorcisms."

THIRTY-NINE

MACK DIDN'T REALIZE THAT LIBRARIES were equipped now with computers and Internet connections that anyone could use. He had taken the bus to the public library downtown and was sitting in front of a computer terminal. His guide to the world of things cyberspace was a gangly youth named Jason who wore two earrings and was lightning fast on the keyboard.

At one point Mack asked him, "Did you take typing lessons?"

Jason turned to him. "Typing lessons?"

"You type fast."

"Never thought about it. Been doing it all my life."

Mack had come to the library to find more information about the weather, and specifically a phenomenon known as the green flash, sometimes called the Amadon Light. The woman behind the information desk had said, "How about the Web?"

"The web?"

"You know, the Internet." Little oblong glasses were perched on the end of her nose.

"Oh, the Internet."

"Jason, one of our volunteers, can show you the ropes if you like."

"All right, then."

With a few swipes of his long fingers, Jason brought up sunsets and actual pictures of the famous green flash.

"Well, isn't that something," Mack said.

"You want these printed off?" He had an earnest face, this young man, and seemed eager to please, despite the earrings.

"I can have a picture of these?"

"Yep." And with one click on a key, a printer started up somewhere in the library. A few minutes later, he returned, a color picture

211

in his hands. "Compliments of the Portland Public Library. Tell your friends."

"Does it cost anything?"

"This one's on me." He smiled.

Mack placed the picture down on the table beside the computer. The green flash at sunset was a well-known phenomenon; he had read about this in some of his other weather books. But the morning flash, the one Katie talked about, was much rarer. And the Amadon Light was why Cos had come to see him yesterday.

"We hear this is where you hold court," Cos had said, sitting down across from him at Mona's. Natasha was with him, which surprised Mack.

"Yeah," Mack said. "I guess I'm here a lot."

"We are told that you are the local weather folklorist."

"I don't know who you've been talking to."

"Actually, it was your friend Mona who informed us. She's been spreading quite the rumors about you, Mr. Sullivan."

Mack glanced over to the kitchen. Mona wasn't there. "You got that from Mona?"

"Mona. And others."

"Well, I don't know." Mack was rubbing his scalp. The fuzzy hair was sticking up as if electrically charged. "I like reading about the weather. It's kind of a hobby, I guess. And the other day a sailor came in here, wanted to know if the weather would clear. I looked at his weather fax. I went outside, and I saw something to the south, felt something to the south of us. Something to the south."

"A cloud the size of a man's hand."

"No." Mack was smiling now. "A clearing the size of a man's hand. And I looked at it, felt the wind, and just knew that we could expect a break in the weather in a few hours. I predicted the next day. And to make a long story short, the weather did clear the following day, just as I'd predicted. I've done a lot of study on the subject. It's a hobby of mine. A hobby of mine."

Natasha's blue-tipped fingers encircled a glass of Coke.

Cos leaned forward. "What I'm interested in concerns something called the Amadon Light, which is presumably a green flash that occurs at sunrise, usually over the ocean."

"I've read about the green flash at sunset. It used to be thought of as an optical illusion, but not anymore. It's a real phenomenon brought on by the refraction of light as the top of the sun hits the top of the horizon, just prior to its disappearing altogether from view. The horizon becomes green for an instant. Just an instant. The merest of instances. If you were to blink, you would miss it. The atmosphere disperses the colors of the spectrum. Those colors with the shorter wavelengths are the last to be seen. Green would be the first to be seen, and it is usually the only one seen, because the atmosphere disperses the other colors in the spectrum, the blue and violet."

"Could this occur at sunrise, Mr. Sullivan?"

"I suppose it could. Because the same factors would be at play, the sun, the colors of the spectrum."

"Fascinating!" said Cos, with an enthusiasm that surprised Mack. "Why are you asking me about this?"

Cos rubbed his nose and sniffed. "Your daughter is convinced that Katie's murder tale had some basis in reality, and also that it had something to do with the Amadon Light. And I'm becoming convinced of that, too."

Mack looked at them, puzzled. "You're paddling the wrong canoe. Katie made up things. She invented all sorts of things—trolls, fairies, the like."

"Sharon and I are convinced there is something to this. There seems to be a ghost haunting Trail's End—"

"You believe those stories!" Mack rammed his coffee mug on the table.

"It may not be a literal ghost, although Natasha here might say otherwise, after what happened the other night. What I'm referring to may be a figurative ghost." Cos looked sadly down into his coffee cup.

"There was so much that Katie wouldn't talk about. Not to me, not to anyone. And I'm beginning to wonder why that was so."

"Perhaps because there was nothing to talk about?" Mack said.

"I was hoping you might be able to shed some light on the green morning light."

"I don't think so."

Yet weather problems grabbed hold of Mack like a bulldog and wouldn't let go. And so here he was, sitting in the library.

"This is interesting stuff you libraries can get, all this information from the colleges," Mack said to Jason.

"Anybody can get this, anybody with a computer and an Internet connection. You don't have to be a library."

"You mean if I had a computer at home, I could look this up anytime I wanted?"

"Yep."

"All this stuff about the weather?"

"Yep."

"Maybe I should get me one of these gadgets."

"You'd have a great time. Lots of old people are getting online these days. Gives 'em something to do."

A mustached man informed them that the library was closing in ten minutes. Mack grabbed up his printed sheets, the few weather books he had checked out, thanked Jason, and headed out to his bus stop.

On the way home he thought about getting a computer. Can you imagine, Rose? They didn't even have these inventions back when you and I were together.

He'd talk to Mona about the best place to buy one. She had one in her office at the restaurant where she kept track of the business. She had never indicated that it was too difficult to master.

FORTY

SHARON WISHED SHE HAD MADE UP some excuse to stay home, like she had to clean out the back bedroom or scrub the kitchen floor. Or wash her hair. But she hadn't, and right now she was sitting in the passenger seat of Elaine Crawford's Toyota. Elaine Crawford, who used to be Elaine Beasly back when they were teenagers. They were on their way to Diane's to "meet some old friends who are just dying to see you."

Three days ago when Diane had called and invited her for lunch at her house, Sharon had demurred. "Oh, I don't know," she had said. "I've got this writing to do. A mystery I'm supposed to get written in a month—well three and a half weeks now. And there's all this family business to take care of. Plus this never-ending ghost thing."

"Did they find Dean yet?" Diane asked quietly.

"No. The lawyer phones every day without fail, sometimes twice a day. I think we're his only clients. First it's, 'I think we've found him,' then it's 'no, we haven't.'"

"We would love it if you could take a break. Elaine really wants to see you again."

"And then there's the cleaning and packing up."

"Here's a deal you can't refuse. You come, and I promise to come to Trail's End and help you clean."

"I don't know."

"It's just an informal group of friends for lunch, a few you'll remember from the old Young People's days—Jackie Patterson, she used to be Jackie Bubrick, you remember her? And Elaine Beasley, who is now Elaine Crawford. She married Ken Crawford, you remember him? And then just a few friends that we've gotten to know since those days, Patsy and Lisa and Janice who live here in Portland. I know you'll love them. When Elaine heard you and I were in town at the same time she was absolutely adamant that I arrange some sort of get-together. Elaine lives in New Hampshire, but will drive up. She could pick you up on her way."

"Did you say Elaine Beasley married Ken Crawford? You mean Kenny Crawford? The Kenny Crawford we were all in love with?"

"Yep."

"Kenny Crawford, the football player Kenny Crawford? The blond hair over his eyes, turtleneck sweater Kenny Crawford?"

Diane was laughing now. "The very one."

Sharon chuckled. "Well, then maybe I *should* come."

"Oh, good."

When they were teenagers, Kenny Crawford had gone to a different church, but they saw him at youth rallies. He was tall, athletic, blond, cute, and all of the girls were in love with him. Sharon would have expected him to end up with someone like Jackie or Diane, one of the beautiful ones, not Elaine. Elaine was a jolly, chubby girl who talked incessantly and spent entire Young People's meetings flopped down on the couch in the youth lounge like a large loose-jointed rag doll. She even had the hair for it—blond, curly—that she wore in two pigtails on either side of her head.

Now Sharon was sitting in the passenger seat of Elaine's Toyota. Elaine was still jolly and chubby and still talked incessantly. In the backseat was Elaine's youngest child, a quiet, thin girl of about twelve named Grace whom Elaine was dropping off at her grandparents' in Portland.

Elaine had enveloped Sharon in a hug when they met at the steps of Trail's End. She had beamed, taken Jeff's hand, and even hugged Natasha, who looked over her shoulder, a surprised look on her face. Afterward, Natasha had smoothed back her hair and examined her nails.

"I'll take real good care of Sharon here. She was always so special to us," Elaine said.

"Well, she's pretty special to us too," Jeff said.

"She was one of the smart ones. We always knew she'd end up being famous."

"Don't worry about getting back soon," Jeff said. "Natasha and I are heading into Augusta. We'll have supper there. Take your time and have fun."

Sharon waved with a cheeriness she did not feel.

On the way to Portland, Elaine brought Sharon up to speed on everyone in the entire church, including the whole story of why and how the church eventually folded.

"It was hymnals. That's the reason. Can you believe it? Hymnals! Well, there were problems, right from when Pastor Harley was diagnosed with Lou Gehrig's. There was difficulty getting a new minister. Pastor Harley'd been with us so long, almost thirty years. And so we kept getting these guest speakers, and then men from the church would speak. You remember Mr. Hedges?" She looked over at Sharon, nearly steering them off the road.

"Vaguely."

"Well, he even spoke. Can you believe it? And you remember how he was? Well, he preached an entire sermon against modern music. Forty-five minutes. Well, that didn't sit right with a lot of people, especially since we were going through this whole hymnal thing then. You remember those old ones from when we were kids? Well, they were still using them long after you left. They were so ratty. Remember when we were kids, we used to sit in church and pull strings out of the bindings and then line them up on the pews in neat little rows?"

Sharon laughed, feeling more and more at ease. "Or write our names in the pew with the strings."

Elaine chuckled. "So, we needed new hymnbooks. That was a given. Anyway," she gestured with her left hand, "there was this group in the church, headed by Mr. Hedges and Mr. Fisher, who just wanted to get replacement copies of those old blue ones. Then there was this other group that wanted a more modern hymnal with some choruses in it. Choruses!" Elaine put a fleshy hand to her chest. "Perish the thought! There was this major fight. I mean major fight. Plus the Hedges-Fisher coalition discovered that you couldn't even buy those old hymnals anymore. They were out of print. Another problem, because now they had to find a hymnbook company that only had the old, and I mean old, hymns. But I think they managed to find one. By this time my parents couldn't stand it and had already left, and we were going to that church on the south side."

"The one Ken Crawford went to." Sharon resisted the urge to call him Kenny.

"Right. That's where we got to know each other. Anyway, the Smiths stuck it out at the old church, so what we heard about the church, we heard from them. And so, anywho, the gist of it was that no one was getting along. Finally, help came in the form of a developer who decided he wanted to build a shopping center on the very spot where our church stood. Actually, I think it was the Lord who looked down and said, 'I've just about had it with you guys, think I'll put up a parking lot.' Then another battle ensued when no one could decide on what they would do with the money from the sale. Buy a new church? Build a new church? Finally, the state had to appoint a lawyer. Can you imagine? Appoint a lawyer to mediate because Christians can't get along. It boggles the thinking. The whole thing was such an absolute mess for a while. And such a bad testimony. You were lucky to be gone for it."

"What finally happened?"

"The lawyers decided that the money would go to some charity or other. By this time there was no church to speak of. When the Smiths left, your father followed them. There were very few people in the original church anyway. Just maybe a few hangers-on."

They were in Portland now, and Grace, who'd been reading a book during the trip, leaned forward and reminded her mother that she had promised to let her buy a CD before they dropped her at her grandma's.

"I haven't forgotten, honey."

Elaine and Sharon waited in the car while Grace hopped out and skipped into the music store. Sharon found out that Elaine and Ken had three kids, Grace being the youngest and a handful. Ken owned two sporting goods stores in the Portsmouth–Kittery area. "He's one of these absolute sports fanatics. Super Bowl Sunday is like unto Christmas at our house. He plays golf, tennis, and skis. And then look at me." Her laugh was hearty. "I'm about as unathletic as they come. He's a great guy, though. Although about fifty pounds lighter than me, if truth be told." Elaine also told her that she baked part time for a small coffee shop. "Just what I need, right? A bakery."

"I love bakeries," Sharon said. "I frequent them often, not being one who enjoys kitchen pursuits."

Grace returned to the car with her purchase, and they drove away. Sharon was about to ask what CD she had bought, when Elaine began to talk about the church they were now attending in Portsmouth. "So different, Sharon, than the church we grew up in. So completely different. Ken's on the board. Our kids love it there."

A few moments later they dropped Grace off, and she went skipping up an old stone walkway to the house Elaine had grown up in, a house Sharon had been inside many times.

"Still the same house," Sharon said.

"Oh, my parents'll never move away. It'll take dynamite underneath them."

"Diane told me that Bud Harley's in prison," said Sharon, when they were back on the main road.

"Such a sad, sad case. Mrs. Harley is now living with the youngest daughter, Karen, in Rhode Island. Although her health is failing. Pretty well bedridden from what I understand."

When they arrived at Diane's, Elaine pulled out a large box from the trunk. "The food has arrived!" she called, carrying the box out in front of her, ta-daing and ta-dumming to the tune of *Pomp and Circumstance* all the way up the steps to Diane's house. In the kitchen

Sharon was introduced to Patsy, Lisa, and Janice and was hugged by Jackie, who seemed thinner than Sharon remembered. Elaine was opening the box and laying out the contents.

"You've got your basic chips, dip, sandwich fixings, deviled eggs, homemade bread, Cheetos, party mix, and tortilla chips with three kinds of salsa. And for the health conscious among us, a fruit salad. All compliments of Susie's Bakery and Deli. Some of the stuff's day old, most of it's nice and fresh."

"We'll never eat all this," Jackie exclaimed. "Not in a million years." Jackie had changed. Her skin no longer had the flawless high school peaches-and-cream complexion Sharon had been envious of. When Sharon was a young teenager and fighting the blemishes of youth, her mother had told her that oily skin was better in the long run. "Those girls with perfect skin? Their skin is the first to age. Oily skin retains its youth much longer. It takes a longer time to dry out." Apparently, her mother had been right. And Jackie's shimmery hair was quite short and a dull brown.

"We will absolute ruin any diets that we may be on," said Patsy, a woman about the size of Elaine. "You always do this to us, Elaine."

"Today is not the day to diet. What we don't eat we'll divide up and take home to our families."

Diane spread out plates and coffee cups on the table while the women chatted, grilling Sharon with questions about her books.

"You guys get together all the time?" Sharon finally asked.

"When we can," Lisa said.

"We try to get together once a month when I'm home from Taiwan," Diane said. "For a Bible study."

"Oh."

"Don't worry," Diane said. "We're not going to have one today."

So, Diane had told them. Now Sharon was probably a line item in a list of prayer requests. That's probably why they invited her here in the first place, to witness to her.

Diane poured coffee, and the women sat down at the table spread with mounds of food. Besides Elaine's contribution, Janice had brought lemon squares, Patsy had bought a dozen sausage rolls at a deli she frequented, and Jackie had made chocolate chip cookies.

Sharon found herself looking into her coffee cup, wishing earnestly that she had her own car here so she could leave whenever she wanted. But no, not only was she here for lunch, after the others left she and Diane were going for supper.

During the afternoon she learned that Patsy had been recently divorced from an abusive husband. She was looking for a job. Lisa was a real-estate agent, and she and her husband, Eddy, had no children. She learned that Jackie had had breast cancer a few years back, and went through a mastectomy. Next, cancer was discovered in her bowel. That was eradicated. Now, a few cancer cells had recently been discovered in her colon. She would be starting a new round of chemo next week. "I just keep trusting the Lord," she said, her hands clasped together.

"I just keep trusting my Lord as I walk along..." Elaine was singing now in that off-key way she always had, waving her coffee cup like a choir conductor. "You remember that golden oldie," she said. And soon all six of them—Diane, Jackie, Elaine, Lisa, Patsy, and Janice—were waving their coffee cups and singing. Sharon knew the song, of course she did, she just chose not to sing. Instead, she methodically spread mustard on a piece of bread.

I just keep trustin' my Lord and he gives a song...

Why had she agreed to come? What did she have in common with these women? She thought of her friend Carolyn, who was smart, funny, and more than slightly irreverent. What would Carolyn say about these women? She tried to imagine.

"Well, Sharon, I think you've outgrown them. What did they say? That you were always the smart one? The thinker? The questioner? Here they are, going through life trusting in something they can't see. Trusting in a myth. Unlike you, Sharon, these women just take everything without asking any questions. And you didn't. You demanded answers, and when answers weren't forthcoming, you left. It's as simple as that. End of story."

Though the storm clouds darken the sky...

Diane raised her hand. "You guys, let's not get carried away here. This lunch is for Sharon, not for us."

After the food was consumed, the women moved into the living room and spent the rest of the afternoon in cheery chatter. Late in the afternoon they began to leave one by one. Elaine left last and not without a big bear hug. "We've just got to keep in touch, Sharon. Diane, you should talk her into joining our e-mail group."

"E-mail group?"

"We keep in touch by e-mail when I go away," Diane said. "We've set up a mailing list. It's kind of like our own online Bible study. Every week we read the same passage of Scripture, then we talk about it all week, and pray with each other—"

Here it comes, thought Sharon.

"The only rule is you have to be honest. That's the one rule."

"I don't think so," Sharon said. "I'm pretty busy."

FORTY-ONE

"I DON'T THINK I WANT TO GO after all." Natasha was seated in the kitchen, still in the T-shirt she had slept in.

"Why not, Tash? We'll have fun," her father said. "You've never been to Augusta."

"I know, but..." She looked at the bulk of him standing there in the doorway, his trench coat over his arm, his umbrella in the other, and could read the disappointment there. "But what will I do there?"

"You can help me in my pursuit of the burial site. I'm going to the library, the land registry, the place where they record births and deaths, and mental hospitals. And then I thought just the two of us could go to some place like the Olive Garden for lunch or something. It'll be fun."

She shook her head. "I'm just not feeling very well."

"You sick?"

"No. I'm just so tired."

He stood there twirling the umbrella. "I was kind of looking forward to just the two of us."

"I need some time to be alone."

"You were out with Cos the other day."

"He always needs people to drive him. And with Cos I don't have to, like, *be* anything."

"You don't have to be anything with me."

"I already am something. I'm your daughter."

"I don't make demands of you, Natasha."

She sighed. "No, Dad, you're a great guy, really. Just right now I have no energy."

"Your mother and I are worried about you. Your mother thinks you're too thin."

"I'm fine, Dad. I'm not too thin. In case you're worried, I don't have anorexia, plus I hate throwing up and would never do it on purpose."

"Well, that's good then."

"Dad, I'm sorry, I've just got to be by myself for a while longer. Could we go some other time?"

After he left, Natasha sat without moving for half an hour. She always did this, disappointed people who cared about her. But she couldn't go. She really was too tired. Even driving Cos to see her grandfather had taken too much energy. She had sat there in the booth in that little restaurant and thought to herself that Cos had more energy than she did, going on and on excitedly about some light, when staring down into the Coke Cos bought for her, it was all she could do to keep her eyes open.

I should cry now. I should finally allow myself to cry. This would be a good time. I'm all alone here. Nobody will be back for hours.

But she couldn't. She didn't. Her face, like the rest of her body, remained impassive, still as granite.

She gazed down at her wrists lying motionless in her lap, at the tiny bones, the blue veins. She had eaten little since yesterday's breakfast. Maybe a few crackers is all. She wondered, was anorexia a disease you caught when food required too much energy to consume? She wished there was at least a television here. She could lie down in front of it, the way she had in Ireland when Jordan was with Laureena, and watch and watch until the day passed.

The phone rang. She ignored it. It rang again. She continued to ignore it. *Will you stop ringing!* she shouted at it. Some time later, although she was not aware of how much time had passed, she fixed herself a piece of toast and ate an apple. She felt a little better. Taking her dishes to the sink—*Why* didn't they have a dishwasher? Didn't these old people *believe* in them?—she heard a sound in the tiny downstairs bathroom. This whole ghost thing was getting rather old. Every morning they went downstairs to something new. Sometimes the chime clock was wound up and going. This morning Doreen's bell was on top of it. Her mother had been so upset, and still was, when the ballerina had been broken. Now here was this noise coming from the bathroom.

"If you really are a ghost *show yourself,*" Natasha yelled. "Move something across the kitchen counter like a *real ghost!* You are pretty *lame* as a ghost! Did you know that?"

Still the scraping in the bathroom continued. When she opened the bathroom door, she found herself staring into the face of the cleaning lady on the other side of the window. She was trying to force open the window, her chipmunk face screwed into determination. Natasha leaned against the doorjamb, crossed her arms across her chest, and watched her. When Doreen finally looked up at Natasha, she began to scream, "Let me in! Let me in!"

Natasha mouthed the words, "What? What? I can't hear you."

"In! I want to come in!"

"You want to come in through the window?" Natasha shouted.

The woman motioned toward the door. "Come to the door. Open the door."

"Huh? I can't hear you."

"The door! The back door! Open it! Please!"

"Oh, the door? You want me to open the door?"

"Yes, please."

At the back door Natasha said, "Are you here to clean?"

"Oh, no. No, no." She was shaking her head, the spiral curls springing off in all directions. "Last time I was here I forgot something. My bag. Yes, my bag. I left it, I think, in the back room. May I come in and see if I can find it?"

"Do you normally climb through windows?"

The woman pursed her lips. "I phoned and when no one was here, I knew I could get in that way. I knew I'd left it unlatched when I cleaned."

Natasha opened the door and the woman bustled past her talking about how she couldn't lose that bag, not in a million years, that it had all her identification in it, and her money, plus her special papers, and she had to be at Mr. Cosman's in ten minutes, and her bag better be here.

Natasha followed her into the little bedroom off the kitchen and leaned against the door while Doreen began rifling through already packed cardboard boxes.

"You think you accidentally packed your bag into one of those boxes?"

"You never know. You never know."

Natasha continued to stare at her.

"I would feel much better," Doreen said, "if you weren't standing there watching me like a hawk, as if I'm some common criminal."

"I live here."

"I grew up in this house, too. I just as much belong here as your mother, and I belong here more than you do," she said while tossing the box contents onto the single bed. "Came here to be a live-in when I was younger than you, and lived here all this time. Right in this room. I've a right to these things, as much as your mother, if not more so. Now my bag has gone. It's not here. Someone must've walked off with it. That's the only thing that could've happened. The only explanation. I left my bag in this house and someone walked off with it."

"You think I would take your bag?"

The woman snorted, reached into her pocket for a tissue and blew her nose. Natasha had no idea why her mother had hired this woman. She was nosy and a busybody. A few days ago, Natasha had seen Doreen standing with her ear against the wall while her mother and father talked in the adjoining room. Natasha had come up behind her. "Hear anything interesting?" The woman had jumped and clasped her hand to her breast, and said, "Oh me, oh my. Do you want to give an old woman a heart attack? I've got a weak heart to begin with. I was just leaning my old bones against the wall resting a minute."

"Right," said Natasha, a gleeful smile on her lips.

The woman was still flinging this and that onto the bed. A ripped jigsaw puzzle box split apart sending little puzzle pieces all over the pink bedspread with the pink flowers.

"Maybe the ghost took it," Natasha said.

The woman placed her hand on her chest. "Please, my heart's not strong."

"Or Mildred. Maybe Mildred took it."

"Mildred?" Doreen looked up.

"Nope. Mildred has an alibi. She's in jail. Yep, Mildred got busted."

"You don't know what you're saying."

"The police carted off Mildred to jail for taking an unlawful bath in our bathtub and for unlawfully bedding down in someone else's bed."

"You shouldn't joke about Mildred. You don't know about her. You don't know that she is not to be argued against."

"I sort of liked the old scarepeople."

The little woman screwed up her face. Her neck was scrawny and veined; a little mouse head on top of that scrawny chicken neck. She pointed her finger at Natasha. "No one in this house will escape God's judgment."

After the lady left, Natasha showered and decided to go for a walk. The previous evening she'd found a small sketchbook within the pages of a 1958 *National Geographic*, and she wanted to show it to Cos. She made her way up the wet sand and knocked on the back door. Doreen answered.

"Did you find your bag?" Natasha said.

Doreen crossed both arms across her chest and said, "It was here at Mr. Cosman's all along."

"Imagine that."

From inside she heard Cos's voice. "Who's there, Doreen? Who is it?"

"It's just that girl."

Cos rose, saw her, and a wide smile crossed his face. "Come in, come in, then. And what brings you out on a very miserable day such as today?"

"I wanted to show you this book. I wondered if it was Katie's. I didn't know Katie was interested in drawing."

From the kitchen, Natasha could see Doreen crane forward to see what she had brought. She deliberately turned her back on her and handed the book to Cos. Nosy old bat.

"Where did you find this?" he said, fingering through it.

"Inside one of those old magazines on the sunporch."

"This is someone's artwork. It isn't Katie's, although I've seen artwork similar to this in style on occasion in amongst Katie's things." He flipped through the pages. "Very good. Someone's a good artist. Someone with the initial of D."

"D? Let me see," said Natasha, bending down to get a better look. "That looks like Trail's End, but I've never seen that big log down there."

"And who do you suppose that young woman is? She's in a lot of the pictures in this book."

"But you never see her face. She's always got a hand in front of it or her hair blown across it."

"She looks lovely," Cos said.

From the kitchen alcove came a strangled sound. One of Doreen's arms was clasped to her chest, another was reaching for a kitchen chair.

"Are you all right?" asked Cos, rising, alarmed.

She staggered into the living room. "It's just my old heart. Giving me trouble. Ready to give out any minute." She was gasping for breath.

"Natasha will drive you to the hospital immediately," Cos said.

"No, it'll pass. It always does." Doreen breathed in and out several times and plopped into a chair next to them. "Feeling better already. There. This happens betimes."

"No, I absolutely insist that Natasha drive you immediately to the hospital. Heart trouble is nothing to fool around with, Miss Cutcheon."

"No, I'm fine now, see. This happens and it's nothing to worry about. I've got my medicine."

"No, Doreen, Natasha will drive you in my car."

"I can drive myself. Truly, I can. If I could have the rest of the day off, though. Drive myself home and get a good rest. Just overworked I am. Overtired. Wasn't my heart at all, just a bit of breathlessness. I'll make up the hours when I come on Tuesday. By then I should be feeling right as rain."

"I am uneasy about this. If you are ill…"

"Oh, I'm perfectly fine. Look at me. Just like before." She stood up and began twirling around on the rug.

"Well, then, I absolutely insist then that you go home and rest."

"That I will do, Mr. Cosman."

"She's a strange lady," Natasha said after Doreen left. She had put the kettle on.

"She's had a hard life," Cos said. "I think that all the sadness in her youth is manifesting itself now that she is older. But I worry about her. She's far too young to have a heart condition."

"How old is she?"

"She's not at all old, late fifties, early sixties at most." Cos laughed. "Although that seems old to you, does it not?"

"Maybe a bit."

"Old is a feeling, not an age. Katie used to say that."

"Sometimes I feel old," said Natasha, carrying the tea and two cups in on a platter.

"I expect you do. There are times when I have felt old. There are times when I have felt young. I expect you know what I'm talking about."

She nodded. "I came here to Maine with all of these things that need figuring out, and all my mother wants to talk about is my future. Get an education. Find a job. Get an education. Find a job. Get a degree. Get two degrees. Get three degrees. My mother defines her whole life by her job; so does my dad. They can't see that people should be people first, and their jobs second. I look at someone like you who doesn't even have a job anymore, so you can't be defined by it, yet you are who you are."

"You have wisdom for one so young."

"I wish."

"I have a limited earthly future. I can only look to the past or to the present. There are too many of us elderly who look only to the past, remembering, remembering, complaining when things aren't like they used to be, boring people with long stories of yesteryear. Katie and I decided never to do that. We could look to the past and lament it—it had dealt us a cruel blow—but that does no good. So we decided we would look to the present, to what we had right at this minute. We seldom talked about the past. I expect you are trying to look to the present, but are being urged to look to the future."

"I don't always understand you."

"I expect someday you will." He leaned forward. "Where's that book then? Let's have another look at that book."

But when they searched for it, it was gone.

FORTY-TWO

THE RESTAURANT DIANE CHOSE was in the downtown section of Portland. It was a tiny one that looked as if it had once been an old house and was now refurbished into a homey café.

Diane and Sharon sat at a table beside the window and were silent. All afternoon the women had filled Sharon in on every single person in the church—what they were doing, where they were, whom they had married, what their children were doing. What more was there to say?

A waitress brought a basket of rolls. When she left, Diane said, "I'm sorry if anything that happened this afternoon or anything that was said made you feel uncomfortable."

"No."

"I looked at your face when Elaine started singing." She placed her hands on the table. "All of these women, we've been through a lot. Patsy's divorce from an abusive husband, Jackie's health. She's been fighting cancer practically her whole adult life."

"I didn't know that."

Diane reached for a roll and buttered it. "They wanted to see you, though. That was the reason for the party. When I told them you were in town, they absolutely demanded that we have a special lunch with you as the guest of honor. Elaine volunteered to coordinate the whole thing."

"I'm just different from them."

The waitress took their order and quickly returned with their salads.

"Can I ask you a personal question?" Diane said.

"Depends on how personal."

"Okay, I'll ask it, and if you don't want to answer it, you can just say it's none of my business."

231

"Fair enough."

Diane leaned forward. "Why did you leave the faith?"

"You mean besides the rules, the hypocrisy, the empty ritual, the dishonesty, the artificial culture, the fact that even the wrong political party was suspect; not to mention that women were supposed to live their lives through their husbands and children? You mean besides all that?"

"I didn't ask you why you left our church. I asked you why you left the faith."

"To me they were one and the same." Sharon felt a tightness in her chest, a closing in her throat. Most likely, at this very minute, all of the women were in a group somewhere praying. She knew how the system worked. She took a bite of her roll and could barely swallow it.

Diane was quiet. She was mixing salad dressing throughout her little bowl of greens. Finally she looked up. "Remember those pens?"

"Pens?"

"The witnessing pens."

"Witnessing pens?" Sharon looked at her, a forkful of salad in midair.

"Oh, Sharon, how could you forget the witnessing pens?"

Sharon looked at her blankly.

"You've just got to remember them. When you clicked them not only did the color of the ink change, but the color of the pen itself. And there was this Bible verse on them. Can't even remember what it was now."

"Vaguely."

"And how we weren't supposed to take a pen unless we covenanted before God that we would use them to witness that week in school. By clicking them you could run through the complete plan of salvation—black for sin, red for salvation, and so forth. I remember that when the black side was clicked, the pen didn't work. We were supposed to witness every time a classmate came up and said, 'Say, I see you have a pen with a Bible verse.'" Diane laughed. "I mean how often do you go up to people in real life and ask them about what's written on their pens? 'Say, I see you have First National Bank written on your pen, would you care to explain that to me?'"

Despite herself, Sharon laughed out loud, nearly choking on a mouthful of salad.

"I remember practicing and practicing," Diane said, "like we were supposed to. We practiced on each other, and then we were supposed to practice when we got home in front of the mirror, and then that week we were to write down how many people we explained the plan of salvation to using the pen."

Sharon waited.

"I remember going home that night and feeling overwhelmed. Here was another thing I had to do. Another thing I had to get right. Another thing I had to mark off my list. My Bible was full of lists."

"Mine too," Sharon said quietly.

"I spoke to exactly one person that week, my chemistry lab partner, a girl named Barbara Vogel."

"I remember Barb Vogel."

"The class valedictorian. And all I said was, 'You want to see a cool pen?' and I clicked it for her a few times and that was the extent of my witnessing. I counted it on my sheet."

"What did Barb say?"

"Nothing. She kind of looked at me like I was nuts. Which I was."

They were silent while the waitress took their salad bowls and brought the main course. Then Diane said, "I guess I'm saying that back then I thought we were doing the right thing. We all thought we were. Probably the Young People's leaders who gave us the pens, the people that invented them, the company that manufactured them, they probably all thought they were doing the right thing. I just know that that night after I marked Barb Vogel on my list, and we all prayed for her, I went home and cried myself to sleep, certain that God was angry with me. And, no matter how hard I tried, I couldn't bring myself to carry my Bible on top of my books. Remember, that was one of the rules, too. If you were a Christian, you walked around school all day with your Bible on top of your books. When you got to class, the Bible was to be placed on top of the desk, not stacked in those metal racks underneath."

"Bud Harley carried his Bible on top of his books, I remember," Sharon said. "And look what happened to him."

"The only thing I learned in all my years at Young People's was that I would never be a good enough Christian."

"But you always seemed to have it all together. I used to envy you."

"I was a good actor. I've always been a good actor. I guess a better question would be the opposite of the one I asked you. Despite all the magic pens, despite the artificial culture, why did I stay in the church?"

Sharon spooned sour cream on her baked potato.

"The thing that bothers me," Diane said, "is that I see the same things happening in the youth groups of my own children. No, they don't have to walk around with their Bible on top of their books, and they're even allowed to go to the prom now—that rule was changed—but I see other rules they're under. Things they've made up for themselves. And it makes me want to say to them, 'Come out from under that bondage!'"

"Why did you stay then?" Sharon asked.

"I guess there was a part of me that knew that beyond all the trick pens and the endless lists, the rules, that there was reality. That if I could get past the phoniness I would find it.

"When Jesus died, God tore down the veil separating the Holy of Holies from the Holy Place. No longer are we under the law, not anymore, but here we are, every generation of people, getting up on stepladders with hammers and nails and staple guns in our hands to make sure the veil stays up there where it belongs. As fast as Christ tears it down, we tack it back up again."

"Do you know that little white church in Beach Haven?" Sharon said.

"I think so. Your aunt went there, right?"

"Yes. I met the minister. I don't know him well, but he seems genuine. I was thinking about going there some Sunday, but I'm hesitant to go back to the whole church scene again, afraid that the same thing might happen all over again."

"I understand."

Sharon laughed. "But Jeff is bound and determined to hire him."

"Hire him?"

"To perform an exorcism on our ghost."

"That ghost of yours is still wreaking havoc?"

"As soon as we hear a noise, Jeff is downstairs like a shot. But by then the ghost is gone, and all he sees is a chair rocking or the painting on the wall turned upside down. Once Jeff stayed downstairs, but of course the ghost didn't show up that night. It's starting to scare me. We came down one morning and the ballerina music box was broken."

Diane leaned back. "I'm too pragmatic, too skeptical for my own good, sometimes. I tend to believe in the most rational explanation. And the most rational explanation right now is that someone wants to frighten you. If you want, Ron and I can come and help you post a watch. I just bet you that your ghost is nothing more than someone playing a prank."

FORTY-THREE

Jeff knew where Little Mary was buried. He was going to drive there. Tonight. He just wanted to let her know. He'd get a motel somewhere. He expected to be back sometime tomorrow morning. Maybe early. Hopefully, not late. But this couldn't wait. Some interesting facts were emerging. She would find all of this very interesting.

Sharon listened to all of this as breathless sputters on the answering machine when she got home later that evening. Then she went into the parlor where Natasha was sitting in the dark, ringing the tiny bell.

"I thought you were going with Dad."

"I decided not to."

"What are you doing sitting here in the dark?"

"I was waiting for the ghost. Trying to summon him or her up. Thought maybe the bell might do it. I was thinking we should get one of those television shows to come here, those ones that go around doing stories on haunted houses." Natasha rose, placed the bell back on the mantle. "Did they really ring these things?"

"Yep."

"This was Doreen's bell, right?"

Sharon took off her jacket and placed it over the back of the couch. "When I was a little girl I remember my Aunt Hilda used to ring that bell and Doreen would come running and she'd say, 'yes, ma'am' in this very refined way that Hilda taught her."

Natasha shivered theatrically. "Aunt Hilda, now there was one scary lady."

"I don't think you ever met her, did you?"

"No, but she sounds scary. I remember Aunt Katie, though, I think. Not too much though. And I think I remember Doreen. I remember this woman who was maybe younger than Aunt Katie. I remember her standing washing dishes, dusting this room with one of those feather dusters. But I don't remember talking to her or anything. Was she as weird then as she is now?"

"Her brother says she has Alzheimer's. But she doesn't seem all that forgetful."

"Just weird. Like this morning. I'm sitting here, right? And I hear this noise, like a scraping at the bathroom window. Turns out it's Doreen and she's trying to break in the house. So then I go in there and I'm like staring at her, and she's making this face at me through the window. And I'm like, why don't you go to the door like other people, lady? So when I get up and let her in she's got this lame story about how she left her bag in the bedroom. So I let her in, and next thing I know she's going through the boxes that you packed. I mean, like her bag's really going to be in those boxes, right?"

"Did she find her bag?"

Natasha drew her knees up to her chest and the chair rocked back and forth, squawking on the wood floor. "She found it at Mr. Cosman's. I mean, here she is standing here, practically accusing me of stealing her precious bag, like I want her bag. So then, later I'm over at Mr. Cosman's, right? And I'm showing him this little book of drawings that I found in one of the magazines. And all of a sudden she's going ballistic in the kitchen, going on about her heart. And so there's this big commotion, Mr. Cosman trying to get me to take her to the hospital, and she's all, no, no, I'm fine, and by the time it was all over and she left, the book was gone. She took the book, Mom! That's the only explanation. What would she want with an old book of drawings? I repeat, she is one strange lady."

"What kind of a book was it?"

"This really tiny little sketchbook. With drawings of this house and the beach and a girl. What's with her anyway? Always going on about the judgment of God, like God is going to strike her dead any minute or something."

Sharon remembered Doreen bent low in the front of the little white chapel, crying, praying.

"She had some kind of a sad background, and Hilda and Katie took her in. She seems so tortured. I guess she'd spent some time in a psychiatric ward before that."

"Well, it didn't work."

Natasha hugged her arms around her chest. Sharon noticed the thinness of her daughter, the blue nails at the end of the skinny fingers.

"Have you eaten today?" Sharon asked her.

"Yeah, I ate."

"What exactly did you eat?"

"I went over to Mr. Cosman's. We ate there."

"Oh, he fixed you a meal, did he?"

"I ate some of those baby cookies he always has."

"That's what you've eaten all day? Baby cookies?"

"And some toast. Mom, I'm okay."

There was something about the girl that suddenly looked so small, so vulnerable, so frail as she sat in the wooden rocking chair, her thin knees drawn up to her chest, the chair squeaking. There were so many secret places to her. Sharon wanted to say, If I seem distant, Natasha, if I seem like I don't understand, that maybe I'm pushing you and always have, it's because I had no one pushing me. My mother died and I had to find my way in life. That's why Natasha. And if I complain about you not eating, it's because I love you. I want the best for you. These are the things I want to tell you, Natasha, these are the things I want you to know.

"I'm going to make you a sandwich," Sharon said.

"I don't want a sandwich, Mom."

"You need to eat something," Sharon said, walking toward the kitchen.

"I don't want anything."

But Sharon was already in the kitchen, clanking knives, forks, sandwich fixings, can opener. When she returned, sandwich on a plate, Natasha was lying in the daybed, blankets to her chin.

"I'll just leave it here on the floor. It's your favorite, tuna fish salad on white."

"Thanks."

"You sure you're all right in this room?"

"I like it."

"It's so cold in here."

"I like cold places."

"What will you do now?"

"Eat the sandwich. Maybe read a bit. I'm all right."

Back in the kitchen, Sharon turned on the radio, washed the few dishes, and wiped down the counter and stove. There was an interview with a Maine author, and it served to take Sharon's mind off her daughter, off Dean and Jeff and her father. Off Katie and Cos and Hilda.

An hour later Sharon secured all the locks and went into the parlor where she wrapped herself in a brown, knitted afghan. She took Katie's Bible from the coffee table, and by the light of a dim lamp, began leafing through it again. There was the picture again, of the throne. She thought of the sketchbook Natasha had found. Was it the same artist? She'd love to look at that sketchbook.

Sharon was flipping through pages, reading Katie's margin notes. Underneath Psalm 46 she had written:

I have learned that the name of that light is the Amadon Light. That is an Irish term. I have not seen this light. D has seen it, but D knows what to look for. Even though I am up most mornings before dawn I still have not seen this light, this light that D is so obsessed with.

And then the entry ended, or rather, Katie had run out of room at the bottom of the page. She turned a page in the Bible, but Katie had written no more about the light.

✔ ✔ ✔

In the morning, Jeff found her sleeping on the couch, the afghan wound around her. He sat down beside her and put his arm on her shoulder. "I've got some amazing information. Absolutely amazing. I may drive to Portland today and talk to Marina Makepeace again."

He told her he had seen where Little Mary was buried. He had driven there. Turns out she was buried in a churchyard on an island off the coast of northern Maine. A fluke that he found it. A real fluke. There happened to be a note taped to the death certificate. The note was written by George Peter Koch, stating that even though her burial place was supposed to be a secret, he felt compelled to add this note. And then his signature.

"Wow." Sharon was rubbing the sleep from her eyes.

"Then since I knew you were gone all day, I decided to drive up there. It was farther than I figured. I took a ferry over to the island and talked to a woman there named Martha. She told me—she showed me, in fact—where Mary Sullivan is buried. She said it was the strangest thing. Two men and two women arrived with a coffin. They wanted to bury the body there on the island. Martha's father told them that the cemetery was for island people and people who went to the church. Well, I guess they were persistent because it was allowed. They hired a few island men to dig the grave and make the gravestone. The islanders insisted on a grave marker, even though the party of four hadn't considered this important.

Near as I can figure this party of four was your grandfather, grandmother, your Aunt Hilda, and possibly George Koch. I think it was your Aunt Hilda who went because Martha said there was a younger woman in the party who had with her a very tiny baby. Martha and her father, who was the minister of that church, assumed the baby was hers. But then the woman started offering to give the baby away. 'Surely there must be a nice young couple on the island who can't have children and would like this baby,' she said. I guess

Martha's father let them have it, telling the young woman that what kind of a woman was she to want to give away her flesh and blood, and they wanted none of this bad blood on their island. Then the four of them went to the coffee shop to try to give away the baby. Well, I guess the entire island had been forewarned because no one wanted any part of this." Jeff paused. "I saw the grave, Sharon. I walked right beside it. I took a picture of it."

Sharon sat up, wrapping the blanket around her. "Why would she be buried way up there?"

"I have a new theory. I've been thinking about it all the way home. I think Little Mary was pregnant."

Sharon stared at him. "Pregnant?"

"Sure, why not? It fits. She's pregnant out of wedlock. She dies in childbirth, and the baby Hilda was trying to give away would have been Mary's baby. And here's what else I think: I think Doreen may be Little Mary's illegitimate daughter."

"Doreen!" Sharon's eyes went wide. She sat up straighter.

"Think about it. The timing is right. Doreen just happened to show up around eighteen years later, in 1958, as an eighteen-year-old. She could've been that little baby Hilda and your grandparents were so eager to get rid of. Well, maybe they did manage to get rid of her and then somehow when she was a teenager, she found out her parentage and came back to claim her rightful place in the family."

"But why would she accept the place of a servant rather than an heir."

"I don't know." Jeff rubbed his eyes. "Not all of the puzzle pieces fit. That's why I want to go back to Portland, to visit Marina and see if she's any more lucid today." He put his arm around her. "Now tell me about your day with your old friends."

"It was...nice."

"Nice?"

"Yeah. Nice."

FORTY-FOUR

"HOW MANY TIMES MUST THIS be hashed over?" Mack said. "I've already told you everything I know."

"I know, and we're sorry." Jeff held up his hands.

He really was a large man, Mack thought, and he felt dwarfed standing beside him.

"Dad, Jeff has a new theory. We want to run it by you."

Sharon was leaning against a kitchen counter in a yellow rain slicker that looked oddly familiar, although he couldn't place it.

Jeff walked back and forth in Mack's kitchen, his trench coat billowing out behind him as he talked. George Peter Koch had left a note taped to the old death certificate. He had found Little Mary's grave on a small island off the northern part of the state. Lambs Island was its name. Was that name familiar? Had he ever come across that name before?

No, that name was not familiar to Mack. He shook his head and said nothing.

Jeff showed him a copy of the note. "I thought maybe she had been committed. That was my theory at first, but here's what I think now: I think that Mary was pregnant and died giving birth, and the baby she gave birth to was Doreen."

Mack sat down heavily on a kitchen chair. Pregnant? Little Mary?

Jeff paced and pointed with his fingers as he talked. "I went to that island I talked about. I spoke with a woman there who was just a girl at the time. She said four people arrived on the island with a coffin and one of them, a woman—I'm thinking this was your sister Hilda— she was carrying a newborn baby and, get this, she was trying her darnedest to give it away." Jeff stopped his walking and looked at him. "Was she pregnant, Mack? Do you remember? Was Little Mary pregnant? What happened on the day she died?"

Mack ran a damp hand over his face. "I don't know," he kept saying. "I don't remember. Believe me."

From the living room, the weather channel was predicting yet more rain. The day Little Mary had died was a day much like this one, misty and gray. And wasn't it just about this time of year, too? Mack placed his hands on the table and looked down at them.

"She was crying," Mack said to them. "I remember her screams that day. They frightened me. I left and went to the uncles'. Hilda arranged it."

Jeff and Sharon sat down across from him at the kitchen table.

If he shut his eyes, he could still remember those screams, her wails. His grim-faced father had taken him quickly to the uncles', not even stopping to let him bring his jacket.

"What's the matter with Little Mary?" Mack had asked his father. "What's wrong? What's *wrong!*"

His father said nothing.

At the uncles' Mackie went up the stairs and looked out the bedroom window and prayed for his sister. A few hours later, Hilda dropped off a bag with some of his clothes. "He'll need to stay for a few days."

Mack had watched from the top of the stairs.

"What if I say we can't keep him?" Uncle Ambrose had said. "What if I say take care of your own little brother. This is about Mary, right?"

"We just need for him to stay here."

Uncle Ambrose took the pipe he kept in his top pocket and began examining it. "And tell me," he said in a loud voice. "What are you going to do with the baby? Going to pretend it doesn't exist? Little hard to hide something like that, wouldn't you say?"

Hilda turned. Her shoes clicked on the wooden porch when she walked.

"I knew it," said Jeff, pounding the table with his fist, startling Mack. "I knew it. I say we go to Doreen. See what she knows."

"I'd go careful with Doreen," Mack said. "I'd go careful. She's not quite right anymore. Mind's failing a bit. You know that."

Jeff smiled. Jeff always smiled. "We'll be careful and kind."

After they left, Mack put on his tweed cap and rain coat and grabbed his umbrella. He was intending to stop in at Mona's for lunch, but ended up walking right past when he glanced in and saw a young couple, people he didn't even know, sitting at his regular booth. He felt a drop on his hand and looked up. More rain. Not a breeze ruffled the still air. No, it wouldn't clear for some time now. Not for some time. He continued walking, thinking about Little Mary and about Dean. Both cancers.

"It was Hilda." He said it out loud as he walked the slick pavement, his shoes squawking with the wet. "Hilda," he said again. "All Hilda." The name felt like poison on his tongue. Hilda had arranged Little Mary's confinement. Hilda had arranged for him to stay at the .uncles'. Hilda had arranged for Little Mary to be buried on some obscure island.

Hilda had even arranged Dean's leaving.

The blowout between Mack and his son had begun a full week before Dean walked out the door. Mack had wanted Dean to get some help, to pray more, to beseech God to change the situation. Didn't his father realize, Dean had argued, that he had already tried all of those things? Didn't he know? Couldn't he at least try to understand? Just for once? To come down from that high horse?

"It was your mother's death," Mack said. "It affected us all."

Hilda had shown up in the midst of this. She was happening by with a pot roast and some potatoes and a few loaves of homemade bread. Hilda did this, brought food to widows and orphans. The backseat of her car was filled with baskets for the poor that day. When she heard the argument, when she understood the situation, she told her brother that Dean would have to be put out immediately. "He's a cancer, Mack, that needs plucking out. You know what has to be done."

And Hilda should know, Mack thought. Hilda was a prayer warrior; she often told people this. And since his own prayers didn't seem to be making it much beyond his ceiling in those days, he listened to her.

Dean left the next day.

The problem was that no matter how much Mack prayed, the decision to send Dean away had never felt right. It didn't then. It didn't now. He had to remind himself that God's harsh judgments never *feel* right, but they must be meted out just the same.

"Never trust your feelings, Mack," Hilda always said. "Trust your faith."

Mack heard footsteps beside him. He slowed and looked around.

"Hilda? Who are you talking about?" It was Mona, and she was hurrying to keep step with him. "I can hear you half down the block, mumbling, calling."

"Just thinking," he said.

"Who's Hilda?"

"My older sister, long dead now." He offered half of his umbrella.

"Ah, it sounds like to me," she said, her voice breathless, "that she's come back to haunt."

"Maybe. Maybe she has. Maybe she never left. What're you walking in the rain for anyway, Mona?"

"This is my afternoon off. Andy always covers for me so I can have my one night off. And then what happens? My daughter, she borrows my car. Doesn't realize. So I'm on my feet all day and then have to walk home. Mandy, she says, 'Take a cab, Nana.' I say, 'Mandy, those taxi cabs, they cost money.' Young people, no understanding of money. None at all."

"If we walk to my house, I could give you a lift home. I'm just around the corner."

She waved her hand. "I know where you live, Mack."

Her hair had come loose from her silk scarf and was blowing around her face. It was soft hair, not hard, metallic gray stiff curls like the hair on Doreen and some of the ladies in church.

"Oh, I put you to so much trouble," she said.

"It's no trouble, really."

"Ach, you're a friend, Mack. Anybody tell you that?"

"Maybe if you haven't had lunch we could go someplace."

"Oh, let me tell you something. That sounds good. Eat someplace not the café. Oh, that sounds wonderful. First, let me change out of these clothes. I get covered in food spills."

Over lunch, which happened to be the same restaurant Jeff and Sharon took him to the first night they were here, Mack told Mona all about Jeff's new Little Mary theory.

She smiled, scrunching up her eyes. She had put red on her cheeks and lips, and it looked nice, not Jezebel-like at all. He had never allowed Rose to wear any makeup. Maybe he should have.

"First he thinks she's crazy, no? And now, he thinks she had a baby?" When Mona talked, her whole face became expressive.

"And he thinks that Doreen is her daughter."

"That little, funny woman, the one always hanging around you? She could be your niece?"

Mack frowned. "The whole thing was so secret. So secret. Nobody talked about it."

"Ach, Mack, don't you remember? Back then, back in our day, people did everything back then to protect good names. Nobody wanted any skeletons to come dancing out of the closets. Sorry thing is, most families had them. And now here, twenty, thirty years later, here they come all tumbling out."

FORTY-FIVE

"WHERE DO THEY COME UP with these names?" Sharon said. "Shady Rest Nursing Home. How absolutely boring. How totally unoriginal. It probably took a committee all of five minutes to name this place."

"I'll tell you, this place isn't very exciting, as you shall see." Jeff pulled the rental into one of the parking spaces marked visitor parking. "Only six slots for visitor parking. That should tell you something."

They were told at the desk by a young nurse with large round glasses that Marina Makepeace had been quite agitated since Jeff had been to see her. "There was some difficulty. It's marked in her chart." She licked her lips nervously. She looked no older than Natasha.

"What kind of difficulty?" Jeff asked.

"Oh, she rambles. She does that sometimes. After you left she went on and on about her father. About how he committed suicide. She says these things, makes thing up like that. Maybe before I let you in, I should call someone, see if it's all right. Since you are strangers."

"We're not strangers," Sharon said. "She was my aunt's best friend."

The nurse looked at them, her hand resting on the phone.

"My aunt died under mysterious circumstances. And right now Mrs. Makepeace is the only person who might know something about this death." Sharon paused. "No one's calling it murder. Not yet. But I think Mrs. Makepeace would rather talk to us than to the FBI. They can be brusque and bad-tempered and most of them get out of bed on the wrong side, if you know what I mean. Or would you prefer the police come in here? That can be arranged, if you or your superiors would prefer. The FBI would be very interested in knowing what's going on in this place, I can assure you."

Out of the corner of her eye she could see Jeff looking down at her, eyebrows arched above his glasses.

The nurse breathed deeply, put her hand to her chest, looked at them both. "The FBI?" she asked in a whisper.

"The FBI," Sharon said emphatically. "Even maybe the CIA."

"The CIA?" The nurse looked around her. "Maybe, first, I should see how she is. Maybe tell her you're here. Wait here."

They watched her scurry nervously down the hall.

Jeff started laughing. He took off his glasses, wiped them on his shirt. "The FBI, Sharon? The *FBI*? Brusque and bad-tempered? That's a scene right out of *The Gates of Hell*, if I'm not mistaken. This whole scene was, as a matter of fact. Lifted right out of your book." He was still laughing. "Complete with the young and wide-eyed nurse-receptionist."

"I'll have you know, Jeff Colebrook, that was my very best Summer Whitney imitation. I practice in front of mirrors. For readings."

"But you were pushing it a bit with the CIA. Your editor is right. You *should* turn this whole thing into a Summer Whitney mystery."

"Maybe I will, maybe I won't."

The nurse returned and led them down a narrow, sour-smelling hall lined with old people in wheelchairs, people nobody wanted anymore.

"She's in and out, you know," the nurse said. "Sometimes she's very lucid, and sometimes she goes on and on."

Marina Makepeace was sitting in an easy chair beside the window. A multicolored afghan was draped around her shoulders. There was something wrong about it. The colors were childish and crayonlike, out of place in this square, grimy room; all wrong on that tiny, colorless body.

The nurse knelt down. "You have visitors, Mrs. Makepeace. The niece of an old friend and her husband are here to see you."

Marina made no comment when she saw Jeff, just her mouth moved in her shrunken, puckered face. Sharon perched herself on the corner of the unmade bed.

"Marina," said Jeff, sitting down in the only other chair in the room, a plastic industrial-use chair. "Do you remember me?"

"Of course I remember you. What do you think I am, stupid?"

Sharon was startled by the strength and lucidness in her voice.

"We have a few more questions we'd like to ask you about Little Mary."

"Little Mary. She hated that name. Never knew how the whole ridiculous thing got started. Probably that beast of a sister it was who gave her that hideous name."

"Do you remember if Mary had a boyfriend?" Jeff asked.

"We both had plenty of gentlemen callers."

"Do you remember a special one?"

Marina sucked in her dry lips, looked out the window onto a shabby courtyard, cheerless in the rain. She nodded.

"Do you remember a name?"

"David. David. David. David."

"David?" He turned to Sharon.

"The boy who lived with Hilda and Katie? But that would've been impossible. He would've been far too young."

"What are you whispering about, young lady?"

Sharon turned to her. "It was *David?*"

"David." She nodded. "David. David. David. But of course, no one was good enough for the Sullivan girls. That's why they were all three single. Single till the day they died. Not like me. I've outlived three husbands." She lifted up a finger. "First there was Art. Died when he was only forty-eight. Keeled over right in front of me. Never knew what hit him. Right on the kitchen floor. I hear this thump, and I go in, and there he is sprawled out, holding on to my green-and-white checkered dish towel. Couldn't pry it out of his fingers. Then," she held up two fingers, "there was husband number two. Name of Will. Oh, I loved Will, and he loved me. Name of Will Ford. Died of cancer." She shook her head. "Terrible way to go. Had to change his diapers in the end. Then I married Vern Makepeace. Biggest mistake of my life. He was a drinking man. In the church and all, and still a drinking man. Beat me sometimes. Imagine, says he's a churchgoer, beats me, drinks. Shouldn't complain, two out of three ain't bad. Happiest day of my life, the day he died…."

"Mrs. Makepeace," Jeff said. "Who was David?"

"My father drank poison. One year after it happened."

All three spoke at the same time. Jeff said, "Who's David?" Sharon said, "What happened?" and the nurse said, "Oh, Mrs. Makepeace, you know that's not true."

"He drank poison." She was nodding her head up and down, exaggerated movements.

"Who was David?" Jeff asked again.

"David Backfisch."

"Tell us about the day Mary died." Jeff spoke so quietly that Sharon had to strain to hear. His notebook was opened on his lap, his pen poised.

Marina's gnarled fingers picked away at a loose crayon-red thread. "They fetched my father. He was a druggist, you know. Hilda came, then Katie stayed. Then my father drank poison one year later."

"Mary was pregnant?"

Marina blinked at him. "That wasn't acceptable then. They weren't allowed to be married in the church. Gerard wouldn't allow it."

"And the father of Mary's baby was someone named David Backfisch?"

"Poor Mary. We were school chums. Had almost the same name, that's why I think we became chums."

"But Mary died in childbirth."

Marina stared at him.

"But her baby lived," Jeff said.

Marina was twisting the piece of red yarn around her fingers.

"Mrs. Makepeace," the nurse said, "we don't want to ruin that beautiful blanket that your granddaughter made for you, now do we?"

Marina shooed the nurse's hands away and said to Jeff, "They treat you like children around here, blubbering, mindless, drooling children."

"Her baby was Doreen," Jeff said.

"Doreen, the servant girl?" Marina shook her head slowly. "Doreen? No one told me that. We left the church then, did you know that? After my father drank his poison, we left."

Later Jeff and Sharon stopped at the motel to see Doreen, but she wasn't there. The long, stringy orange cat had stretched himself out on the window ledge and stared at them through amber eyes, his tail moving slowly back and forth.

"I don't like cats," Sharon said. "They can see right into your soul. Did you know that some cultures say cats are the true demon spirits, the spirits of the departed dead?"

"Looking at that thing, I can almost believe it."

At the front desk, Russ Cutcheon squinted at them and told them that Doreen was working and unavailable to talk. "You fellas want to talk to her, you can do it sometime when she's not working."

"Maybe we'll come back then," Jeff said. "When will she be free, do you know?"

"What do you want to talk to her about?"

"We'll find her another time," Sharon said.

"What is it you need to know? Maybe I can help."

"We just need to see her."

"But what did you want to talk to her about?"

"We'll find her later."

They walked to their car, and as they drove out of the parking lot, Russ followed them with his eyes, his large arms folded across his chest. He did not move until they had driven away.

"He's weird," Sharon said.

"Awfully protective of his sister, I'd say. One wonders why poor little Doreen needs so much protection. First there was Hilda and now her brother."

FORTY-SIX

NATASHA WAS THROWING THINGS into her backpack and her small duffle: loose socks in the corners, her nail polish, her hats one inside the other, the T-shirts. Jordan's Irish sweater. This whole mother-daughter thing just wasn't working out. She'd been on her own for too long to go back to mommy and daddy. Besides, this place was as boring as a cemetery. It sort of did remind her of a graveyard, too, all wet and rainy, like funerals in movies.

When she had gotten up that morning, the thought of leaving began playing around in her head. She counted out her cash. Two hundred and twelve dollars American. Not a lot, but enough if she were careful. She'd work odd jobs for cash if she needed to. That's what she and Jordan did all through Europe. Nothing permanent. That's how they met Laureena…She pushed that thought to the back of her mind and continued shoving clothes into her backpack. She didn't have one of those—whatchamacallit—green cards, just her Canadian passport, her British Columbia driver's license, her Social Insurance number, and her B.C. Health Care card.

She scribbled a quick note to her parents, folded it, and placed it on top of the computer.

> *Dear Mom and Dad,*
> *I've decided to take off for a while. It's nothing to do with you. I'm heading south. I'll catch up with you again. I'll call or write when I'm settled.*
> *Tash*

The daybed made up, her belongings in the two bags she had brought in with her just a week or so ago, she walked out the back door. But first, she'd say good-bye to Cos. Odd, she thought, that visiting with Cos was the only bright spot in this Maine adventure.

Doreen answered her knock, and Natasha just stood there, holding onto her bags.

"Oh, it's you," Doreen said.

"Is Mr. Cosman here?"

"Well, of course, he's here. Where else would he be?"

"Is that you, Natasha? Come in, come in then." He had been sitting beside the window, a pair of binoculars around his neck.

She entered and leaned her bags against the wall. "I wanted to return your poetry book."

"Oh, you could have kept it longer. I'm in no need of it at this moment. And," he looked at Doreen and smiled, "Doreen has found your sketchbook, haven't you, Doreen? The very next day. It had gotten itself shoved way under a cushion of the couch."

"Funny," said Natasha looking evenly at Doreen, "I checked there. Ran my hand way under all the cushions and everything."

"Well, you must've missed it," Doreen said, "'cause there it was, next day, plain as day, right there."

"Imagine that," Natasha said.

"The book is here on the coffee table, Natasha, should you wish to take it back to Trail's End."

Natasha sat down across from Cos and said so quietly that she hoped Doreen couldn't hear, "Actually, I'm not going back to Trail's End. It's time for me to move on."

He put his big hands on his knees. "You're leaving? Oh my." He paused and squinted at her. "That's quite a becoming hat, Natasha."

She touched it. "Thanks. It's one of my favorites. I got this one in Edinburgh."

"Ah, Scotland. You have traveled the British Isles extensively, I see."

"I guess." She rose. "Well, I guess I should be on my way, then. It was nice getting to know you. Thank you for teaching me about poetry and all."

"How will you be getting to where you are going? Have you a mode of transportation?"

"Hitchhike."

Cos smiled and his ears wiggled. "There is a long history to hitch-hiking. That's how I got to Philadelphia, you know."

"Seriously?" She sat back down on the couch.

"As soon as it was made known that I was no longer welcome in Katie's presence, or in anyone's presence at Trail's End, I packed a small carpetbag and hitchhiked. When I arrived in Philadelphia I found a room at the YMCA and then found a position teaching high school English literature. That's where I met Isy. She was also a teacher."

"Very romantic."

"You seem a true gypsy."

She laughed, took off her hat, and ran her hands through her hair. "When I find what I'm looking for I'll drop you a line."

"You do that, Natasha. But don't wait too long. I'm an old man."

She looked at him.

"Your parents will miss you, I presume. Did they try to keep you from going?"

"They don't know I'm leaving."

He winked. "I left without a word to my parents, as well."

"I left them a note. So it's not like totally without a word."

"You like leaving quickly."

Natasha traced her fingers over the rose in her denim hat. "I left Jordan that way. He was out making a delivery with Laureena, and I just packed up and left." She looked up at him. "But he never came after me. He never even tried to find me."

"Do you think your parents will come after you?"

"I don't know."

"But you will be upset if they don't try."

She shrugged, fingered her hat.

"Mr. Cosman, will you be having lunch?" Doreen was standing in the doorway, a can of furniture oil in her hand.

"Lunch. What a magnificent idea. Natasha, you will stay?"

"I don't know."

"But, my dear ladies, I'm afraid there's not too much in this house. I haven't had a chance to do the shopping. Natasha, will you be so kind as to take my car and fetch us something. Sandwiches. There's money in that bowl by the door."

"I could also do your shopping for you if you give me a list."

"Oh, we'll tend to that later. Doreen ofttimes does my shopping."

Natasha grabbed a twenty-dollar bill, put on her jacket and hat, and drove away, glad for something to do. It was pouring now. She'd wait until this downpour passed. It was harder getting rides in the rain. Nobody wanted a wet, drippy body messing up their upholstery. At the Irving she bought three ham sandwiches, a big bag of chips, a few apples, and some cans of Coke.

When she got back to Cos's, her parents' rental was parked there. She sat in Cos's car for a few seconds, breathing deeply before she went in. Were they upset that she wanted to leave? Would they try to make her stay? Enroll her in a university?

Her parents, however, barely glanced at her when she entered the room. They were sitting in a corner deep in conversation with Doreen, who kept swallowing and patting the curls in her springy hair.

Cos, who was not part of the little conversation in the corner, waved her in. "I shall have to send you out for more sandwiches. Your parents have arrived."

"Did you phone them?" She looked at him accusingly.

"Oh my dear, Natasha, I would never presume to enter into your business. I didn't phone them. The thought never crossed my mind, surely."

Her mother looked up. "Oh, hello, Natasha."

"Hi," she said uncertainly.

"We wondered where you were."

"You came for me?"

"Came for you?"

"You got my note?"

"What note?"

"I left a note."

"Oh, we must've missed it. We were in and out. But we appreciate you letting us know where you'll be."

Natasha placed the sandwiches on the counter.

"We keep coming across a name." Her father, who hadn't even said hello to her yet, was leaning toward Doreen talking intensely. "A specific name. David."

Doreen let out a little yelp. Natasha jumped and dropped the bag of chips on the floor. No one noticed, except for Cos, who said quietly, "How about you and I have some of that tea? Let them talk."

"I'll make it," she said turning to the sink.

Her father was talking. "David was Little Mary's boyfriend. That we have found out. His name was David Backfisch. We got that information from Marina Makepeace, an old friend of Little Mary's. We checked into the Backfisch name, and it turns out that yes, there was a David Backfisch, dead now, who would've been about the same age as Little Mary. No one could verify if this David Backfisch was Little Mary's lover, but the dates and the localities match."

Doreen was twisting a dust rag in her lap. "I don't know who this person you talk about is. Little Mary?" She shook her head vigorously.

"Doreen," Sharon said gently. "Do you know anything about your mother?"

The woman jerked her head up, dropped the rag onto the floor, reached to pick it up. "My mother?"

"Yes, your mother."

"Why do you want to know about my mother?" She was running one little shaky finger around her left ear.

"Because we have information connecting Little Mary with your mother."

She looked genuinely confused. "I don't understand. Who is Little Mary?" She was tugging on her earlobe now.

"I don't know any other way to ask this: Were you adopted?"

"Adopted?"

"Yes, adopted."

Doreen shook her head.

"Where is your mother now?"

"My mother is dead. A few years ago. She was seventy-nine."

"That was your real mother? And Russ Cutcheon is your real brother?"

Doreen looked from one to the other.

"We have reason to believe," Sharon said carefully, "that Hilda's younger sister, Little Mary, may have been your biological mother."

"That is crazy talk." Her eyes widened. "This is God's judgment, isn't it? Coming back."

In the kitchen Natasha rolled her eyes and Cos smiled.

"Hilda said that eventually it would come. No matter where I was, no matter how much penitence was made. Despite everything. God's judgment." She began whimpering, twisting the rag.

"Doreen," said Sharon moving closer to her. "Tell us, who is David?"

She looked at them, and suddenly she was back to herself. "David? Why, David is my cat."

FORTY-SEVEN

SHARON HAD TAKEN KATIE'S OLD BIBLE, the red cloth book, David's baby book, the sketchbook Natasha had found, and Katie's school scribbler to the coffee shop where she could look through them away from the ringing phone. The lawyers were giving her daily updates on Dean's whereabouts, and she didn't want to be there if Marge phoned asking how the new Summer Whitney was coming along. Three weeks! Now she had only three weeks to write it! The thought made her want to throw up.

She pulled her hair back into a ponytail, tried not to think about her Summer Whitney deadline, and arranged the books and her notebook on the small, round table. The sketchbook was filled with drawings signed by D. All of the drawings in the Bible were signed by D. D, whoever he or she was, was quite artistic. Doreen? Although nothing would surprise Sharon now, the idea of Doreen doing up these pictures seemed unlikely, especially since Doreen and Katie weren't very close. And Katie spoke very affectionately about D.

Did D stand for David Backfisch, Little Mary's boyfriend, the father of her illegitimate child? Or did D stand for David, the orphan boy who lived with Hilda and Katie for a while? And why did Doreen name her cat David? And why did Doreen blanch when the name David was mentioned? Sharon sat quietly and looked out at the rain, thinking, thinking. There was one picture in her mind: Sharon as a very young child, sitting on her mother's lap in the parlor, and a teenage boy sitting on the couch across from them, his hands in his lap, nodding his head, nodding his head. That's what she remembered, that he nodded his head, his pale hair falling forward. Nodding. Nodding. Then someone saying David. And he looked up.

The memory faded.

Another idea surfaced, and she wrote it down. Doreen and David.

She wrote the two names together on her pad. Twins? Yet, Jeff said only one baby was offered to island residents.

Carefully, page by page, Sharon went through the faded blue baby book. He was named only David Thomas in the book. No middle name. Or was Thomas his middle name and Sullivan his rightful last name? Backfisch? She fingered the little curl of light hair taped into the baby book. She looked through the book for a date. Nothing. Sharon took another sip of coffee and on the back page found something. A tiny square of paper was taped on all four sides into the book. She undid the tape and pulled out the piece of paper. And read:

David Thomas Sullivan, born March 5, 1940, was dedicated to the Lord today in a private ceremony, performed by me and seen only by God. I took him down to the ocean and gave him to the Lord. He was not permitted to be dedicated in the church, because of his illegitimacy. Tomorrow he goes to his foster home.
Katie

March 5, 1940. The date Little Mary died. Surely, if twins had been born, Katie would have mentioned them. Unless—she didn't know. Unless Doreen was adopted out right away. But David? Where was he now?

Then Sharon remembered something. Hurriedly, she stacked her things, placed them in her satchel, paid for her coffee, and left.

She parked the rental a few buildings away from the Drift Inn Motel and made her way to the room they had stayed in. She looked through a slit in the curtains. Unoccupied. On the wall, she saw what she was looking for.

Carefully, looking to see if she was being observed, she walked to the motel office. It was empty. She opened the door slowly, very slowly, taking care not to let the bell jangle. In the distance she heard a television. Slowly, carefully, the way she had described Summer doing it a thousand times, she tiptoed behind the counter and took down from the board the key to room 14. She left as carefully as she had come.

A few minutes later Sharon was standing in the middle of room 14, shivering, hugging her arms around her. The familiar cold; the skimpy towels; the two queen-size beds; the scant hangers; the wood smell of the place; all so familiar. But her interest was the drawings on the wall and one in particular. There they were, the lighthouse, the abandoned beach house, and the side view of a girl bent over in the sand. She pulled the curtains shut and unhooked the drawing of the girl from the wall. With the small knife she always carried, she undid the backing from the frame and pulled out the drawing. Yes, it was the same girl she had seen in Natasha's book, drawn in many different poses. She turned it over and along the bottom was one word: "Doreen."

Another picture came to Sharon—Doreen kneeling at the front of the church, head bowed. Doreen, bending over the mop at Cos's. Doreen as a young girl bent over the tea service, long hair covering her face. Doreen, reaching down to fluff the cushions on the couch behind Hilda. The same stoop to the shoulders. She placed the drawing in her bag and left the room key on the dresser.

"Okay, Jeff," said Sharon when she returned to Trail's End. "Look at this and tell me who it is."

He took the picture and stared down at it. "Who is it?"

"You tell me."

"I have absolutely no idea." He handed it back to her.

"This," she said triumphantly, "is Doreen. The girl in all these pictures is Doreen."

"So Doreen is the mysterious artist with the initial D, and she drew pictures of herself?"

"That could be, or they could be David's pictures. You have your theories, now let me tell you mine: I think Little Mary had twins, David and Doreen. For some reason an adoptive family was found for Doreen, but not for David, so David was moved from foster home to foster home. And ended up spending time here with my aunts. And then, he found out who his sister was and went looking for her. That's my theory."

He held the picture up. "But what happened to David?"

"That's the part of the mystery I don't have figured out yet." She put the drawing back down on the table.

"Where'd you find this anyway? Here at the house?"

"It was on the wall of the motel room we stayed in. Remember?"

"Russ Cutcheon let you take it?"

"Not exactly."

"How'd you get it then?" He eyed her.

"I did my best Summer Whitney imitation and sneaked into his office, took the key from the board behind the desk, went over to the room we were in, and took it off the wall."

"You stole it?"

"Borrowed it, Jeff. That's all. These are identical to the pictures in the sketchbook Natasha found, and I was hoping there was a name or something on the one in the motel, and I was right. I hope to have it hanging on the wall before he even notices it's gone."

"You could get into trouble for that, Sharon. You're not invincible like Summer Whitney, you know."

"People break into this place regularly, and so far nobody's gotten into any trouble that I can see."

"Sharon, you just can't go around doing that."

"It's already done, Jeff."

He shook his head. "We should go talk to Doreen. Demand a straight answer."

"And have her go on and on about the judgment of God? Nuh-uh. Plus she swears that she wasn't adopted."

"I'm in the middle of checking that out as we speak."

"Did you talk to Natasha?"

"We had a long talk. She still wants to leave, but not right away. For now, Cos has hired her, so she's staying."

"Cos!"

"To buy his groceries, take him places. To the doctor's. Some light cleaning."

"Oh, so she'll get the use of his car. Clever girl." Sharon placed the picture on top of the other Katie mementos.

"Another thing before I forget—the lawyers called again. They're pretty sure they're getting closer to finding Dean. He's changed his name. They're going to call later today if anything pans out."

They heard a car drive in and then a knocking on the back door. They were surprised to see Ron and Diane standing there.

"We were out for a drive," Diane said, "and we happened to come by this way."

"Well, come in," Jeff said. "We were about to put the coffee on."

"Actually, we're lying," Ron said. "We're taking you up on your offer, Sharon, to help you find your ghost."

FORTY-EIGHT

"THIS ONLY NEED BE TEMPORARY," Cos assured her. "As soon as you are ready to leave, you may."

"I don't mind helping. I need to save up some money anyway." Natasha was wiping the kitchen counter with a dishcloth.

"I think a nice cup of tea would be the order of the day, don't you, Natasha?"

"I'll put the kettle on."

"And some of those cookies."

"Yep."

Cos was listening to his record player. Classical music. Loud. Very loud. Old people, they complained about young people's music being loud, well, she could barely hear a word he was saying. She walked over and turned it down just a little.

"I've had this record, Natasha, for I don't know how long. It's beautiful, don't you agree? Italian baroque. Corelli's concerto in F major."

"They don't call them records anymore, Mr. Cosman."

"Oh, I know. I should get one of those," he waved his hand, "those compact disc playing machines. I'm very out of fashion, I'm afraid."

"No, I mean they don't call them records anymore, even when they are records. They're called vinyl now."

"Vinyl? Vinyl. Oh my."

"Some purists even say they have a better sound than CDs."

"Well, my word."

"There's kind of an underground revival in vinyl," she said, wringing the rag in the sink. Today she wore a long-brimmed, flowered baseball cap.

"Isn't that something," he said. "What goes around comes around, as they say."

"So you see, you're not old-fashioned at all."

"Well, I thank you, my dear. I thank you. You are very kind."

"Tea's ready."

They sat across from each other by the front window and drank tea and ate arrowroots in the darkened living room. Sometimes he kept the lights off so he could see the birds, the gulls, the ships out on the sea.

He said, "It is when you stand at the edge of the sea and gaze out that you realize your mortality."

Natasha took a sip of her tea. It was still too hot.

"Though inland far we be, our souls have sight of that immortal sea, which brought us hither."

"Tennyson."

He looked at her, a smile brightening his large face. "Guess again."

"Dylan Thomas."

"No, no, no, no." He waved his hand in front of his face, as if shooing away a fly. "Way before Dylan Thomas."

"Longfellow."

"You're just guessing. Think. Think."

"I give up." She lifted her hands in mock surrender.

"Wordsworth. William Wordsworth." He paused, then stared out at the sea and began reciting:

Strange fits of passion I have known
And I will dare to tell,
But in the lover's ear alone;
What once to me befell.
When she I loved look'd every day
Fresh as a rose in June
I to her cottage bent my way,
Beneath an evening moon.

For several minutes Natasha said nothing, just sipped her tea. Finally, she said, "You were talking about Katie, right?"

He leaned forward. "Funny how one remembers those old lines, when things more recent are forgotten. I can't remember what I had for breakfast yesterday, but I can remember as clear as summer the way Katie looked when I first saw her. I was courting Hilda, of course. Katie brought in the tea. She wore a beige dress, Katie did, which came to about midcalf." He motioned with his hand to his leg. "And some clunky black strap sandals. I guess they were the fashion then. And her hair was done up with pins, but not expertly because one side was slightly higher than the other. She wore a bright yellow apron, frilly, that tied up behind her neck. The apron was quite large on her, and I surmised that it belonged to their mother, who was much stouter than all three of her daughters. Katie wasn't beautiful. Oh, not like the starlets of the era, but there was an impishness about her. Something about the way she stood there, bending down and offering tea to her sister, that made her so very appealing. After she left I said to Hilda, 'I didn't know you had a sister.' And Hilda hmphed at me."

"She hmphed at you."

"Grunted, hmphed, you know. Then she made a disparaging remark about her sister having her head in the clouds or some such. And all of a sudden, at that moment, I fell in love with Katie, and Hilda suddenly was long forgotten to me."

"Wow."

He leaned forward and said quietly, "I think if Hilda had said something like, 'Oh yes, that's my sister. She's quite a character, but we all love her,' my feelings for Hilda would have remained unchanged."

Natasha brought her knees up on the chair and hugged them to her chest. "How did you manage to see Katie after that? Did you call her every night? Was it like that?"

He laughed. "My dear, the telephone, that modern invention, we did not use them the way we do today. No, I wrote her a letter."

"A letter? A person lives in the same town and you wrote a *letter?*"

"It was done then."

"That is so romantic."

The record player finished, and Cos started to get up.

"I'll get it," Natasha said. She turned the record over and placed the needle at the beginning. Once again, the sounds of the baroque concerto filled the room.

"Horribly barbaric, wasn't it, but that's what people did then. Ofttimes the postcards would be mere invitations. 'Shall we have lunch on Friday?' Things of that nature."

"Mail service must've been better then."

Cos laughed. "That night in my room I wrote her a short letter asking if I might call on her betimes. In a sentence or two, I explained that I was a horribly fickle person, but I found I had lost feeling for Hilda. I posted it the next day. Four days later—I know because I counted them—I received a letter by return post."

"Mail service *was* better then."

"She wrote that she would be delighted to be called on by one such as myself, and then she mentioned a time when she knew Hilda would be off visiting the sick and her father would be at work. So, I went. We sat on a rock out there on the beach—you can't quite see it from here, it's a bit around the bend. And we talked and talked. It seemed we had an immediate connection. For hours we sat there and talked. All the more surreptitious because neither Hilda nor Gerard knew of our clandestine meeting."

"But Katie's mother knew?"

"Pearl? Pearl was a sweetheart. And of course, her younger sister, Little Mary, was at home. But Mary, she was a sweetheart, too. Gerard and Hilda ran them, I'm afraid. We met and courted after that. And finally, her parents, it seemed, came around a bit, perhaps. Although Hilda never did fully accept the situation, I expect."

"You guys were mean to her."

"On the contrary. We tried to include her. We took her on motor trips. I tried to get my cousin interested in her, but she was a bit stiff for him."

"Stiff?"

"Unyielding. Set in her ways. She was younger than you are now, Natasha, but dressed and acted like a mature woman."

"How long did you know Katie for?"

"Eighteen months. We were to be married."

"When you were married to your wife all those years, did you ever think about Katie?"

"Oh, of course, but I loved my Isy. It's nothing like that. We had our life and family in Philadelphia. Our children. Oh my, children do keep one busy. I fully thought that Katie had married some fine young fellow of her father's choosing. And I hoped she had found love."

"But you came back looking for her after your wife died?"

"No. It was for the sea that I came. When one has grown up by the sea, and then moves inland, something is missing. Something is lost. Something is not quite right with one. 'The sea! The sea! The open sea! The blue, the fresh, the ever free!'" He paused. "I came back not to rekindle a romance with Katie. In truth, I fully expected Katie to be passed on by then. I, on the other hand, come from healthy stock." He smiled and his ears wiggled. "I've chosen my ancestors well. My mother lived to ninety-seven, my father to ninety-two, my sister at age eighty-nine still lives on her own in southern New Jersey, not a hint of senility. She still walks to church every single Sunday. No, I didn't come back for Katie, I came for the sea. To end my life where it all began. It was just happy luck that we found each other again."

"Why didn't you and Katie get married then?"

He pursed his lips. "I don't know. We meant to, this time, but never got around to it, I suppose. Her health was quite frail in those last years. I took care of her."

"That is so romantic." Natasha hugged her knees. After a pause she told him all about Jordan and Ireland and leaving him and Laureena.

At the end he said, "I will not insult you by saying that you will love again, although that is a surety, but I will say that time heals and that your experience will bring you closer to understanding."

"Understanding what?"

"Yourself. And as you grow to understand yourself, I know you will grow in an understanding of God."

"You're talking about religion."

"I never talk about religion. Hilda spoke of religion. She was a very religious person. She visited the sick. She dutifully made up and carried baskets to the poor. When one is religious, one does things. But when one has faith in God, one just is."

"My mother raised me to make up my own mind about God. She said she didn't want to raise me the way she was raised, in the hypocrisy of organized religion."

"What about your dad?"

"Same as Mom. My grandparents on my father's side of the family, I think they go to church, but my dad doesn't. But he doesn't go on and on about 'organized religion' like my mom. I'm glad they're allowing me to make up my own mind."

"Your parents have tried to instill within you the values of hard work, honesty, morals; but they are values with no base." He poured milk into his tea. "And values with no base are no values at all. Your mother has a strong belief in God."

Natasha shook her head and folded her legs underneath her. "You're talking about someone else's mother now."

"Look at the books she wrote, all with religious themes: *Fallen from Grace*, about a minister who commits murders; *Though He Slay Me*, about a pedophile priest who kills children; *The Gates of Hell*, about a survivalist cult that engages in some very weird practices; *Nothing but the Blood*, about a serial killer who lays out his victims as if they'd been crucified; *A Wretch Like Me*, about anti-Semitism taken to the utmost. I could go on. All with religious themes. All with a strong moral base. Good definitely wins out over evil in the end. Katie and I used to talk about this at length. No, your mother believes in God, even if she doesn't admit it to herself. She rejected the religion of her youth, but not the God of the values by which she was raised."

Natasha took an arrowroot and sat back. "I may not always get along with them, but I appreciate the way I was raised. Now, I'm to the age where I can choose what I want to believe in."

"A young person raised without having to make a choice will make a choice for nothing."

"I'm choosing to be happy."

"An admirable goal."

"I have an uncle who also left the church. I guess that both of them in that family found it a bit stifling."

"Ah, yes, Dean. Katie loved that boy. She was grieved when he left and although at one point she hired a sleuth, she never did locate him. He sent her one postcard from California. Said he was moving on and he'd write to her at a later time. He never did."

"My family has a lot of skeletons, doesn't it?"

"All families do."

"You and Katie went to church?"

"We did, yes, we did. But not out of obligation."

"My mom says you went to that church across from the museum. The little white one?"

"Indeed."

"Do they believe the way you do?"

He rubbed his head. "Churches, I'm afraid, are made up of people, and people, I've seen, often behave in rather imperfect ways. So no, it's not perfect, but we attempt to love and obey God. That's what counts."

"If you need someone to drive you to church, I could come with you sometime."

"That would be wonderful."

FORTY-NINE

DIANE HELD THE PICTURE UP to the light. "Do you think this green line's supposed to be here?"

"What green line?" Sharon asked.

"All around the edges of the bottom." Diane flattened the picture out on the kitchen table and ran her forefinger along the lower edge. Encircling the letter *D* was a splatter of green paint which ran halfway up the sides. It looked like a mistake, as if the artist had finished and stood back to admire his work, unaware that his brush still dripped green paint. Except there was no other green on the picture. It was a pen and ink drawing.

"The Amadon Light," said Sharon, remembering. "My aunt talked about the green light, how D had seen it, how he had known what to look for. He drew another picture of it. It's in the lobby of the Drift Inn. I didn't take that one."

"Where is this David now? Do we know what happened to him?" asked Ron, who was leaning against the sink, holding a huge mug of coffee.

"He's dead." Jeff was walking in from the kitchen. "Augusta's faxing up a copy of the death certificate. I've got to go pick it up at the public library. They've been kind enough to receive it for me. I also want to check out what they have on microfilm about his death, if anything. I also have information about Doreen."

"You've been busy," Sharon said.

"I like research. I miss it. This newspaper stuff gets in your blood." He pushed his glasses up on his nose. "But here's what I found out— Doreen is not Little Mary's child. Doreen was born in 1941, a year after Little Mary died. So that settles that."

"So her child is David," Diane said, "and David died, but we're not sure how."

"That's what I'm going to find out."

"I'm going with you," Sharon said.

"Let's all go," Diane said.

At the public library downtown, the four of them pulled up chairs to the microfilm monitor. The death certificate said he died April 10, 1958, so they took out microfilm for that date. They quickly found what they were looking for in the April 14 edition of the paper.

Youth Dead

The body of David Thomas, age eighteen, was found on the beach near Beach Haven, twenty miles south of Portland. The youth was apparently riding his bicycle along the beach when he fell off, hit his head, and was knocked unconscious. He drowned in the rain and incoming tide. Foul play is not suspected.

"This fits with the body on the beach stories," Sharon said.

Jeff moved the microfilm ahead. "That's odd. Nothing about a funeral. Those sorts of things are always in the paper."

"That's not so odd," Sharon said. "It seems that the Sullivans were famous for not providing funerals for those family members they decided didn't deserve them. I mean, if they were going to rot in hell anyway, why give them a send-off?"

Diane looked at her.

"It's true, Diane. Little Mary wasn't given a funeral. Apparently she had so shamed the precious family name that they didn't even bury her with the other Sullivans. She's buried on some obscure island up north somewhere. I'm willing to bet that David was buried in the same place."

"Or maybe he was cremated," Ron said.

"I doubt that. There were some things even the Sullivans wouldn't do, and they didn't believe in cremation. Something about the body being left in one piece for the last trumpet or something."

"No, nothing about a funeral," Jeff said. "That's all, just this one little article. No police investigation, nothing."

The four of them made their way out of the library and walked the few blocks to the Portland Public Market, where they bought coffees and pastries and sat on a stone hearth beside a fireplace there and talked. Jeff pulled out his notebook.

"Okay, what do we have so far? Little Mary gets pregnant. The father was someone named David Backfisch. Something goes wrong and she dies in childbirth."

"Maybe it was the castor oil," Sharon said.

"The what?" Diane asked.

"Castor oil. My father said she was given castor oil."

"What for? As some kind of a pregnancy tonic or something?"

"I think it was to get rid of the baby. I researched that once for a Summer Whitney book. Back then it was believed that large doses of castor oil would terminate a pregnancy. Other herbs were used as well, but castor oil could be readily obtained through a pharmacy. Usually, it had the opposite affect. It made the mother quite ill, especially in large doses, but the baby—well, the baby fared just fine, thank you very much."

"And George Koch, Marina's father, was a pharmacist," said Jeff, pointing with his pen. "He also went to the same church as the Sullivans. He could've supplied this."

"Plus, don't forget, he signed the death certificate," Sharon said.

"And accompanied the family to the island where they buried Little Mary."

"And then being filled with remorse, he killed himself a year after it happened."

"Sort of like Judas," Ron said.

"I don't remember the Kochs," Diane said. "You said they went to our church?"

"I think the family left after George died," Sharon said. "Marina said something about that."

272

"But why would Mr. Koch do such a thing—help to terminate a pregnancy? Not to mention sign a death certificate, which is illegal."

"Wake up and smell the coffee, Diane. My grandfather, the pillar of the church, had our illustrious George Koch under his thumb. The more I learn about the famous Gerard Sullivan, the more I think he pulled the strings in that church. Look what he did to Cos. He could've sent David Backfisch running, too. Maybe George Koch was facing a few lean times himself. Maybe in order to survive, he supplied my grandparents with castor oil for Little Mary. All to keep the precious Sullivan name unsullied in the eyes of God."

"Not unsullied in the eyes of God," said Ron, interlacing his hands behind his head and leaning against the stone wall. "Unsullied in the eyes of the church maybe, but not unsullied in the eyes of God."

Diane fiddled with the lapels on her jacket. "I'm still confused. There are two Davids?"

"Mary could've named her baby David after his father," Jeff said.

"Before she died," Diane said. "How sad. So much sadness in this world."

"When I was a child," Sharon said, "Hilda constantly spoke of this poor orphan boy named David that they took in. It seemed to be this point of contention between Hilda and Katie, because whenever Hilda would mention David, Katie would get this gleam in her eye and start telling a troll story. Or a ghost story."

"Those sisters, they didn't get along, did they?"

Sharon laughed out loud. "That's like saying, Hurricane Mitch, that was a pretty bad storm, wasn't it?"

"Something else worth checking out is the foster homes David went to," Jeff said.

"And there's one more question," Sharon said. "Was David murdered? And by whom? And did Katie suspect? And if she knew, or did suspect, why didn't she tell anyone?"

"That's four questions," Ron said.

"Okay, four questions."

"Hey," he said, pointing, "that looks like honest-to-goodness snow out that window."

"No, couldn't possibly be. This is spring."

"I know what snow looks like and that looks like snow."

"This is unbelievable."

Before they left the market, they bought fresh fish, cheese, cartons of homemade soup, and some organic produce.

When they got back to Trail's End, Natasha was bent over the card table organizing jigsaw puzzle pieces by color.

Ron pulled up a chair beside her. "That's not the way to do it," he said. "First, you have to get the side pieces. Corner pieces are the easiest, so you look for them first. Then you have to get the straight pieces, and then you start organizing by color."

"I never did one of these before. We never had them when I was a kid."

"That's because that's all we ever did," said Sharon, laughing from the doorway. "Every single Sunday afternoon of my entire childhood was spent putting together jigsaw puzzles at this very card table in this very parlor. I vowed that my home would be a jigsaw-puzzle-free zone."

"Like it was a God-free zone." Natasha said this quietly, as she reached for a straight piece.

"Natasha…." Jeff said.

"I've found a corner." Natasha held up a tiny piece with her blue fingernails. "The upper right, if I'm not mistaken."

"Good," Ron said. "That'll give us a basis to work from. One needs to have a plan. A strategy in all of this."

"I'll heat up some of that soup," Sharon said.

A chorus of yeses.

Sharon filled up the coffee percolator with water. While it heated, she leaned her head against a kitchen cabinet and closed her eyes. A God-free zone? What was that all about? Didn't Natasha know what she'd been saved from? All the rules? No dances, no movies, no television, no makeup, no going to the Beatles movies even when everybody in the entire school, that's all they talked about? No high school prom, no graduation party (well, except for the church one, where they bobbed for apples and played Twister)? No listening to rock-and-roll music on the radio (there were entire books about the evils of rock-and-roll)? Having to bring in notes—incessantly bringing in notes—to school, excusing us from social dance and from sex education and from reading certain novels for English class. Notes exempting us from going on class trips to see Shakespeare plays. God-free zone, Natasha? Give me a break. I saved you from all of that!

Besides, nothing you ever did was good enough. If you witnessed to a dozen people, you were reminded, "What about that thirteenth person?" You were encouraged to leave gospel tracts everywhere because you never knew who would happen by, pick one up, and get saved. Sharon left tracts behind the toilet stalls in the school bathroom or stuffed into the toilet paper holders. One never knew.

I saved you from that, Natasha. I *saved* you!

When the soup was heated through, Sharon put it in bowls and carried it out on a tray she found in the cupboard. In the parlor, four heads were bent over the puzzle.

She laid the tray down on the coffee table and looked out the window at the rain on the beach. Her eyes went to the picture above the mantle. The Last Supper, twelve heads, plus Jesus, sitting along a table. Sometimes when she was a very young child she would look up into the eyes of Jesus and imagine that he was looking down at her, just at her; and that his outstretched arms were only for her. When Hilda and Katie and Dean and her parents were gone, she'd sit on the couch and look up at the painting. "Jesus," she'd say, "could you please make Daddy not mad at me? He says I was mean to Dean and I wasn't," or "Jesus, could you make it sunny tomorrow for the picnic?"

or "Even though Hilda yells at me, I know you still love me." It was something she felt, something she instinctively knew.

But as she grew to adulthood, she came to understand that there were conditions to his love. All your sins had to be repented of. A quick "forgive me all my sins" wasn't good enough. You had to list them daily, making sure you didn't forget one thing. Listing them on a sheet of paper was good; as you read them off to God, you could cross them out because if you forgot one thing, it might be held against you for all eternity. And you had to do all the required things: witnessing from door to door, reading the Bible every single morning, going to church every Sunday and Wednesday. After a while she didn't look at the picture of Jesus anymore.

She was looking up at it now.

In the corner Diane shouted "Yes!" and placed a piece of the puzzle down with a "Ta-da." And then Natasha stood up and started punching the air with her fist shouting, "Di-ane! Di-ane! Di-ane!" until the little purple hat fell off her head. Diane scooped it up in her hands, laughing.

Sharon looked over at Diane, this person who had seemingly come through all of this unscathed.

"Sharon, you all right?" Ron was looking at her.

"Oh fine, just thinking. Remembering. That very puzzle." She chuckled.

"Kind of tacky, isn't it?"

"Tacky isn't the word."

When the phone rang, Sharon went to the kitchen to answer it.

A few minutes later she stood beside the kitchen window and looked out at the darkness. They had found him. They had found her baby brother.

FIFTY

Recently the lawyers had started phoning Mack with questions about his son. We're looking for information that would help us locate his whereabouts, they would say. What is his mother's maiden name? they asked. They often take the mother's maiden name.

"You mean my wife's maiden name?"

"Ah, yes. That would be it."

He told them, but they kept calling, now with updates on the investigation.

He would listen and answer their questions and then talk to Mona about it, who would listen, her head cocked to one side.

"What will I do if they find him?" he would say.

"Do you want to see him, or do you not want to see him? You have to decide for yourself."

He would rub his hand across his head. "I don't know. There's a part of me that wants to and a part of me that's afraid. What if he hasn't changed? What if he's still the same?"

"If he hasn't, he hasn't. Is that your problem, or is it his?"

"I don't know, I just don't know."

But tonight he wasn't talking to Mona, he was saying these words out loud to Rose's picture on the mantle. A few minutes before, that fellow from the lawyers' office had phoned. They had found Dean. They had absolutely found Dean. Everything matched.

"And you're positive?" he asked.

"We have experience in this sort of thing. The identification fits. Our private investigator checked him out pretty thoroughly. Ah, he has changed his name, legally, to Aidan Dean Fahey."

"Aidan is his middle name. It was my father-in-law's name. Fahey was his name, my wife's maiden name. So Aidan Fahey would be his grandfather."

"Ah, yes. What did we tell you? They do that a lot. Do you want to know about him?"

"What?" Mack took off his glasses and rubbed the bridge of his nose.

"To know about him, where he works, those things. Our investigator found out a bit about him."

"Uh…" Mack felt his chest tighten. He felt warm. What if he hadn't changed? What if…. He needed to sit down. He clutched at his chest. He rubbed a glistening line of sweat off of his forehead and wondered if this is what happened to you when you had a heart attack.

"Mr. Sullivan?"

"Yeah…"

"Your son, Dean, or rather Aidan now. He is, ah, an animator for a computer firm out in California. Quite a successful one, from the sounds of it. Aidan himself has done work on these new animated movies that are so popular now."

"Aidan."

"What's that?"

"His name is Aidan."

"We told you that. Yes."

The tightness was lessening. He moved his hand away from his chest. From on top of the mantel Rose smiled down on him.

"Would you like to talk to him?"

"What? Is he there?" For one horrible moment he thought that Dean was right in the lawyer's office in Maine, sitting next to this lawyer, his hand ready to take the phone.

"Mr. Sullivan, are you okay?"

"Yes."

"You sound so…"

"This is quite a shock."

"Yes. Ah. Well, I have his phone number. Do you have a piece of paper?"

"A what?"

"A piece of paper. To write down his number."

"Hold on a minute." Mack's hands were trembling as he found a pencil and a scrap of paper. He jotted down the number as it was read to him.

"Do I call him, Rose?" he said out loud. "Do I call him?" In the distance on the TV, the weather forecaster, clad in a shiny yellow rain slicker and sou'wester, was smilingly predicting still no end in sight for the rain. "And those little white things you saw in the sky this afternoon? Yes, my friends, that was honest-to-goodness snow. Might as well make the best of it. It'll be here for a while longer."

I had to put him out. If your eye offends thee, pluck it out. If your son offends thee, put him out.

He was kneeling beside the old couch now. He didn't know how that happened. He was talking to the lawyer, watching the yellow-slickered man on the television one minute, and then the next he was on his knees, crying, hands clasped together, great heaving sobs that wracked his body and made his chest feel tight again. Never before had he allowed himself to cry for his son. Never once.

It was dusk when he picked up his keys, got into his car, and headed down to Trail's End. When Sharon answered the door, he said, "There's something you have to know about your brother."

FIFTY-ONE

"DAD, ARE YOU OKAY?"

He entered and looked around. He heard the jigsaw puzzlers in the other room and momentarily looked confused. "I didn't know you had company."

"Oh, it's just Ron and Diane. Are you sure you're okay?"

"I thought I was." He stood in the doorway, his wet coat hanging limp on his narrow shoulders, as though he had grabbed someone else's coat by mistake, someone much larger. For a brief moment, Sharon wanted to put her arms around him, comfort him.

"You said something about Dean?"

He nodded.

"I know about Dean," Sharon began. "The lawyers just called me. They found him. I have his number. Did you drive all the way here to tell me that?"

He opened his mouth to say something, then closed it again. There was something very odd about his face; his cheeks were too bright.

"Dad, what is it? Do you need to sit down? Here, give me your coat."

Sharon slid his coat off his arms, as if he were a child, and led him to a chair. From the other room, she could hear Diane say, "Here it is, the middle piece of the blue sky. And I found it la-de-da!" And Natasha answering back, "You go, girl!"

Sharon poured her father a cup of coffee and set it down in front of him and waited.

"This is hard for me," he said. "So very hard." He stared down at the coffee as if he didn't quite know what to do with it. "We were so sure we had it right, all of us were."

"What, Dad? Did you talk to Dean?"

He shook his head. "I need to talk to you first."

"Is Dean all right?"

"I've come to tell you…I need to tell you why Dean left. The real reason."

Sharon looked at him and waited.

"It was my fault he left. I made him leave. I've only told one other person the real reason. Not even Fred." He ran his hand across his head. "No one from church. They would've thought less of me, having a son like that, and I couldn't risk that. Only Mona."

"Mona from the café?"

"Yes." He paused. "I told her." Sharon got up and closed the door to the kitchen.

Her father folded his fingers together and placed his hands on the table. "It was your mother's death, I think. He was so attached to her, more than you were, Sharon. You were the independent one, always knew your own mind, never needed anyone else. But Dean was different. He would wake up from bad dreams and cry and cry. Your mother, well…she would go into his room and hold him and rock him and sing to him until he fell asleep again. I didn't do that. I told Rose, I said, 'That boy has to grow up sometime. He has to learn to be a man.'"

"I remember you did that when Mom died, sometimes."

He looked at his hands. "You remember how Dean was?" He looked over at her, a pleading look in his rheumy eyes.

"You're talking about his suicide attempts."

"I wasn't there for him when he needed me most. I failed him." He paused. "About a week before he left he came to me and told me…this is difficult." He looked at her. "He came to me and said that he thought he was a…um…a homosexual. That's what he told me."

Sharon stared at him.

"I didn't know what to do. You can't imagine my devastation. I couldn't go to Pastor Harley. Imagine what he would think of me if I were to tell him something like that, that I didn't do my duty as a father, so my son turns out like that. There was no one I could go to. No one in the church. And very little written about it then. I looked in the library when no one could see what I was reading. I was trying to find some help for him, you see. I eventually found this clinic in Boston, far enough away from Portland so no one here would need to know. They used shock treatments or something."

"Oh, Dad."

"Then Hilda found out."

"Hilda."

"After she talked to me, I knew there was only one course of action. He had to be put out. That's what I thought then, that I needed to do the thing God commanded and put him out. So I demanded that he leave. And he did."

After a long silence, Sharon said, "We have a long history of that in this family."

His trembling hands were palm down on the table and there were tears on his face.

FIFTY-TWO

IT WAS QUITE A GANG OF THEM that stayed over that night at Trail's End. Natasha's grandfather took the small upstairs bedroom with the single bed, and Ron and Diane took the upstairs bedroom with the double bed, the one Sharon had wanted Natasha to move into. The little room off the kitchen was Command Central, that's what Ron was calling it. Ron and Diane, who'd moved their car three blocks away to dupe the ghost, were taking the first shift. At 2:00 A.M. her parents would take over the night watch. Her grandfather had gone to bed early, and her mother was uncharacteristically quiet, but the rest of them, Ron, Diane, and her father, had talked into the night, making plans.

She would never admit it to friends, but Natasha had had a good time this evening. She never would have thought that piecing together a jigsaw puzzle could be fun. But it was the campiness of it, the tacky picture they had chosen to work on, a stereotypical landscape. And Diane was constantly cracking jokes; half the time Natasha couldn't tell if the lady was serious or if she was pulling someone's leg. "Oh, this is such a beautiful picture. I'd love to glue it on a board and frame it when we're finished."

They had completed it as far as they could. A few key pieces were missing. The blue sky had a few patches of brown table showing through.

Later on, her mother and grandfather told them the lawyer had found her uncle. In the morning her grandfather was going to call him. Maybe it was the presence of Ron and Diane, but she noticed her grandfather didn't complain about the heat or the cold or the food or the tea. He didn't look at her like she was from outer space. At one point, he even asked her about Ireland. She was surprised he even knew she'd been there.

"Your grandmother was Irish," he said.

"That makes me part Irish."

"If I'd have known you were going, I would've given you the names of her people to look up. They're from County Cork."

"I was there."

"Are you thinking of going back?"

She shook her head.

"I'm maybe thinking of going there," he said. "Visit my wife's people. I've never been. Maybe I'll go after all of this is over."

After all of what is over, she wanted to ask. He was fiddling with the tweed wool cap he always wore.

"That's a neat hat," she said.

"You like hats?"

"Sort of, yeah."

"Would you like this one? I've got others." He handed it to her.

"Wow, thanks. Yeah."

Her father and Ron were sitting across from each other and writing down notes on a piece of paper, planning the night's strategy. They had her parents' cell phone at the ready, and Ron had brought a flashlight the size of Maine from his car.

"What if the ghost doesn't show up tonight?" her mother asked.

"We stay here until it does," Ron said.

"What about your kids?"

"Matthew is just as happy being there by himself, and Heather and Jonathan are in Connecticut with my brother and their kids."

"I think we should make popcorn," Natasha said. "Do we have any popcorn, Mom?"

"I absolutely do not have a clue. You can look around. If there is any, it's probably quite old."

Natasha and Diane had rummaged around the cupboards until they found a quarter of a jar, a pot, and some oil. Then they had all shared a huge bowl of popcorn, all except her grandfather, who had gone to bed early.

🐦 🐦 🐦

The clatter awoke her. Voices. Yelling. And the sound of running. Hurriedly, she pulled on a pair of sweatpants, grabbed her glasses, and ran into the kitchen to see Ron and her father struggling to subdue a man Natasha thought she recognized. Diane was dialing 911.

He was a gray-haired man with jowly cheeks and a very red face. Whether that was from Ron holding him so tightly from behind, Natasha couldn't tell. And then she remembered. This was the man from the motel, the one who grumpily told her where she could find her parents!

"Who is he?" Ron asked.

"Doreen's brother," her father said. "The manager of the Drift Inn Motel. Name of Mr. Russ Cutcheon."

"This is a mistake. It's a mistake." The man was sputtering. "Please don't call the police. Please. Just let me go. I had to protect Doreen, couldn't you see?"

"And you've come into our house every night and moved things around? This is all part of your protection of her?" her father asked.

"And broke the ballerina?" Sharon said.

"That was a mistake. It dropped out of my hands. I'm not a criminal. I would never hurt anyone."

"Ron, be easy on him," Diane said.

"He's a burglar."

"I never stole anything. The Colebrooks can vouch for that."

"Why?" her mother asked. "Why did you do this? Come in, move the clock, set the chair to rocking?"

"I had to."

"Why?"

"To scare you fellas away."

"Why?"

"To protect her."

"From what?" her father asked.

"In case you would find something. Let me go, you're hurting my neck!"

"Find what?" her mother asked.

"Something about Doreen. About the death." He sputtered some more. "She's not stable. I had to take care of her."

"How'd you get in night after night?" her father asked.

"Doreen's key. She keeps it by her door."

"What death?" her mother asked. "What death are you talking about?"

"Let me go."

Ron did, and the man stumbled to the floor, then scrambled to his feet and ran for the door. Her father grabbed him.

"The police are on their way," said Diane from the phone.

"What death?" her mother asked again.

"There was no one else to protect her. It had to be me. Especially when Hilda died. I had to be the one."

"Protect her from what, Mr. Cutcheon?" her mother asked. "Why do people need to protect her?"

He shook his head. "It was an accident. She didn't mean it." He sputtered and wiped his mouth.

"What was an accident?"

"I can't talk about it." He looked utterly helpless. His head was in his hands, and Natasha had to strain to hear him. "Before David died, she was a pretty girl, so small and so pretty. They were in love. David called her his fairy queen, and that's what she was like, a little waif. He drew pictures of her. I have some of them."

"They weren't twins," her mother said. "They were lovers."

"Not lovers, nothing like that. They were boyfriend and girl-friend."

"How did they meet?" her father asked.

"My parents were his foster parents for a time. That's where they fell in love." Russ sighed. "It was in the summer. He told Doreen he was taking the bus down to Trail's End, that he had found something out about his true parents. You have to know something, that kid was always trying to find his parents. Quite a daydreamer, too. Used to get up early every morning and go down to the ocean to look at some light. The kid was a bit bonkers, and I told Doreen so. Anyway, he asked her to come to Trail's End, where he was living with Hilda and Katie for the summer. They got into some sort of a fight on the beach. I don't know how or why because Doreen and David were two of the nicest kids you'd ever meet, but I guess she pushed him. He fell, hit his head, and died."

From the doorway into the kitchen her grandfather said one word. "No."

They stared at him.

"It's time the lying stopped. Doreen didn't do it. Doreen didn't kill David." He paused, put his hand on the doorjamb. "Hilda did."

In the distance were police sirens.

FIFTY-THREE

"HILDA?" ALL SIX OF THEM TURNED toward him.

"I remember David," he said, moving into the room rubbing the sleep out of his eyes with his knubby fingers. "I remember him."

Mack walked into the room and leaned heavily against the fireplace, jarring the little bell, which plinked wildly. From his wallet, he pulled out the worn news clipping, the one he'd kept for so many years. He handed it to Jeff, who opened it up and stared down at it.

"What is that?" Sharon asked.

"Read it," Mack demanded.

"We've already seen this. At the library on microfilm," Jeff said.

"Read it anyway."

Jeff read, "Youth Dead. The body of David Thomas, age eighteen, was found on the beach near Beach Haven, twenty miles south of Portland. The youth was apparently riding his bicycle along the beach when he fell off, hit his head, and was knocked unconscious. He drowned in the rain and incoming tide." He looked at Mack when he finished. "Foul play is not suspected."

Mack sat down on Grandma Pearl's rocking chair. "Hilda knew something about this, that's what I suspected. I even went to her once, but of course she said nothing. Denied everything."

"She was protecting my sister," Russ said. "Of course she said nothing."

"But why would she protect a young girl she barely knew?"

Russ stared at Mack, dumbfounded.

"Hilda didn't know Doreen. Not well, anyway. I used to wonder about that, why did Hilda so willingly take in a complete stranger? I think Katie had the same suspicions I did, but of course we didn't talk about it. Hilda was always doing these works of charity." He had trouble keeping the venom out of his voice. "We were told that little

David was from a local orphanage, but the only person who really seemed to care for him was Katie. I remember Katie—oh, she would've been in her late twenties by this time—I remember her carrying the baby around. When David was not even a year old, my father said he couldn't live with us anymore. That broke Katie's heart. I think she was prepared to raise that child all on her own. I remember standing at the top of the stairs and watching my father literally grab the baby from Katie's arms. David was crying, Katie was crying, and my father was yelling that he would not raise this unlawfully begotten son. I thought he meant that any child from an orphanage was unlawfully begotten. And then I saw my sister down on her knees begging our father to leave David here, that he was just a child and had nothing to do with any of this. I remember it was a rainy day, like today, and as soon as my father saw me standing there he ordered me back to my room. So I went."

"But David came back," Sharon said, "because I have a vague memory of him."

Mack nodded. "Several times. Hilda hated the boy, Katie loved him, and I ignored him. After our father died, it was easier for David to visit. Hilda didn't want him around, but she didn't have the clout our father did. Although she tried. When David died, I cut this article out of the paper. It always seemed important, but I could never figure out why. I never could. But now I know who David was."

"Little Mary's baby." Jeff said it for him.

Mack looked at him, eyes wide. "You knew?"

"We just figured it out. The woman on the island where Little Mary is buried said they were trying to give away a baby. That would've been David." Jeff passed the article back to Mack. "You think Hilda killed him?"

Mack nodded. "A feeling. Only a feeling. Something I've never been able to shake. I always felt she had something to do with that boy's death. But I never could figure it out. Never could pin it down."

"I think we should talk to Doreen," Jeff said.

"No!" Russ said.

"But if what Mack says is true, Doreen may have had nothing to do with it," Diane said. "Wouldn't she want to know the truth?"

"She was there. She remembers pushing him off the bike." He choked on his words, turned to Mack.

"We need to talk to Doreen." Jeff was adamant.

"No!"

"We could talk to the police, I suppose," Sharon said. "They're here now."

Russ looked at her.

"We're talking about a murder. Last time I checked, the police were still interested in solving them."

He held up his hand. "Okay, okay, we go to see Doreen tomorrow. Just get me off the hook here."

FIFTY-FOUR

AT NINE O'CLOCK THE FOLLOWING MORNING, after a night of no sleep, after telling the police that the entire thing with Russ was a misunderstanding, something they'd take care of, Russ, Sharon, Jeff, and Mack were sitting in Doreen's little motel apartment. Doreen sat on an old upholstered chair, her feet swinging back and forth in child's moccasins, not quite touching the floor. She was biting a fingernail on her left hand. The cat, David, had sprawled his long orange body across her lap. She looked like the Doreen of Sharon's childhood, the young woman who stood in front of Hilda, biting her fingernails, waiting for instructions. Sharon wondered how much Doreen was comprehending of what Russ and Jeff were saying.

"Doreen, we'd like you to tell us about the day David died," Jeff said.

For a long time no one spoke. Doreen stroked the animal's fur and hummed quietly. They waited. "But he's not dead," she said. "He's right here with me. On my lap."

"Not the cat, Doreen. Your friend, David, from a long time ago."

She looked up, her hand stopping in midstroke.

"It's okay, Doreen," Russ said. "You can talk about him."

"But Hilda's not here."

"But I am. And I know it's okay to talk about it."

"But what if I can't remember?"

"Just tell us as much as you can."

"Hilda said that no one would know, that for as long as Hilda was alive, no one would know."

"Know what?" Sharon asked impatiently.

"Hilda knew I didn't mean it. The others…the others wouldn't understand. Hilda knew that. Hilda stayed with him and told me to fetch his bicycle. She said that would be the best explanation."

"He wasn't riding his bicycle when it happened? You always told me he was," Russ said.

Doreen shook her head.

"He was in bad shape, so much pain. A twisted ankle can do that, you know." She smoothed the cat's fur. He was purring so loudly that Sharon had difficulty hearing Doreen's soft voice. "Hilda knew I didn't mean it. She was the only one who knew that."

All of them were silent. Mack was staring at her, his mouth open. Russ had his hand on her shoulder.

Jeff leaned forward and said, "Can you tell us what happened? Start at the beginning if you can."

"So long ago." She bit her lip and stroked the cat's ears. "David was my special friend. He used to draw me. In pictures. I have some of them. Some are here at the motel. He always wanted me to pose. But I never let him draw my face." She was smiling now, eyes bright. "I never thought I was pretty enough. David said I was, but still, I wouldn't let him draw my face. So he drew the back of me and the side of me. We wanted to get married. We were so young then. When he came to live with us, we were both fourteen. Oh, such a long time ago."

"What about the day he died?" Sharon said.

"He wrote me a letter. He always addressed his letters to me, he called me Mildred."

"Mildred! Why?"

"That was our code word. One of his favorite foster mothers was named Mildred. He said that Mildred would be our code word. Whenever he said the word Mildred, it meant that we were supposed to meet on the beach by the rock. So as soon as I got the letter, I knew. I still have the letter. I keep it in my bag. I thought I lost it once." She was stroking the cat's long, wagging tail. "But I only left it at Mr. Cosman's. I thought that girl took it. But I still have it. I took the bus." The cat, David, bolted from her lap. "I can't remember."

"Try," Jeff whispered. "Just try."

Doreen was wagging her head back and forth. "I went to the beach. To our special place. There was a log there. We used to sit on that log for hours and hours. He told me all about things. All sorts of things. He wanted to be an artist. He was going to draw the light." She stared past them and was quiet.

"But what about that day?" Russ asked.

"David wanted to tell me something about his real mother. About how his real mother died. And something about Hilda. He started to get real serious when he talked about Hilda. But then he told me he'd seen the magic light that morning, and that was a good sign. Not a bad sign. He was going to paint that afternoon. We were so happy that day.

"We got up from the log, and we were walking. We were sort of jostling each other, you know. And I pushed him. Maybe I pushed him a little too hard, because he fell and hurt his ankle. We were both laughing. I remember falling into the sand next to him. And he was clutching his ankle. But then when he tried to get up, he couldn't. Sprained his ankle, he did. So I said I'd run for Hilda. When Hilda and me got back he was in real pain. Ankle was so swole he couldn't even get up. Hilda bent down and looked at him, then she told me to go fetch his bicycle. I said, 'Pardon me, miss, but he ain't going to be able to ride no bicycle.' But she told me to go, so I go. By the time I got back he was...he was..." She put her hands to both cheeks. "He was dead. I couldn't believe it. I couldn't understand it. We tried so hard, Hilda and I did, to revive him. Hilda said that for a little bit of a thing I was strong, didn't know my own strength, that I had pushed him a bit too hard. When he fell, he hit his head, as well. I couldn't understand that, because we were laughing and talking just a bit before. Hilda said that sometimes that happens. A person with a head injury can be fine one minute and then dead the next. She'd seen that happen, she said."

"Did he ever get a chance to tell you about his real mother?" Sharon asked.

She shook her head.

"You didn't kill him, Doreen," said Mack, rising. "You had nothing to do with his death. Didn't you realize that?"

Doreen was looking past them out her window into the motel parking lot. "Hilda believed me. She knew I didn't do it on purpose. She understood. She took me in out of the goodness of her heart. She made up the story about the bicycle. So no one would blame me. Hilda arranged it."

"Doreen, you never told me that," Russ said.

"I know. I couldn't. I been so ashamed."

"You didn't kill him," he said. "You didn't kill him."

"So Hilda kills David," Sharon said, "so David wouldn't tell anyone what he had discovered, that Hilda had been in on the plan to poison Little Mary with castor oil, to get rid of David. All for what, so that the precious Sullivan name wouldn't be besmirched?"

Doreen looked up at her brother. "Are they going to take me to the police now?"

FIFTY-FIVE

"MAY I SPEAK TO DE—TO AIDAN, ah, Aidan Fahey, please?"

Sharon hoped alternately that first, he was there, and then that he wasn't. It would be nice to talk to him, but it would be so much easier to leave a sunny, breezy message on his machine. Why is it that when you would rather leave a message, a real person answers, and when you need to talk to a real person, you get snarled up with voice-mail jail.

A real person answered. "May I tell him who's calling please?" The connection to California was remarkably clear.

"This is Sharon Colebrook. Sullivan Colebrook."

"Oh my goodness! Are you the Sharon Sullivan Colebrook of Summer Whitney fame?"

"Yes."

"Oh my goodness, well, you must be calling about the television pilot. I'll get you through to Mr. Fahey right away. I have to tell you, though, that I've read absolutely every single one of your books. Every one! I said to my husband, Jake, I told him that one of my dreams is to visit Canada and go to all the places that Summer has been to. And it's all Mr. Fahey's fault. He makes us read them. He buys them hard-cover, and I mean who actually buys books in hardcover? Plus, he has this scrapbook of all your reviews. You have a big fan there, that I can tell you. He's the one single-handedly pulling this television thing off. He's got such neat ideas about animation."

"It's your company that's doing this program?" Sharon touched her hand to her face.

"Isn't that what you're calling about?"

"I had no idea."

"Well, we are an animation firm. But don't you worry. It's such a neat concept. Real actors with some animation. And it was Mr. Fahey who found funding for this project. Just a minute, I think his line's free."

Sharon waited.

"Aidan Fahey here."

"Dean?"

There was silence. Then, "Who is this?"

"This is your sister. Sharon."

"Sharon!"

"It's been a long time."

"It certainly has."

"How are you?"

"I'm good. Real good."

"I'm calling from Maine. Trail's End."

"Good old Trail's End. The lawyers got a hold of me."

"So I guess I have you to thank." Sharon paused. "You're the one who's behind this bid to put Summer Whitney on television."

"Oh, that."

"I had no idea it was you. Not in my wildest dreams."

"We'd lost touch."

Sharon laughed. "Yeah, like around twenty-five years ago!"

"I talked with Dad last night."

"You did?"

"He called."

"Really?" Sharon ran her hand through her hair. "He told us why you left. I didn't know that before."

"We must have talked for an hour. He apologized. For sending me away."

"He did?"

"He did. It was good to hear his voice. To know he's all right and everything."

"Wow."

"It's been so long. I know a little bit about you. I keep up with the reviews."

"Your secretary told me."

"Administrative assistant. Did she talk your ear off?"

"Not quite." Sharon laughed.

They talked then. Dean told Sharon about what he'd been doing since he left Portland, and she filled him in on her life.

"Beautiful place, Victoria," he said.

"You've been there?"

"Actually, to Vancouver, to a conference."

"You should have visited."

"It's funny. I knew you were living there because of the back of your book, but I couldn't bring myself to. A bunch of us took the ferry over to the island. I've never told anyone that you were my sister."

"I understand."

"I'm anxious to see you all. Meet you all. Your husband, your daughter."

"We are too. I've spent some time with Diane here."

"Diane." His voice became quiet. "That was a long time ago, wasn't it? A different life."

"She's a sweet person."

"She always was."

After they hung up, Sharon went outside. It was warm. The clouds had lifted temporarily. She found a dry spot on the log and sat and looked at the ocean with Katie's old Bible on her lap.

FIFTY-SIX

"I NEVER QUITE FINISHED ANSWERING your question about why I stayed in the church."

"I thought you did."

"There was more I wanted to say."

Diane and Sharon were walking along the beach. The sun had come out, the clouds had gone, and the sky looked like a piece of blue fabric stretched tight and pinned in all corners. Sharon had picked up a piece of driftwood and was using it as a walking stick.

"At first maybe it was because I wasn't brave enough to leave," Diane said. "I envied you, your courage to just pack up and leave. After one year of Bible school, to say you've just had enough."

Sharon poked her stick into the soft sand.

Diane continued, "I went forward during a missions conference at Bible school and dedicated my life to the Lord for missionary service. I thought that if I became a missionary, then I would finally become one of the spiritual ones, that I wouldn't have to struggle so much. You remember those missionaries, Sharon, when we were kids and they'd come to church and set up these displays of little trinkets in the back, baskets and whatnot? They were always so spiritual. They had found the secret. I wanted what they had."

A gull cried overhead.

"At Bible school I met Ron who also felt God's call to the mission field. We ended up getting married and going to Taiwan."

"So," Sharon said, "you found that elusive answer."

"No." Diane paused. "Not at first. Not until much later. At first I was absolutely appalled at the conditions." She shook her head.

"In the country?"

"No. With the missionaries. I saw missionaries living in opulence. Gated houses, with servants. Living totally apart from the Taiwanese people. I saw…I saw…" Diane's mouth became a thin line. "I saw missionaries fight over things, not even important things. I saw missionaries in our group jockeying for positions of control on the board. I remember one time, the field director of our little mission group was a church planter. When Ron and I first got there, we went to his house and there were these absolutely amazing framed photographs all over the walls. He had quite a collection of cameras and loved to go out into the villages and take photos. And he was good at it. I said to him, 'Oh, you must love photography,' or something to that effect, and he said that yes, he did. And that what he would love to do more than anything was to have his own photography studio. 'How come you came to Taiwan, then?' I asked him. He said, 'Because somebody has to do it. I hate it here, but I do it.' He *hated* it, Sharon." She stopped and pushed her hair away from her face.

"When we first went, Ron and I were so wide-eyed and innocent and young. It was gradually, so gradually that we came to see all this. I guess it all came to a head one evening. We used to have these weekly mission group prayer meetings, attendance required. Well, they were always the same: you sat around a circle, our director would take requests, and then we would all pray around the circle, one after the other. Missionaries are supposed to be spiritual enough to be comfortable praying out loud, even though I never have been. Still am not to this day. The prayer requests were always the same too. 'Pray for Mr. Cho, he's very close to accepting the Lord' or 'Pray for Suzanne Su' or 'Pray for our maid, Mrs. Wu, we've invited her to church.' Always so safe, always outside of ourselves. They never prayed, 'God, give me the strength to work here' or 'Give me a vision for your kingdom' or even, 'God, be merciful to me, a sinner.'

"One prayer meeting night I was pretty down. I'd just gotten a letter from Elaine so I knew about Pastor Harley's illness, Bud Harley being arrested, and the church shutting down. Plus I was pregnant with Matthew, so I was sick and hot on top of everything. I remember sitting there in this little living room at the director's house with all his beautiful photography on the wall. The prayer requests were all listed—innocuous things, people I didn't know. I could tell that soon it would be my turn to pray. And I couldn't. I can't explain it but I just couldn't, Sharon. So about two people ahead of me, I got up and went to the bathroom. I stayed in there, crying and crying. Then I washed my face and went out. By this time the prayer meeting was over and it was time for food. I told Ron I was sick, and we left early.

"When we got to our little apartment, I went into the bathroom and I threw up. I kept throwing up and I just couldn't stop. Ron was so concerned, kept asking if I wanted him to phone the doctor. I said no. But it was like all the misery, all the stuff I'd seen, all the stuff I'd learned was getting to me. Here I was, a born-again Christian missionary, with all these little old ladies back home supporting me from their pension checks, and I didn't even know if I believed in God anymore."

"What did you do?"

"Nothing. Not right away. That feeling lasted a long time. It wasn't something I magically got over with a quick prayer. I learned to act the part, I'm ashamed to say. All spiritual on the outside, but dead on the inside. I'd write these wonderful, glowing prayer letters home, and no one knew. Nobody could tell but Ron. He was struggling, too. We would talk a lot about it.

"After four years we came home to Maine and still had to act the part, the whole trinkets in the back of the church thing. But I was finding it harder and harder to pretend. One night we had Elaine and Ken over, and I don't know how it happened, but suddenly we were unburdening ourselves on this poor couple. Turns out they had been feeling the same. We talked and talked. They've become our dearest friends. We began a group, we called ourselves the Searcher's Group. We studied the Bible, we prayed, but one of the ground rules we decided on was that we would be totally honest. It was that year at home that really refreshed me. We still have that group, about seven of us, but when we're away we meet by e-mail. We did go back to

Taiwan, as you know, and everything was different."

"In what way?"

"We started by being honest with ourselves and with God. We prayed, 'God, we're going back, but we're not sure of anything, nothing at all.' When we got back there something strange began to happen. I began to look at people through God's eyes. I began to realize that the problem was with me, not the missionaries, not the people in the church, all those I had labeled and judged as hypocrites. I began to see them all in a slightly different light. I watched the photographer bend down and ruffle a Taiwanese child's hair. I saw not hatred there, but love, and I asked him about it. 'The place gets to me sometimes,' he said, 'but I don't hate the people. I love the people. I love them. I couldn't leave them. That's what keeps us here.'

"And I began to find and talk to missionaries who *were* really dedicated, people who would travel over rough roads to bring medical supplies to inland communities, individuals who spent tireless hours talking to people, listening to their tears, caring for their children, taking blankets to the cold and homeless, visiting the elderly and lonely, taking in families broken apart by violence, ministering hours to people in the hospitals, street people, the business people who hide themselves in their high-rises, but are lonely and searching. Sure, there were problems with the mission board. Still are. And when we go back we'll probably have to deal with a whole new crop of them, but what I guess I'm trying to do is to look at people the way Christ does. Even people like the Hedges and the Fishers were only trying to do their best, and I was so quick to judge them.

"And more important, I'm learning how to worship God. I'm discovering that my highest calling is to worship Him, not mark off points in my Bible or even witness. That falls second to worship."

Sharon shaded her eyes against the sun and gazed past Diane out to the calm sea. "Looks like you found the elusive God you were looking for."

"Does it make sense for me to say that I know God, that I love

God, that God has forgiven me, yet my life continues to be one long search for God?"

Sharon felt the warmth of the sun on her shoulder. Out on the sea, a ship was making its way across the horizon.

"Maybe my life has been a search, too, without my even realizing." Sharon threw the piece of driftwood into the water. "Cos told me that he can see in all my books a search for God, rightness, and morality."

Diane nodded. "I agree with him. Your books are all very moral. High moral themes, where good always triumphs over evil."

"I certainly didn't intend them to be. I just wrote them." After a while Sharon said, "Dean flies in tomorrow."

"Dean is finally coming home. That's great."

"After all these years."

"I hope I have a chance to see him. When I think of what the church did to Dean…I bet the majority of gay men living without families in our cities come from families where they were told they weren't welcome. Wounded, so wounded and hurting."

Sharon nodded.

"But healing can come with Jesus Christ. I know it can. Is he staying at Trail's End?"

"No, he's staying in Portland with my dad. My dad is different now somehow. He told me it had to do with the prodigal son."

"Dean is the prodigal son?"

Sharon shook her head. "No, that's not exactly what he said. He said he was the prodigal father. He had thrown his son out of the house, and that if Jesus had thrown everyone out of his house who had ever done anything wrong, then all of us'd be cast out."

"True. But we do it all the time. Even if we don't throw them out physically, like Dean or your Aunt Mary, we throw them out in our thinking. Judge them, like I did. Like I still do. I hope the visit goes well for your family."

"I've never seen my father so excited," Sharon said. "You'd think the queen was visiting. His lady friend is—"

Diane put up her hand. "Hold the phone," she said laughing. "Your dad has a lady friend?"

"Well, I don't know if it's a real lady friend. It's that Mona from the café down the street from where he lives. Mona and her granddaughter are doing the cooking for this big family dinner. My dad called me last night, read me the menu over the phone, wanted to know if I thought it was all right. He said, 'Do you think someone from California will like Mona's Yankee pot roast? Do you think he's a vegetarian? I've heard that people from California are vegetarians.' I told him I thought pot roast would be great. And then to top things off, Mona gave him this old shortwave radio that had belonged to her late husband. My dad's in his glory now, spends all his time listening to sailors. He's planning to get his shortwave license so he can talk to them. I guess he's quite good at figuring out the weather. He's also getting a computer. One of Mona's sons is in the computer business."

"Wow."

In the distance Ron was walking toward them. Diane looked at her watch. "Ron's probably chomping at the bit right now. We've got to drive Matthew down for that college interview."

"I hope things work out for him. I've got to get back to the house, too. Natasha will be home from driving Cos to town, and I promised Jeff I'd give him advice on this article he's writing."

"We'll keep in touch," Diane said. "I've got your e-mail."

FIFTY-SEVEN

Katie was an honest person. She was a good person. She looked for the best in people. When I was little and Aunt Hilda had just scolded me, Katie would pat my hand and say, "Oh, that's just Hilda. Pay no mind."

Katie was my teacher. It was from her that I learned the value and importance of stories. It is from her that I discovered the wonderful gift of imagining. Katie was impish, a tease, and I loved her for that. I loved her extravagant stories. I loved thinking about trolls and fairies and strange goings-on underneath the beach. I loved the fact that she took the time to dress Mildred and stand her in the garden, complete with blue handbag, when any old wooden scarecrow would have done.

Katie looked for the best in people. When my own mysteries and stories began appearing in magazines, she was my cheerleader. She urged me on to new heights in my writing. She looked for the best in her sister Hilda. She could not believe that her own sister could be capable of such treachery.

And when others ignored him, she took David, her baby sister's illegitimate child, and loved him like her own. I believe her lifelong anxiety around children stems from the loss of him. She would not allow herself to love a child again, not the way she had loved David.

But Katie was not perfect. A perfect woman would have sought the truth no matter what the consequences. A totally honest person would have taken the doubts she had about Hilda, Little Mary, and David's death and spread them out on the table, instead of inventing stories around them. It saddens me that she could not confide these things to Cos, her dearest friend.

"I wish I could take back all of the hurt I have dealt to

people," she wrote once in a letter to me, the closest she came to revealing anything of herself. I believe she was speaking here of Doreen. I think she may have realized too late how much her stories had hurt that young woman, especially when Doreen fled from her in fear when Hilda died.

I think of the sadness that Hilda and Gerard caused. Hilda murdered David, and then began convincing Doreen, little by little, that she was responsible for his death. I believe that George Koch did commit suicide, as his daughter suggests. I believe he was so overcome with remorse that he felt this was the only way out. Jeff has checked the death records, and George died by an overdose of a headache medication he was taking.

But so much of this is conjecture. There are so many unanswered questions. It will forever remain like the jigsaw puzzle on the card table in the parlor with the pieces missing from the sky.

We haven't gone to the police with any of this. What would be the point when all of the principals are dead? Only Doreen is alive, and Doreen and Russ are finding help through a counselor, referred to them by Rev. Barry Brannin of the church Katie and Cos went to.

To all of my Summer Whitney fans, I apologize. I could not follow the advice of my editor, nor of my husband, and incorporate these facts into a mystery. I tried, but could not. I wanted to tell the true story of my family: of Katie, of Little Mary, of her son David, of Doreen, of Dean, of all of us who have been so hurt by lies, by pretense, by the struggle to maintain appearances, to all of us injured when we confuse what is important with what is not.

I needed to write the true story, and I have done that.

I have done that here.

Sharon Sullivan Colebrook